alana candler,
marked for murder

aLana canDLeR,
MaRKeD FOR MURDeR

A NOVEL
JOANIE BRUCE

AMBASSADOR INTERNATIONAL
GREENVILLE, SOUTH CAROLINA & BELFAST, NORTHERN IRELAND

www.ambassador-international.com

Alana Candler, Marked for Murder

This is a fictional work. Names, characters, places and incidents either are the product of the author's imagination or are used fictitiously. Any resemblance to actual persons, living or dead, events or locations is entirely coincidental.

ISBN: 978-1-62020-130-5
eISBN: 978-1-62020-182-4

Unless otherwise indicated, Scripture taken from the King James Version of the Holy Bible. Public Domain.

Cover design and typesetting: Matthew Mulder
E-book conversion: Anna Riebe

AMBASSADOR INTERNATIONAL
Emerald House
427 Wade Hampton Blvd.
Greenville, SC 29609, USA
www.ambassador-international.com

AMBASSADOR BOOKS
The Mount
2 Woodstock Link
Belfast, BT6 8DD, Northern Ireland, UK
www.ambassadormedia.co.uk

The colophon is a trademark of Ambassador

I would like to dedicate this book to my parents,
James and Beth Franklin, for always teaching me I could be
or do anything I wanted to be or do, and to my
husband and children, Ben, Katy, Kristy, and David for
standing behind me while I did them.

Acknowledgments:

To my Lord and Savior, Jesus Christ: Thank you for the ability you've given me to share Your Gospel with everyone who likes to read.

PROLOGUE

THE PENTHOUSE APARTMENT WAS PILLAGED.
   Evidence of a break-in and burglary littered the room. The entertainment center in the corner of the den sat empty—raw wires and forgotten USB cables were barely visible behind the shelf where the video system once stood.

Glass lay scattered around the china cabinet where fine bone china had been displayed, and a pedestal in the corner that once held a rare Ming Dynasty vase stood empty.

Contents of drawers in the master bedroom lay scattered around the room. The jewelry closet held nothing but a few pieces of costume jewelry and a beaded necklace lovingly crafted by a grandchild.

The contrast in the living room was palpable—nothing was out of place.

The wind blew softly through the billowing curtains, and the fans whirred quietly overhead. The grandfather clock in the hall chimed a soft melody marking the midnight hour.

One thing in the middle of the room electrified the air, marring the calm.

A body.

A body—wrapped in a blood-soaked sheet.

A body—lying in pools of blood—staining the carpet red.

Beside the body was a newspaper released the week before. The headline read, "Sheet Murderer Strikes Again."

ONE

"Preserve me, O God; for in Thee do I put my trust."

Psalm 16:1

ALANA CANDLER GLANCED AT THE rearview mirror for the umpteenth time. The shadowy SUV she thought was following her finally turned off the lonesome road as she sped on ahead, trying to separate herself from the shadow behind her. A relieved sigh escaped her lips, and the tension in her head was released in the puff of air.

Stretching her neck from side to side relieved the tense muscles as she strained to see through the driving rain.

This downpour was getting worse!

She cranked up the radio speakers, hoping the loud strains of the new Casting Crowns' tune would jumpstart her sleepy brain as she slowed the car to a crawl. Finishing the trip tonight would be a nightmare. The storm was vicious, and the howling winds were trying to force her compact car off the road.

A bright blue and green sign flashed ahead—Lakeside Hotel.

The word "hotel" perked up her senses. Oh, how she craved the luxury of a bed for the night! Should she stop?

The sharp pains in her temple from lack of sleep and worry about the possible stalker following her all the way from the city of Landeville made up her mind.

The deluge of rain increased, and dime-size hail pelted her windshield. She cringed and quickly jerked her Nissan into the turning lane and up under the hotel's covered entryway.

A few hours of sleep, and she'd feel more like driving home in the morning.

Next to her car, a white box truck was parked with the motor running. She could see the ghostly shadow of a person behind the wheel. Fingers of anxiety traveled up her spine and spread across her back.

He just pulled in to get out of the hail, Alana. She chided herself as she slid out of the seat, locked her door dutifully, and darted through the door of the hotel.

Ignoring her, the hotel attendant faced the other direction with the phone pressed against his ear—enjoying his phone conversation. Tapping her fingers on her arms, she tried not to burn a hole in the back of his head by impatiently staring.

The wallpaper surrounding the information desk was a cheery, floral print, and the carpet was plush and inviting. A cherrywood table covered with a lacey cloth sat on one side of the information desk with a copy of a newspaper sprawled across the top. The headlines read, "Serial Killer Still At Large."

Alana uncontrollably shivered and turned away from the newspaper to stare at the rain falling in sheets down the front of the building. The distorted image of the man in the box truck brazenly watched her. Shrinking back, she shifted her position further behind the drapes. Uneasiness settled on her shoulders, and she tensed.

The lightning in the distance flashed through the windows, and for a second, it cast a glow on the room.

She counted to gauge the distance of the storm.

One one-thousand, two one-thousand...

At ten one-thousand, the thunder boomed so loudly it rattled a vase standing on the counter in front of her.

Two miles away.

"I'm sorry to keep you waiting."

Alana jumped at the voice behind her.

"Did you wish to register?"

The accent of the man behind the desk sounded almost soothing as he crooned the question. His smile and soft-spoken speech scattered the butterflies in her stomach, and she smiled in response.

"Yes, please. Do you have a single room?"

The frown that replaced the smile on those weathered cheeks was forced and misleading. Even though his words expressed sorrow for not being able to accommodate her wishes, her hobby of reading body language told her he was lying.

His blinking increased and the higher-pitched tone of his voice gave him away as he explained—the hotel was full. It seemed all he had left were double rooms with two queen-size beds.

A rush of air followed a scowl as she agreed to pay extra for the larger room. His lying bothered her, but she had no choice if she wanted a room.

An application appeared before her, and she filled out the information.

Name:	*Alana Joy Candler*
Address:	*3890 Ridgeview Drive, apt 201*
	Ross, Tennessee, 25144
Phone number:	*865-555-7880*
Occupation:	*Photographer*
Driver's License#:	*555731*
Age:	*27*
Marital status:	*Single*
Vehicle Description:	*Make/Model: Nissan Sentra*
Color:	*white*
Year:	*2007*
Tag#:	*172blm*

As he scanned her information, the surprise on his face was accented by his double take of the paper. Slowly he raised his head and stared at her—his eyebrows twitching.

"You are a photographer?" His accent, more pronounced

than before, and the half-closed position of his eyelids rang alarm bells in her head.

"Yes, freelance mostly."

His interest in her profession was confusing. Maybe he assumed Alana couldn't afford a room. "I'll pay with cash, please," she said by way of explanation as she grabbed one of the hundred dollar bills in her purse.

This fact did nothing to alter the unreadable gleam in his eyes as he spoke quietly. "Would you excuse me for a minute?"

He left through a door behind him, and when he returned, the glow in his eyes was frightening. Never fully looking her in the face, he turned and pulled a key from the box behind him.

"It seems we do have a single room available." Honey almost dripped from the words as he said them and handed her the invoice with the amount scribbled at the bottom.

Alana paid him and reluctantly took the plastic key card from his hands.

"Room three-thirteen. Top floor. Last room on the end." As he gave her the directions, he pointed to the right side of the hotel. "Elevator's at the end of the building."

"Thank you," she said.

She could imagine him watching her as she left through the automatic doors and got into her car parked at the curb out front.

The box truck had disappeared. Where had it gone? It wasn't in the parking lot, and it was still raining too hard to drive safely on the road.

Immediately, Alana reached over and locked all the doors. Shivering in spite of the hot muggy air, she pulled down the drive to the end of the hotel building.

Five minutes later, she still sat in her car—staring at the whopping number of *four* cars in the hotel parking lot. Hadn't the manager said the hotel was full?

Her uneasiness escalated when she realized the third floor room with three-thirteen painted on the door was at the end of the long walkway and stood by itself—a good forty feet from the other rooms and at least two hundred feet from the last car in the parking lot.

"Why am I nervous?" She mused aloud to the weathered dashboard. "What can happen? After all, there *are* locks on the doors."

Gulping a couple of deep breaths, Alana unlocked her door and gathered her purse, overnight bag, and camera case. Grasping the hotel key firmly in her hand, she locked her car and ran through the downpour toward the elevator.

While she waited for the elevator doors to close, a dark SUV, like the one following her, pulled into the hotel parking lot and froze in the middle of the exit lane. The shadow of a man inside leaned forward and gazed through the driving rain in her direction.

Alana shivered and ducked into the corner of the elevator—hidden behind the elevator walls. Thankful when the doors finally closed, she sank against the cool metal. Her heart thumped in her chest.

After reaching the third floor landing, Alana rushed through the door of room three-thirteen and slammed the door behind her. The dead bolt scraped as she snapped it tight and hurried to the window—peering through the blinds into the parking lot.

Her heart was beating as if it would come out of her chest, and her breath came in painful gulps. She made herself inhale deeply and evenly to gain control of her breathing and then strained to see if the SUV followed and parked in the lot below.

No SUVs lurked in the dim lot as far as she could see. Relieved, she stared at the ceiling and gave herself a pep talk. This was an ordinary hotel room. She would spend one night and be on her way in the morning. There was nothing to make her think otherwise.

Yeah, right! Only a weird hotel manager who looked at her like she could be his next meal and a shadowy stalker following her in an SUV. That's all. Nothing unusual!

She took another deep breath to calm her racing heart and then turned for the first time to survey the room.

The picture above the bed immediately drew her attention. It was an eerie arrangement of colors. The background was a peaceful country scene, but transparent circles of purple, yellow, and blue looked like angry raindrops splattered all over the picture. It spoke, in its own way, of agitation and unrest and matched her mood perfectly.

The same nauseating purple in the picture was an accent color in the comforter on the bed, and the lamps on either side had yellow shades.

The room was cold and uninviting. In her opinion, even a single basket of artificial flowers would have added a touch of coziness, but the only accessories in the stark room were a clock and a phone.

A phone!

She threw her bag on the bed and picked up the receiver. If she hadn't left her charger at home, she would have been able to use her cell phone.

"Hello. May I help you?" A woman's voice picked up the call.

"Uh, this is Alana Candler in room three-thirteen. I'd like an outside line, please."

"I'm sorry, Ms. Candler. The outside phone lines are down because of the storm. Would you like me to call you when they're open again?"

Alana licked her lips and answered in a raspy voice. "Yes, please."

Was she really surprised? This whole day was like one big nightmare. She hung up the phone and sat down on the bed, feeling trapped.

She searched in her overnight bag for the book she'd grabbed at the last minute from her apartment that morning, hoping it would reduce her nerves from a boiling point to a simmer.

Murder in the Bayou was splashed across the cover. She quickly thrust it back into her bag.

No way! That was definitely *not* what she needed to read tonight—her imagination was wild enough already!

Digging deeper into her bag, her fingertips touched the worn leather of her Bible. It hadn't been read much lately, but she'd been busy. She sat down in the soft recliner and opened the pages to the calming book of Psalms—she would read for a while and make sure no dark stranger showed up on her doorstep.

When the clock on the other side of the bed read 1:15, her heavy eyelids begged her to get a shower and go to bed. She picked up a pamphlet advertising the waterfalls a couple of miles away and stuck it in her Bible to bookmark the page.

It was quiet outside. The storm had finally passed. Her nerves were calmer, and she convinced herself the uneasiness she felt when she arrived was because of an overactive imagination and the horrifying job she completed in the city of Landeville, Tennessee.

Noise from the television would help dispel some of the cobwebs of isolation, so she punched the number of a cable news station on the remote and pulled her gown from her bag. The pungent odors of pine-scented cleanser and potpourri assaulted her nostrils as soon as she stepped into the tiny bathroom. They reminded her of similar scents she'd spent all day trying to ignore. It triggered an immediate reaction, and sweat popped out on her forehead.

Unbidden, her thoughts raced back to the events of the last twenty-four hours, and she shivered. Closing her eyes could not shut out the disturbing images she photographed of the last victim murdered by the madman terrorizing the city of Landeville.

The victim was a woman. She was stabbed in one of the most exclusive apartment houses in the city. Her costly possessions were stolen, and the apartment was ransacked.

Alana was asked to take crime scene photos because of the heavy workload of the police photographers and because some sort of flu bug had wiped out half of the city police force—not to mention the fact that her brother, Brad Candler, was the Landeville City Police Chief.

Brad called in the middle of the night and begged for help. She drove the four-hour trip from Ross to Landeville at 4:00 a.m.

yesterday morning and spent the rest of the day taking pictures.

Her mind flew back to the gruesome images she snapped. Taking pictures of a dead person was hard enough, but taking pictures of a bloody sheet wrapped around the body, mummy style, was unsettling.

There had been a series of murders in the last few weeks—all using the same method. All widows, all wealthy, and all five of them were wrapped mummy style and stabbed through the sheet.

When she finally finished acquiring the pictures Brad asked her to take, she downloaded the pictures to her laptop and printed two duplicate CDs. One she dropped off at the police station and the other she mailed to her apartment in Ross. Then she started the long trip home. After driving for almost an hour, her fatigued brain finally noticed the SUV following her.

Had it been following her since leaving the city, or did creeping fatigue cause her to imagine a stalker? She rebuked herself for not accepting Brad's offer to spend the night with him, his wife Lisa, and their three children. It was ridiculous to assume she could make it without sleep for two nights in a row.

Ignoring the odor in the small bathroom, she confronted herself in the mirror.

"Just brush your teeth, Alana, and stop thinking!"

Reaching for the faucet to heat up the water in the shower, she paused when the dialogue from the television suddenly became deafening. The voice of the newscaster blared in the other room.

Had someone … turned up the volume?

A cold chill ran through her veins as she inched open the door to the bedroom and listened. Out of the corner of her eye, she saw a shadow move in front of the bed and toward her.

She slammed the bathroom door and pushed the button lock. Frantically glancing around the small room, she realized there was nothing she could use to defend herself. She crouched low inside the tub and wrapped the shower curtain around her. Her heart pounded against her rib cage.

Lord, please protect me.

Suddenly, the bathroom door burst open, and she screamed. A hooded figure dressed in black forced the shower curtain from her rigid hands. Flames of fear coursed through her veins as she was forced back against the tub and a white cloth pressed against her face. Screaming into the cloth and clawing at her attacker, Alana could only see glowering eyes above her—dark and sinister. His bushy eyebrows were drawn together in anger. A strong, sweet smell filled Alana's lungs as she struggled and screamed against the cloth. Gradually her limbs became weak, and her mind refused to function. Then, the creeping numbness squeezed out the presence of everything near, and the world around her slowly disappeared.

TWO

W AS THAT THE SOUND OF water running?
Her hazy brain balked at trying to figure out where the sound was coming from—until Alana felt her toes tingling with cold. In spite of her confusion, she could tell her feet were wet, and when she kicked her feet slightly, they made a swishing sound.

Was she in the pool at her parents' home? No, that was sold long ago.

Water swirling around her ankles forced her eyes open. A blurry steering wheel loomed in front of her, and even in her muddled state of mind, she recognized the dashboard of her car.

Her car was in water!

She tried to focus her vision as the water came up to her knees. With numb fingers, she felt to see if she still had on her seat belt. The latch was sitting by itself on the seat. She reached to open the door then gasped at what she saw.

Outside the window was a solid wall of water. Bubbles floated by her window as the water replaced pockets of air in the car. The headlights of her car were still burning, and the wavy beam cast an eerie shaft of light through the murky water.

She grabbed the door handle and frantically tried to open the door. It was either stuck tight or forced shut by the pressure of the water.

"Help! Somebody, help me!" she cried hopelessly as she scooted over to the passenger side and tried in vain to force open the door. Her voice broke, and the shaky sound vibrated back at her.

"Lord, please help me!" she prayed. The water now reached

her waist. Tears fell down her face as she tried to find a hard object to bust open the window. There was nothing loose in the car ... nothing on the seats or the floorboard ... nothing in the glove compartment.

She had to get out!

As the water reached her shoulders, she pulled her feet up to bust the glass with her shoes. The soft-soles made no impact. Limply she tried to shatter the glass with her feet, then her hands, pounding on the unyielding glass with her fists.

Nothing.

When the water filled up the pocket of air in the front seat, she pushed herself to the back seat and tried to open the back door. It wouldn't budge. The water continued rising until it reached her neck and crept toward the highest part of the roof.

She took a deep breath of air and watched the last pocket of air fill up with water. Jerking on the door handle and clawing at the glass with her hands, her lungs fought to hold the last stale breath of air. The faces of her family flashed through her mind.

Please, Lord, comfort my family.

She closed her eyes and prayed. When she could hold the air no longer, her lungs forced out the stale air. She uncontrollably opened her mouth and breathed in the murky lake water.

THREE

J AYDN HOLBROOK FLUNG HIMSELF INTO his Lexus and blew
out an irritated breath of air. Dropping back against the seat, he
glared at the apartment building where he had just stormed out the
door.

Patricia was impossible! It was hard to remember why she had
charmed him in the first place.

He pushed the starter button and cranked the motor of his car.
The long ride home would be murder. It would take more than
an hour, and he was already tired and emotionally spent. Patricia's
insistence on his attending a party that didn't begin until ten o'clock
angered him. That was four hours ago.

He released a ragged sigh and pulled out onto the deserted street.
The time on his dash clock flashed neon green in front of him. It
was now after two a.m. No wonder they quarreled.

Even as the thought flew through his head, he knew it wasn't
true. They quarreled on every date they shared lately, and this latest
argument had nothing to do with the late hour. Despite a nagging
ache, he admitted their relationship was rocky—at best.

Her slender face and golden blond hair rose like a ghost from
the depths of his mind and floated in front of him.

As a model, Patricia Langley was vivacious and beautiful, but
when her attitude and character seeped through the facade of the
beauty on the outside, she lost her charm—big time.

The stoplight turned yellow, and he slowed his car to a stop—
giving him much too much time to think.

Making the decision to break his attachment with Patricia wasn't going to happen overnight—not because he'd miss her beauty or personality—but because he longed for someone special to come home to at night.

Someone who would tantalize him with intelligent conversation.

Someone who would enjoy watching *Indiana Jones* movies while eating bowls of caramel popcorn on the sofa.

Was Patricia that someone?

Did he really want to give up on the two years they'd spent together?

Would this red light never change?

When the light finally turned green, he made a right turn onto a deserted road that would take him across Lake Morgan. Confused, negative thoughts trapped his logic, and he traveled for a while in silence.

As he turned the corner toward home and headed across the four-lane bridge, his headlights caught the reflection of something in the water.

Probably night fishermen.

He continued across the bridge, but turned his head curiously to glance over the edge. What he saw caused him to draw in a sharp breath and do a double take.

That looked like the roof of a car!

Jamming his foot on the brakes in the middle of the bridge, he backed up to the edge of the road. Then pulling a flashlight out of the glove compartment, he slid down the muddy embankment.

As he peered into the waters below, he heard an engine come to life behind him. A dark vehicle, hidden at the edge of a dense stand of trees, made a U-turn in the road and rapidly headed in the other direction—slinging gravel everywhere. Jaydn stared at the back of the truck as it disappeared. The headlights flashed on just before it went out of sight.

He didn't have time to figure out what that was all about. The city of Landeville was almost five miles away, and it would take the emergency crews too long to get here. He needed to see if there was still someone in that car.

In the light of his headlights illuminating the top of the sub-merging car, he picked up his phone and began jerking off his coat and shoes.

"Nine-one-one operator. What is the nature of your emergency?"

"Yes, I'd like to report a car in Lake Morgan at the Sam Monroe Bridge."

"A car?"

"Yes! A car!"

"Is there someone in the car, sir?"

"I don't know, but I'm about to find out. Send help."

He snapped the phone shut and ran to the edge of the lake. After taking a deep breath, he dove into the water just as the trunk of the car went completely under.

The flashlight he still held in his hand went dead as the water closed over it, and he pushed it away in the water. He took another deep breath and swam down as close as he could to what he hoped was the driver's side window. When he pulled on the handle of the door, it jerked open in his hands. His tall frame barely fit inside the small opening, but he pushed inside the car and felt around for a body.

There was nothing there.

Relief flooded his emotions as he backed his large frame out of the car and pushed his body up toward the lights at the top of the water. When his head broke the surface, he gasped for a lungful of air.

The short elation he felt disappeared, however, when logic reminded him there might be someone in the back seat. He pictured a baby's car seat with a toddler still strapped inside. Groaning at the possibility, he shook his head in determination, then took two more deep breaths and blew them out slowly. The third breath he held and then dove once again into the shadowy depths.

When he pulled the back door to jerk it open, the handle bit into his hand, but the door wouldn't budge. With an attitude close to anger, he swam back to the front door and once again pushed his tiring limbs into the car. This time when his hands floated around in the area of the back seat, they met something soft, cold, and still.

A body!

The adrenalin in his system took over, and with super human effort, he pulled the small form of the person he was trying to rescue up into the front seat and out the door. The journey up seemed to take forever. His lungs were begging for air. At the same time, he was trying to remember how long a body could live without oxygen. He only had a few precious moments if he was going to save this person's life.

When he finally felt the cool air of the night around his head, his aching lungs gasped, and he breathed in the welcome oxygen. The accident victim lay limp in his arms.

A woman.

Her blond hair spread and floated in the water around her as he tugged her the short distance through the water to the edge of the lake. Gently, he lowered her to the wet ground, and in the headlights of his car, he watched her chest to see if she was breathing. Desperately, he placed his ear next to her mouth, hoping he would feel a puff of air.

Nothing!

The vein in her neck showed no signs of life-saving, pulsing blood pumping from her heart.

He quickly turned her over to push the water from her lungs. Then, after checking her mouth to make sure the airway was clear, he covered her mouth with his and began forcing air from his lungs into hers.

Fear and desperation had a chokehold on his soul, but he couldn't let that stop him now. His CPR training pushed its way forward into his thoughts.

Two quick breaths. Then press.

One, two, three, four, five …

When he reached thirty, he checked again for a heartbeat.

"Come on, breathe!"

Two more breaths. Then press.

Though it was less than a minute, it seemed like hours before he heard the screaming siren in the distance and watched an ambulance pull off the road beside him.

Finally! Someone trained had arrived to take over the responsibility for this woman's life. Jaydn blew out a relieved breath. Shirking responsibility wasn't something he normally allowed himself, but being accountable for whether a person lived or died—that made his heart stutter.

A police car pulled in behind the ambulance as two paramedics rushed toward him. One of the paramedics, tall and muscular, leaned around Jaydn's hands as he continued administering compressions and checked for vital signs.

The paramedic looked at Jaydn and shook his head.

"Can you keep up the mouth-to-mouth while I administer the compressions?"

Jaydn nodded and moved to the woman's head.

The other paramedic began pulling equipment from the ambulance and set up radio communication with the hospital. Jaydn waited quietly while the first paramedic administered the compressions. Then he breathed into the woman's lungs again.

"How long was she without oxygen? Do you know?" The paramedic puffed out his question as he continued the compressions.

Jaydn shook his head. "I have no idea. The car was sinking when I drove by … maybe not too long."

He leaned over for two more breaths, but the second paramedic waved him back. The man placed the stethoscope on her chest and listened.

"I'm getting a faint pulse."

Placing a portable resuscitator over her mouth, the man squeezed twice.

Suddenly, the woman coughed and drew a trembling breath on her own. Jaydn sat back on his heels and let out a relieved breath. He watched the two men hurry to surround the young woman with more attention. An IV was inserted in her arm, and her face was covered with an oxygen mask. Then they stabilized her and lifted her into the ambulance. Jaydn stood uncertainly, puzzled about what to do next.

The paramedic driving the ambulance told him quickly. "Sir, you'll need to come with us to the hospital so they can get your information. Can you meet us at Landeville Memorial?"

Jaydn nodded and walked over to his car. He stood staring as the ambulance pulled out into the road.

"Are you all right, sir?" The policeman beside him handed him a towel.

"Yes," he nodded unsteadily as he rubbed the towel through his hair.

"Do you know who she is?"

Jaydn shook his head. "No. I've never seen her before."

It seemed odd when he said it—even to himself. She was a stranger, and yet he'd been consumed with an earnest desire to see breath return to her lifeless body. Something melted inside his heart as he thought about saving her life.

A red and white wrecker pulled up beside the bridge, and the policeman spoke to Jaydn. "I have to stay here a little longer. Okay if I get your statement at the hospital?"

Jaydn nodded and got into his car.

When he reached the hospital, the nurse at the information desk asked Jaydn to have a seat in the waiting room. He sat down slowly on one of the orange hard-back seats.

He was sitting in the same position ten minutes later when the same policeman pushed through the double doors and walked up to the desk. The nurse listened carefully and then pointed to Jaydn sitting slumped in the uncomfortable chair. Jaydn tried to gather his rickety thoughts as the officer stepped over to him and nodded.

"Evening, sir. Are you okay?"

Jaydn nodded but stared at the officer's uniform, wondering what he could tell the man.

"They said you saved her life. That's a miracle. The nurse says she's waking up now, and she'll be fine."

Jaydn noted the man's look of satisfied approval, and it sank in what he did.

In the two years since he was trained how to perform CPR, he'd never used what he learned. Knowing that he saved a life because of the four-hour class filled him with awe. The relief he felt in know-ing this woman would live because of his actions caused his legs to shake, and he smiled weakly up at the officer.

"Can I get your name, sir?"

Jaydn's lips felt numb, but he mumbled, "Jaydn Holbrook."

The officer looked stunned. "*The* Jaydn Holbrook? Jaydn Ross Holbrook of International Enterprises?"

Jaydn felt his face flush hot as he looked at the officer. "No, that was my dad, but he's gone now. I'm Jaydn *Dean* Holbrook. Can we please *not* make a big deal out of this?"

The officer tried to hide his surprise by lowering his head to study his pad of paper. "Okay, sir. If that's the way you want it, that's the way I'll handle it."

"Thank you," Jaydn said gratefully.

"Can you tell me her name, Mr. Holbrook, or how her car got into the lake?" the officer asked in a business-like manner.

"No. I'm sorry. I don't know her name. When I was crossing the bridge, I noticed a car in the lake and ..." He paused and gazed off into space. His thoughts were muddled. Was he even making sense?

"I understand, sir. Could I get a number where I can reach you if I have any more questions?"

Jaydn tried to recall his cell phone number and watched the man's pencil as he scribbled it down.

After the policeman left, Jaydn walked over to the reception desk and asked the nurse to contact him if there was a change in the patient's condition. She scribbled down his number and agreed.

Jaydn picked up his wet shoes, and walked toward the door. For some reason, making sure the woman survived was all he could think about.

FOUR

THE BLACK FORD EXPLORER SAT along the deserted highway. Anxiety bounced back and forth between the two men in the front seat. The driver leaned back in the seat.

"Do you think it's over yet?"

Sweat appeared on the passenger's upper lip. "I don't know … they got here so fast—"

"The boss ain't gonna like this."

"Maybe he doesn't have to know."

They looked at each other for a minute. Then, the driver sighed.

"I gotta call 'im—one way or the other. Do you want me to tell him or not?"

"He'll find out anyway … if … you know …"

The cell phone on the leather console began playing *Take Me Out to the Ballgame*—injecting more tension into the already tight atmosphere.

The driver stared at the phone vibrating across the console as if it were a snake about to strike. The boss's number flashed across the screen. He blew out a quick breath of air and rubbed his mouth with his hand. Finally, he reached over and picked up the phone.

"May as well get it over with. Boss?"

"Is it done?"

"Yep."

"Any problems?"

"Nope. Went like clockwork, boss."

Silence. "You know I can always tell when you're lying—even over the phone."

The driver frowned—pinching his nose. "Well, boss ... a car drove up afterwards, and—"

"You idiot! Did they see you?"

"No, boss." He hurried to appease the fury burning through the connection. "It was dark, and he couldn't see anything. Some man got out. We got away before he even knew we were there."

The silence on the other end made his chest burn until his boss spoke in a quieter tone. "Get rid of that SUV, anyway. Sell it ... trade it ... burn it if you have to, but get rid of it. Is that clear?"

"Yes, boss. There's somethin' else you should know." The driver looked at the man sitting beside him and dread filled his voice as he whispered into the phone. "We parked the car and walked back to see what was happening. There was an ambulance and a couple of police cars."

The voice on the phone was low, controlled, and infused with fury. "And?"

"And, they put her in the ambulance."

"Was she breathing?"

A pregnant pause.

"We're not sure. They had an IV and a breathing thing on her face ... but they weren't doing CPR."

Curses from the phone filled the air and bounced off the leather interior—making the two men in the car cringe.

"What do you want us to do now, boss? Take care of it at the hospital?"

"No! There'll be too many people there. If she hasn't talked by now, it means she hasn't figured it out. Just wait. See if you can search her apartment, and I'll do what I can. Tell Charlie to get that bomb he's been working on ready. We might need to put it in her apartment. Then go back home until I call you again. And, Gene ... don't make another mistake. Cleaning up after mistakes is messy. None of this would have been necessary if you hadn't flubbed up in the first place."

"Yes, boss," he said simply. If he said more, he'd just add fuel to the fire and get himself in deeper trouble. The boss hated arguing, and he hated mistakes.

FIVE

POLICE CHIEF BRAD CANDLER LEANED back in his desk chair across from Criminal Investigator Bo Watson and pursed his lips. Patience was not one of his virtues. Getting Bo to fill him in on the facts he gathered from the hotel where Alana was abducted was like pushing wet noodles down a hot stretch of asphalt.

Trying to be patient, he reminded himself of their training at the police academy—the drills, the exercises, pushing their bodies to the limit. Bo possessed a tremendous amount of stamina and was always there to encourage and prod Brad further. That bond forged a lasting friendship that ignored their differences.

Even though their personalities were as different as the black and white cars they drove at the academy, Brad still compared their friendship to the comfortable fit of a broken-in pair of tennis shoes. In spite of the fact that they were good friends, he admitted Bo sometimes pushed his buttons.

Bo, redheaded and hot tempered, enjoyed life to the fullest and made impulsive decisions that were a little on the daring side. Because his personality was so laid back, he never advanced far in the ranks and was always left behind when it came time for promotions.

Brad worked hard at being conscientious, reliable, and systematic in his investigations. He tried to overlook much of Bo's impulsive behavior, and when Brad became chief of the Landeville City Police Department, he was happy to promote Bo to primary crime scene investigator.

Finally, Brad's irritation spewed out of his mouth.

"Are you telling me the manager said she wasn't even there?"

Bo nodded. "Yep. He said no single women checked into the hotel at all yesterday, and he didn't seem interested in letting us check out the hotel room Alana said she stayed in. He said it was *occupied*."

Brad stood up and paced the floor. "That's unbelievable!" He couldn't think—couldn't even imagine what that revelation might be telling them.

Kent McDaniels, Bo's partner, knocked on the door and stuck his head in. Brad waved him into the room.

Brad stopped pacing and tightened his lips. "Get a search warrant, Bo. Check out that room. See if it's like Alana described."

As Bo stood up, Brad nodded at Kent and added, "Kent, go with him. I want every inch of that place searched, fingerprinted, and checked for DNA evidence. Take plenty of pictures. Get addresses and phone numbers of the hotel manager and anyone working last night, and get a list of the customers who slept there and their contact information."

Kent McDaniels, the computer genius of the department, was the thinnest and tallest of all the policemen. His personality was unassuming and shy, but his smoky gray eyes let Brad know he was calm, careful, and deliberate—a man after Brad's own heart. He nodded at Brad and headed out the door behind Bo.

Brad paired hotheaded Bo with level-headed Kent to keep Bo grounded and out of trouble. In turn, Bo was teaching Kent his unfathomable, canny way of solving mysteries. Bo's tendency to slide around the usual way of doing things helped him think outside the box when solving the puzzles that complicated crime scene investigating. As partners, they made a great team.

Scooping up his car keys from the desk, Brad closed the file he was working on, filed it and locked the cabinet, and headed out the door to check on Alana.

Around the corner, Bo was flirting with Brad's secretary at her desk while Kent leaned against the wall—a patient resolve reflected in his eyes.

Brad cleared his throat and pasted an annoyed look on his face.

Looking sheepish, Bo said, "I'm going, I'm going." He grabbed the search warrant request and gave the secretary one last wink before leaving.

Brad turned to his red-faced secretary. "I'm headed to the hospital to check on Alana. I'll be back sometime around lunch."

"Yes, sir."

After obtaining the search warrant for the hotel from Judge Collins, Kent settled into his unmarked police car and waited while Bo made a phone call.

Bo nodded at Kent as he slid into the passenger seat and paused as the radio sounded a tone from the dispatch.

"Dispatch to any available unit near Pine Road—cross street ... Sunset Circle. We have a report of a four-acre brush fire. Possible arson. Witnesses say several juveniles were seen running from the area."

"Maybe you should take that, Kent, since Brad's short-handed. I'll head over to the hotel, and you can join me later."

Kent nodded and reached for the radio. After acknowledging he was ten-seventy-six to the scene, he headed for Pine Road—several miles out in the country.

Bo got into his car parked on the curb, placed the portable strobe light on top of the car, and drove toward the hotel between Landeville and Ross.

SIX

THE CHARACTERISTIC SMELL OF ALCOHOL tickled Alana's nose. Her mouth turned down in a frown, and her head turned into the pillow.

Sounds of movement rustled around her, and she tugged her heavy lids open. Through tiny slits, she saw a white uniform and a man's smiling face.

A warm tenor voice boomed across the foot of her bed. "Hello, young lady. How're you feeling this afternoon?"

The owner of the voice came around to her other side, pulled the thick curtains open, and let the sunshine fill the room. He frowned at her reaction to the bright sunlight. "Still have a headache from the concussion?"

"A little," she said with a squint.

"That'll probably stay with you a while yet. I tried to let you sleep as long as I could." He put one hand on her forehead and smiled.

She glanced at the clock under his arm and was shocked to find she'd slept through lunch. Closing her eyes for sleep the night before only brought back terrifying memories of choking in the shadowy lake water. How could she rest with that memory tugging at her subconscious? As soon as she relaxed enough to sleep, the fastidious nurse came around and flashed a bright light in her eyes until she was convinced her concussion hadn't caused serious problems.

After several miserable hours of restlessness, she finally dozed off only to wake up with a headache that would not go away and a persistent drugged feeling that made her body feel sluggish and feeble.

Now, she sat still as a cold stethoscope was pressed against the bruises on her chest, and she cringed—trying to ignore the dull ache. Being brought back to life had its disadvantages.

The nurse listened to her heartbeat and took her blood pressure. He turned to study the IV machine beside her head and then asked her quietly, "You ready for me to take this out?"

Alana was alert immediately and sat up in bed. "Okay," she whispered. She hated needles and had spent all night trying to ignore the one protruding from her arm. Turning her head, she closed her eyes as he carefully withdrew the needle and placed a tiny bandage over her wound.

"There we go. As good as new."

That was easy for him to say!

The nurse threw the paper in the trash as he walked out the door and told her with a smile, "The doctor will be in shortly. I think he might let you go home today, if you're feeling up to it."

Alana nodded and slumped down in the bed, pressing a hand to her forehead.

"Hey there, munchkin."

Alana dropped her hand and looked up in satisfied pleasure. The first smile of the day spread across her face.

"Brad! You're here! After being here so late, I thought you might not get here until this evening."

"Sure, sis! Nothing could keep me away. That's what brothers are for. How are you feeling?"

Alana didn't answer but watched him amble across the room and perch on the edge of her bed. Dark circles from lack of sleep framed his eyes, and worry lines painted wrinkles in his usually smooth complexion. More gray than normal tinged the edges of his dark brown hair.

A shaft of guilt stabbed her heart. It hurt—knowing she was causing her brother added stress. Being police chief was a demanding job. Constant worry over the latest string of murders and robberies caused him enough stress to last a lifetime. Now the assault she had suffered added to the burden. Not only was it another case to solve, but this one was personal.

Brad reached over and touched her tenderly on the arm— studying her pale face. "You still look a little white to me."

Alana blinked her eyes to hide the strain her headache was causing. "I'm just glad to be here." She paused before adding quietly, "I almost wasn't."

Brad's brown eyes met Alana's, and they shared a warm gaze. He reached over and rubbed her cheek. "I'm glad too." Then, he playfully tweaked her nose. "Hey, I brought you something."

He flipped a brown sack onto the bed.

After carefully opening the top, she smiled with delight. "Clothes!"

Brad made a face and said, "Yeah, your old clothes still smell like lake water, and I figured the hospital wouldn't let you leave with one of their gowns. So, Lisa loaned you those. They might be a little big, but I reckon they'll do." He smiled.

Brad's wife, Lisa, was a petite blond with a strong out-going personality and an athletic build. She was a little bigger than Alana, but the clothes she packed into the sack looked as if they might fit perfectly.

Alana smiled at him warmly. "Thanks, Brad. Brandy promised she'd send me clothes from my apartment in Ross maybe tomorrow, but thanks so much for these. And tell Lisa I said thanks too."

"You'll have a chance to thank her yourself in about thirty minutes. She's coming to take you home with us for a few days. That is, if the doctor says it's okay for you to leave."

"I hate to make her come all the way up here with the kids, but I'd love to get outta here."

"The kids wouldn't miss it! You'd think they hadn't seen you in years instead of just a few weeks."

A little stab of guilt pierced Alana's heart. "I'm sorry I haven't been around lately. It'll be good to see those ragamuffins again. How old is Timmy now?"

Brad closed one eye thoughtfully. "Tomorrow … he'll be

ten months old."

"You're kidding! It seems like yesterday I babysat Rob and Jan while you and Lisa rushed to the hospital."

"They grow up faster than tadpoles in a freshwater pond."

"Please! Don't mention the word pond." Alana closed her eyes, laid her head back on the over-stuffed pillow, and frowned through the pain.

Brad's voice held a grimace. "Sorry. You sure you're okay, Lane?"

"Just a few bruises and a little bit of a lingering headache."

"The doc says you'll be sore for a few days, but soon you'll be as good as new. Did you get any sleep?"

"A little. Brad, what about my car?"

He sucked in a slow breath and shook his head regretfully. "Well, kiddo, we towed your car in this morning. Looks like you're gonna need a new one. The motor's ruined."

Alana closed her eyes. "What about my camera and my luggage at the hotel?"

Brad's gaze plunged to the floor.

"Lane, they weren't at the hotel. They were in the trunk of your car. Your purse, your camera case, and your luggage with the laptop inside. Even your credit cards and the two one hundred dollar bills in your wallet were still there."

"What?" Her brow wrinkled in confusion. "I don't understand. I told you—I gave one of those bills to the man at the hotel to pay for my room." Her voice increased in volume.

Brad rubbed her on the arm. "Calm down, Lane. We're short-handed because of this flu bug, but Bo and Kent are there now talking to the manager. They'll do a thorough job and let us know what they find."

Alana shook her head. "I don't understand. I *was* there. I remember the room number—three-thirteen. I saw the weird picture hanging over the bed. I wouldn't make all these things up, Brad. Go to the hotel and see if it's not just like I described."

"Bo's checking on it, Alana. Be patient. We'll figure it out, I promise."

Thoughts of eyes, dark and sinister, flashed before Alana's eyes. She hoped they would figure it out—and soon.

SEVEN

A LITTLE WHILE LATER, A DULL knock sounded on the hospital door. Chet Fabian and his friend and cruising partner, Elliott Morris, stuck their heads inside the door.

"Can we come in?"

Brad raised his head. "Hey, fellas. Come on in."

Brad shook hands with Chet first and then Elliott as they ambled into the room.

Alana dried the tears from her face as the two policemen crossed the tile floor—both dressed in sharply pressed uniforms. She watched as Chet, the newest rookie of the department, stepped boldly up to the bed. Concern burned above the pudgy, dark circles under his eyes as he patted Alana's arm.

"Alana, I know I'm new at the department, but I want you to know we're gonna find this guy."

Short and rounded, Chet's cocky personality constantly pushed anyone away who might be interested in making friends. His ash-colored hair was slicked down with some kind of men's gel, and his eyes behind the dark-rimmed glasses flashed self-assurance and an all-important attitude. In spite of the showy front, Alana could hear the warmth and determination framing his words.

Once again, tears blurred her vision and clogged her throat so she couldn't speak. She put her hand on Chet's—still resting on her hand—and smiled her appreciation.

Elliott stepped forward and handed her an arrangement of cut flowers—geraniums, daisies, and baby's breath.

"Oh, they're beautiful, Elliott. Thank you." Alana smelled the flowers and placed them on her tray where she could see them.

Elliott stood back, and grinned.

Elliott, tall, blonde, and a little on the aloof side, was a two-year member of Brad's force and was famous for his patience and common sense. Brad told Alana how Elliott tolerated Chet's friendship in spite of his arrogant disposition because of their intertwined backgrounds. After growing up in the same neighborhood—their houses only a block apart—Chet and Elliott shared the same high school classes, the same criminal justice degree in college, and graduated from the police academy on the same day.

Elliott joined the Landeville City Police Department immediately after his graduation, but it was two years before Chet could apply. Alana remembered the day Chet's father had been diagnosed with Alzheimer's disease —the day after Chet walked across the stage to accept his diploma from the police academy. Chet spent two years taking care of his father followed by settling his estate when he died. Two months ago, when Chet came to Brad for a job, Brad paired him with Elliott as partners, and since that time, they'd been inseparable.

Alana saw Chet and Elliott together during their off hours at the tennis courts or out on the golf course. Losing most of the games hadn't diminished Chet's arrogant attitude. He let everyone around him know that he thought his specialty—*mental* strength—was more important than mere *physical* strength.

Chet placed his hands on his hips and sucked in a deep breath. "We gotta get back to work, Alana, but if you need anything, let us know."

Elliott nodded. "Anything, Alana." His voice, though quiet, was full of compassion.

"Thanks, guys. I will."

Brad followed them as they walked to the door, and when they were gone, he turned. "I'm gonna check on that doctor and see what's taking so long. Be back in a minute."

Alana sat back in the bed and rubbed her aching head. She'd be glad to get out of here and back home where she could rest.

Another knock sounded on the door just before Bo stuck his

head in the room. "Can we come in?"

"Hey, Bo. Come on in."

Kent pushed through the door behind Bo and glanced at Alana. A slight nod of his head was his only acknowledgement. Then, in a timid sort of way, he retreated to the corner of the room.

Bo sidled over to the bed. "What do we have here? I hear you've been going for joy rides in the lake and skinny-dippin' in the middle of the night," Bo said with a grin.

Alana's eyes flashed as she stared at the teasing expression on Bo's face. "Believe me, there was nothing joyful about it."

Bo leaned over the bed. "Are you okay?"

"I've felt better, but I'm just glad to be here. Did you talk to the manager at the hotel? Did he confirm I was there?"

Bo's expression slipped a little as he answered. "We're still checking into it, Alana. We'll let you know, okay?"

He pasted a smile on his face and nodded toward Kent. "Before we headed out for duty, we just wanted to check in on you—make sure you're okay. Ain't that right, Kent?"

Kent smiled shyly from the corner and nodded.

"So … how'd all this happen?" Bo asked as he sat on the edge of the bed.

"It's entirely your fault, you know. If you hadn't been out of town this week, I wouldn't have been in Landeville, and I wouldn't be here in this bed."

Bo had the decency to look sheepish. He shrugged. "My cousin was getting' hitched … what can I say? So, you came pretty close to leaving this world, huh?"

Alana nodded.

"How were you able to get out of the car?"

"I was lucky. Some man drove by and saw my car in the lake. God was watching out for me. Most people would have kept on going, or at the most called 9-1-1. Instead, this man jumped in to pull me out. I'm really thankful."

"Yeah, I imagine so."

"Thanks for coming, Bo. Brad and I both appreciate your friendship."

Bo seemed to be embarrassed by the sentiment, and his lop-sided smile didn't quite reach his eyes. Clearing his throat, he asked quietly, "Did you see your attacker?"

Alana shook her head. "I didn't see anything but his eyes—dark and angry." She shivered and shook her head to rid herself of the memory.

"Well," he said absentmindedly, "we're glad you're safe, aren't we, Kent?"

A silent nod came from the corner of the room. Alana had forgotten Kent was there.

"Who was the man who pulled you out? Do you know?" Bo asked.

"No. I never found out, but I'm sure Brad can find out for me. I'll definitely find him and thank him in person."

Bo stood up and stretched his arms to the ceiling. "We better get to work before your brother fires us. Come on, Kent. I'll race you to the car." He grinned and turned toward the bed once more. "Let me know if I can help in any way, okay? Do you need a ride home?"

"No, Lisa's coming to get me. I'll probably go home with them for a couple of days, just for some rest. Thanks for the offer, though."

"If you need a ride back to Ross, let me know, okay?"

"Sure, Bo. Thanks for coming by. See you later, Kent." She sent a half-wave in Kent's direction. Kent lifted a hand and turned toward the door.

EIGHT

O UTSIDE IN THE HALL, BRAD turned away from the nurse's station and saw Bo and Kent leaving Alana's room. He cringed inwardly at Bo's wrinkled sports jacket and ruffled red hair. No matter how many times he suggested Bo dress more carefully, his personality always seemed to assert itself in his clothing. Brad strode forward.

"Did you finish up at the hotel?"

Kent leaned against the wall, his hands in his pockets, waiting for Bo to speak.

Bo ran his fingers through his hair and opened and closed his mouth.

"Spit it out, Bo. Did you or didn't you?"

"I don't know how to tell you this, buddy, but nothing at the hotel checked out like Alana said."

Brad's jaw tightened. "What do you mean it didn't check out?"

"It all differed from what she described, man. There was no room three-thirteen."

"Bo, you know Alana wouldn't lie, and I know she didn't make up all that stuff about the weird picture and being attacked in the bathroom."

"I know Brad, but did you hear what I said? There … was … no … room … three-thirteen."

Brad stood stunned for a moment. "Maybe they changed the number on the door."

Bo shook his head. "Even if they did, the room she described didn't look anything like what I saw. The picture in the last room on that floor next to the elevator is a waterfall in the mountains, not a country farmhouse with weird colors. The walls and carpets are gray, and the lamps are blue, not yellow like Alana said. None of the things she mentioned last night were there."

Frustration combined with weariness from lack of sleep took over. Brad slammed his open hand against the wall. "This is crazy. Someone must have changed the room."

"The color of the walls? And the carpet? Come on, Brad, you know that can't be. There wasn't even a key card programmed with the number three-thirteen."

A nurse in a white uniform passed them with a tray of medicine. The sharp, pungent smell of disinfectant followed her footsteps down the hall, and Brad scrunched his face and watched her pass.

"Man, I hate this place," he whispered. "My parents were in this hospital after the wreck. For hours, we thought they'd make it … then suddenly, they were both gone. I remember the waiting … and the smells." He dropped his head.

Bo's shift in position drew Brad's attention, and he looked up to see Bo—hands on his hips and staring at Alana's open door.

"I need to say something, Brad."

"What?"

Bo scrubbed his face with his hands and then stopped and leveled his gaze at his friend. "I think maybe … I mean, maybe Alana …"

"Maybe Alana … what?"

"Maybe … maybe she dreamed the whole thing after she ran off the road. Maybe the concussion caused her to hallucinate." His words came out on a puff of air.

Brad paced back and forth across the hallway. He clenched and unclenched his hands. His anger was almost to the boiling point as the words spewed out of his mouth.

"Are you crazy? No way! You know how detailed she was about everything. There's no way she could have dreamed something so fantastic."

A tinge of anger flushed Bo's face, and his tone grew louder. "Look man, you're not thinking straight. She's your sister, and you're not looking at this logically. Admit that it could happen. Admit that."

The hair on Brad's forehead jerked as he shook his head back and forth. "Never! I'll never admit to such an absurd idea. There has to be another explanation. We need to dig deeper."

The red hair hanging on Bo's forehead drew attention to the white spots of anger on his face. He raised his shoulders in resignation and walked off toward the elevators.

Kent, looking flustered at the anger filling the hall, nodded at Brad and followed Bo to the elevator.

Brad ran his fingers through his hair and tried to calm down before going back in to see Alana. How was he going to tell her this news? She'd flip if she thought he even considered the possibility she'd dreamed the whole thing up. He took several calming breaths and gently pushed open the smooth wood of her hospital door.

NINE

THE RAISED VOICES OUTSIDE THE hospital door surprised Alana. When she realized it was Brad's voice spewing anger, premonition twisted her heart into knots.

Something was wrong.

That feeling was confirmed when Brad walked into the room and she saw the tight lines on his face.

"What is it, Brad? What's wrong?"

Brad sat on the side of the bed and touched her arm. Alana stared at him—waiting for him to speak.

"Bo said there was no room three-thirteen at the hotel on the Ross highway."

When she finally spoke, her words were barely above a whisper. "That can't be. I was there, Brad. I saw the room number. They must have changed the number on the door."

Brad shook his head. "It's not just the door number, Alana. The pictures on the wall ... the color of the room ... it all differed from what you described."

"Are you saying I'm making it all up?" Her voice was tight.

Brad leaned forward to her and held her gaze—his voice strong and deliberate. "No. I'm not. I'm saying someone went to a lot of trouble to cover up the fact that you were there."

"But, I don't understand. Why would someone do this? If he wanted money, he would have taken my wallet, my camera. If he didn't steal anything, then what did he want?"

Brad's back stiffened, but he didn't look away.

"If he didn't want to rob me, then he wanted to ... what?

Make sure yesterday was my last day on earth?" She stared at Brad, her expression begging him to tell her it wasn't true. "Why, Brad?"

"I'm sorry, honey. I can't answer that. Think carefully. Have you had any threatening calls lately, or anyone angry enough to want revenge for something you might have done?"

Alana rubbed her forehead, laid her head back on the downy pillow, and closed her eyes.

"No."

Then she sat up in bed and cringed when her temples pounded and the bruises on her chest knotted.

"Wait a minute. There was an SUV following me all the way from Landeville last night. I thought it was just my imagination until later. I saw him pull into the hotel parking lot as I was going to my room."

"Did you see the person driving? Man or woman?"

"A man … at least, I think it was a man. I couldn't see his face very well, and he was gone by the time I got into my room."

Brad pulled out a notebook. "Describe the vehicle."

"Dark blue or black. It was raining and hard to see, but I think it was a Ford."

"Was it an Escape?"

Alana knew he was trying to make her smile. Her mouth straight-lined, and she looked at Brad through her lashes. "Funny, funny! No … it looked like … an Expedition maybe?—boxier and bigger than the Escape."

Brad scribbled in his notebook and looked up. "We'll find him, Lane. I promise."

Alana looked at the determination radiating from Brad's eyes and nodded. Her voice became a whisper. "I guess my camera's ruined, isn't it?"

Brad nodded. "Was it the one Mom and Dad gave you for Christmas?"

Alana bit her lip and nodded. Tears blurred her vision and threatened to fall. She could see anger and frustration bubbling in Brad's eyes like lava in a volcano. He knew how much that camera meant to her. It was a special gift. Their parents saved for a year to buy it and gave it to her a week before they died.

When he spoke, his voice was soft with emotion. "It's okay, Lane. Things can be replaced—you can't. I'm glad *you're* okay."

Alana slumped down further in the bed, turning her head slightly away as the tears rolled down her cheeks. "This doesn't make sense, Brad. Why did somebody do this?"

"I don't know, Lane, but if we follow every lead—even something we think might not be important—we'll catch him. Our best forensic team's checking out your car—somebody had to drive it to the lake. Hopefully he left DNA somewhere inside. We dusted the hotel room for prints." He paused, then continued softy. "If you were there, maybe we'll get lucky and find one of your prints somewhere in the room."

She felt the blood drain from her face, and she searched his eyes.

"*If*, Brad? *If* I was there?"

Tears of distress rolled down her checks again. She pulled tightly on his sleeve as she buried her face in his shirt.

Brad's arms wrapped around her and rubbed her head softly. "I believe you, Lane. We just have to find a way to prove it."

He held her and let her cry before he raised her head gently with his hands. "There's so much to be thankful for, munchkin," he said softly. "God took care of you, didn't He? A lot worse could have happened."

Alana nodded and straightened her shoulders. Brad was right. There was still much to be thankful for. She wiped her eyes with the tissue he offered her from the bedside table and made an attempt at a grin through a sea of tears.

"I guess if you can be thankful you have to put up with me a little longer, I can be thankful too."

Brad laughed and leaned down to kiss her on the cheek.

As he opened his mouth to change the subject, Alana suddenly sat up straight.

"Oh no!"

"What's the matter, Lane? Did you think of something?"

"My computer!"

"It can be replaced, Lane."

"No! It had all the pictures I've been taking of the orphanage kids. I hadn't backed up those files yet. Now I'll have to start all over."

"Oh, that reminds me. I talked to Shirley. She said not to worry about missing this week's photo shoot. She'll be happy to dress the kids up again, maybe next week. She's just glad you're okay."

More tears filled her eyes. Going to the orphanage was the highlight of her week. Besides weekly trips to play with the kids and cook them a special meal, she'd been taking a small group aside each week and taking pictures of them. Then, as a special gift, she would edit each image into a caricature of the subject's favorite book character. About half of the children had their own framed caricatures now, but she had been working on the next group with the pictures she'd taken the week before.

Shirley and Darrell Hamlin, the "parents" of all the kids at the orphanage, had such a challenging responsibility—keeping the bills paid on time and providing each child with clothes that fit. Sometimes fun activities were placed on the bottom of the list. Alana's gift to the children—a framed picture of their own face in the funny body of a book character—was something Shirley and Darrell both appreciated.

Brad leaned over to give her a hug, and there was another knock on the door. Her doctor came into the room, followed by one of the nurses.

Alana rested back on the bed, listening while her brother and the doctor discussed the importance of her resting for the next few days and concentrating on the future—not the past.

As the doctor's words blurred into one long speech, a nagging wariness filled the back of her thoughts. The future was hers for the making, but the past was full of black, sinister eyes that appeared before her now. Her blood chilled with the anger she saw in them. No matter how hard she tried to forget the past, she had a feeling it would somehow influence her future. And there might be nothing she could do about it.

TEN

JAYDN STOOD AT HIS OFFICE window, watching the skyline of the city as the sun rose over the peaks of the distant mountains and cast a pink glow on the rooftops of downtown. It was early, and the city was just waking up to truck horns and shops opening for the day. Already, smells of hot pavement and sweet bread cooking at the bakery on the corner wafted up on heat waves and slid through the crevices of the window.

He breathed a deep sigh of relief when he laid the phone back in its cradle. According to a friend at the hospital, the young woman he pulled from the lake would recover completely. She was being released today.

A satisfying warmth spread through his body as an image of the unconscious girl appeared before him. Even in the chaos of the rescue, he had sensed that she was beautiful. Knowing he had saved her life gave him an inner peace like the warmth of the sun rising over the city.

A knock on the door interrupted his musings, and he turned. "Come in."

A short balding man in a creased white shirt sauntered into the room. He threw his suit jacket over the arm of the sofa and draped his rather oversized frame onto the chair in front of the massive desk. As a high-powered lawyer, Steve Reynolds had been employed by Jaydn's company for many years and felt at home in Jaydn's office.

"You sent for me?" His statement came out on a yawn.

Jaydn laughed. "Sorry to get you up so early. I forget you're a night-owl and barely out of bed before ten in the morning."

Steve laughed and glanced at him sideways. "Since you're paying my salary, I can't complain."

Jaydn laughed again. "I have a sticky problem for you to solve." The older man sat up quickly in his seat and leaned forward. Steve loved a challenge and was always up for a fight. Jaydn hid a smile before he continued.

"The city council of Bishop wants us to build a parking garage for city use in downtown Bishop. I believe we have property there that's rented at the moment, but I want you to talk with the tenants and see if they'd be interested in moving. See what you can do to get them out of there—nothing illegal, but I'd like them moved to another location."

Steve nodded. "I'll take care of it." He stood up to leave but turned back around. "Hey, where's Florence this morning? Her desk is a mess, and as long as I've been coming to this office, I've never seen it look that way."

"She's out with the flu. The temp's not very organized. It's been rough."

A heartless grunt burst from Steve's mouth. "*Humph!* Now you see how the rest of us live." He chortled as he walked out the door.

Jaydn sighed and turned back to the mass of paperwork cluttering his desk, wishing his efficient secretary would return.

ELEVEN

"Oh, wow! I almost beat you this time." Chet flipped the tennis towel over his head and wiped the sweat out of his eyes.

Elliott looked at the score sheet in his hand and gaped at his own winning score of sixty-love. He grinned on the inside and shrugged. Chet's bluster was talking again in spite of losing the game.

Elliott picked up his racket and stuffed it into his bag. "Yeah, well, how come you don't show more of that winning spirit at work?"

Chet's smile dissolved into a frown, and he sat down on the bench lining the tennis courts. "I just don't understand it. It's not like me at all. Brad's gonna fire me if I don't stop making so many stupid mistakes." His normally self-assured attitude was taking a beating.

Elliott took a long look at his partner. "Maybe you're trying too hard, Chet. It's not as bad as you're making it sound."

Chet squared his shoulders. "Yeah it is, and Brad's not gonna put up with it much longer. I've gotta do something to show him I'm worth keeping on the force."

Elliot's usual teasing banter was checked when he saw the look of determination on Chet's face. "Be patient, man. The mistakes you've made are normal for rookies. We all made mistakes our first time out of the gates. I made my share."

"Sure enough?"

"Yeah. The worst one was when I gave a ticket to the mayor

for parking in his own parking space."

Some of the discouragement left Chet's face, and he grinned. "For real?"

"Shoot, man! I didn't know he was the mayor. He'd just got elected, and all I knew was that he was parking illegally."

Chet laughed out loud, his round stomach jiggling.

"Yeah, well, arresting the bank president's bodyguard instead of his mugger last week sure made the chief mad. I should've known the man with the muscles and the holster was the bodyguard, not the thief."

Elliott shook his head and hid a smile. "At least I was there to straighten out the mess, Chet. That's why Brad pairs rookies with seasoned officers. So they can learn all the tricks. Don't worry about the chief. His patience is never ending—especially with rookies." He grinned. "Now, are you ready for another round?"

"Nah. I don't think so. Guess my mind's not on tennis today." The sentence came on the back of a huff as he chased a ball rolling across the tennis court. "Have you heard any more clues about Alana's kidnapping?" he asked as he tossed the ball at Elliott to stuff in the bag with the others.

"Not yet. None of the test results have come in from the DNA samples, and they're still trying to prove Alana was in the hotel. If they can prove she was there, then someone at the hotel has to be involved." Elliott jerked up his bag. "Come on, man, I'll take you home."

Together, they grabbed the rest of the loose balls from around the court and headed to a gray Chevy Malibu parked by the curb. Inside the car, Elliott tried to ignore the smell of sweat and hot bodies and concentrated on getting home quickly. After three games of tennis, he was ready to head home, hit the shower, and order a pizza.

As Elliott drove through Chet's rustic neighborhood, the smell of magnolia trees and steaks on the grill wafted through the open windows of the car. Sniffing appreciatively, Elliott turned his head toward a barking dog coming from the driveway of the red house next door to Chet's.

"Hey, Pops!" Chet yelled out the window and waved at the man leaning over a huge Pyrenees dog. The man was without a shirt, and his shorts were ragged and torn with holes in all the wrong places.

Gesturing with a disgusted arm movement, the man shook his head and stomped into the side yard as his dog followed.

Elliott looked at Chet with raised eyebrows. "Pops?"

"Yeah. I call him that 'cause he's got a whole pile of beer cans stashed in his back yard. He's one strange dude."

"You think he's strange because he piles up beer cans?'

"No. I think he's strange 'cause he's strange. I introduced myself to him the day he moved in. He just grunted and turned away like he did just now. He's a recluse, man. He comes home at all hours. Doesn't work a job that I can tell, yet deliveries come to his house constantly. Giant flat-screen TVs, brand new industrial sized appliances. A truck from Williams-Sonoma pulled in last week and delivered a whole new living room suite, including a huge entertainment center."

"Maybe he's got lots of money," said Elliott.

"Living in that icky-colored red house? In this neighborhood? No way. He didn't win the lottery either—I checked. I'm keeping my eye on him. He has a white box truck in the shed behind his house and pulls it out all hours of the night. After a while, some man brings Pops home, and the next day the truck is returned and stashed in the shed again."

"Maybe he's making deliveries or something. You never can tell."

"Right. Two weeks apart? Don't think so. He's strange, I tell ya."

Elliott watched Pops as he played around with the dog—throwing a bone and teaching him to fetch. The dog returned with the bone, and Elliott laughed when the dog dropped it on his owner's toe and made Pops holler. Still, Pops leaned over and praised the dog with rubbing and pats—the dog's tail slapping back and forth.

"Looks like his dog loves him—even if he is weird."

Chet frowned. "You don't believe me, do ya? One of these days, I'm gonna follow that truck and satisfy my curiosity."

Elliott gave him a wary eye. "You better watch out stickin' your nose where it don't belong. It might get cut off."

Chet opened the door and stepped out onto the driveway. "All right, next time he pulls outta that shed, I'm gonna call *you*, and you can come with me."

"No way, man. I'm not stupid."

Chet laughed and closed the door. Elliott gave him a quick wave then pulled back into the road.

Chet lifted a hand toward Elliott as he drove off, and then he turned to study the house next door. Pops and his strange behavior gave him an idea. If he could prove Pops was involved in some kind of crime, he'd win points with the chief.

A plan began to form in his mind. The next time the box truck pulled out of the shed and down the road, he'd be following … a discreet distance behind.

TWELVE

At Brad's house, Alana sipped her coffee and watched in amazement as Lisa ran around the house gathering papers, books, and a glass jar for Jan's science experiment. Clad in jeans and a tee shirt, Lisa looked like she was dressed appropriately for the marathon she was running. Her blond hair was pulled into a ponytail, and she looked like a teenager instead of the mother of three children.

"Jan, I thought I told you to get all this ready yesterday," Lisa said in exasperation to her passive four year old slumped in front of her.

"I did, Mama. But, Rob wanted to do a 'speriment too, an'... an'... he just took mine to use for his."

Lisa gave her a frown as she stuffed a sack lunch into a black backpack. "Well, go and tell your brother that we have to meet the school bus in five minutes."

"Yes, ma'am." The head of curls bobbed up and down as she nodded. She rushed to the bottom of the stairs in the middle of the hall and yelled to the bedrooms above. "Ro-o-o-ob! Mama says get down here!"

Lisa looked in irritated amusement at Alana and shook her head.

"Jan," Lisa said quietly to her daughter. "I could have yelled myself."

Jan cocked her little head full of curls to the side and looked searchingly at her mother. "Then why did you tell me to do it?"

Alana laughed inwardly at the innocent question and tried to hide her expression from the little girl.

A loud banging echoed from the stairs as Rob barreled down the steps three at a time.

"Never mind." Lisa told her daughter as she helped place the backpack on her seven-year-old son's shoulders and shoved them both toward the back door. She turned to Alana.

"Listen for Timmy, will you? He probably won't be up for a while, but I'll be back in a few minutes. The bus stop is at the corner."

Alana nodded and laughed as she watched her sister-in-law push her offspring out the door. Jan's blond head never stopped bobbing as she argued with her older brother about why she should sit in the middle seat. Rob's light brown hair, straight as a board but angled with two stubborn cowlicks, remained perfectly still as he listened calmly and headed toward the *back* seat of the van—his usual place.

As their Chevrolet minivan backed out of the carport, a twinge of jealousy invaded Alana's good spirits. She remembered the happiness in Lisa's face that morning when she greeted Brad after his morning shower.

Alana sighed as the longing for a family and a husband to care for resurfaced. Since her choice of men wasn't the best in the world, that itch for a family had resulted in nothing but disaster so far.

Her first attempt at a serious relationship was with Tom Watting, a self-assured, seemingly perfect individual. After two years of dating, she was sure a proposal was right around the corner.

In her imagination, she'd supplied a house, a family, and even a dog to complete the picture of a marriage with Tom. But when her feelings were pushed to the side gradually, her dreams of the perfect marriage vanished like fog on a sunny day. Tom's work as financial wizard and advisor for his family's multi-billion dollar company became more important to him than her dreams.

Alana used her work in photography as a way of ignoring

the problems with their relationship. The more work she did, the less time she spent thinking about Tom. Her growing lack of interest and attention eventually caused him to search for attention in other places.

Alana's face flushed as she remembered finding him kissing another girl in the restaurant that he had told Alana was their "special place."

Looking back, she realized it wasn't fascination with her job that caused her growing lack of interest in Tom, but the dissatisfaction in their relationship. Being married to a rich executive would have made her miserable. His scheming and borderline dishonest practices would have continually pricked her conscience.

Martin Strands, her second beau, was considered the most handsome man in the tiny town of Bishop, but when the newness of their relationship wore off, he began showing his true colors. As the only son of a wealthy lawyer in town, Martin, the owner of several pool halls, considered himself above the rules of the town and used his power and money to manipulate those around him in order to enforce his own agenda—pleasing himself.

When she broke off their relationship, a sinister side of Martin's personality revealed itself. His anger pushed her even further away—making her thankful God stopped her from making a terrible mistake.

The dream of having a family of her own kindled an ache in her heart that wouldn't go away. When God sent the right man to make that dream a reality, it would take top priority in her life. After her engagement with Martin ended, photography became her life.

Alana sighed deeply and went to get her Bible from the suitcase in her bedroom. Thankful the water didn't reach her Bible inside her waterproof bag, she sat down at the kitchen table facing the window and opened the Bible. After her close brush with death, reading God's Word was a pleasure.

Last night on the local cable station, her favorite television evangelist preached that Christians are commanded to praise God in all circumstances of their lives—both good and bad. She felt guilty for complaining when God truly blessed her in so many ways—as Brad reminded her in the hospital.

No matter what came into her life, she vowed she would remember to praise God, even if it seemed impossible.

It was hard to praise and thank God for being attacked, but according to the preacher on the television, that's what the Bible instructed her to do. The verses in Ephesians spoke to her heart as she read them aloud.

"Giving thanks always for all things unto God and the Father in the name of our Lord Jesus Christ."

Dear Lord, I know I haven't been as close to You lately as I should have been, but I do love You, Lord, and I thank You for taking care of me. Even though You allowed my car and other things to be ruined, You saved my life, and I thank You for that. I thank You also for this man, whoever he is, that jumped in the lake and saved me. Help me find him and thank him in person. Help me learn to be thankful in all things like the verses showed me this morning. In Jesus' name I pray. Amen.

She raised her head and stared out the double-glass patio door at the fine mist covering Lisa's rose garden. The damp and dreary weather that hovered over the city conspired to make her feel lethargic and depressed.

"And now I have to replace my car … and my camera." A groan escaped her lips.

Suddenly, the sound of her griping filled her heart with shame. "You're really something, Alana Joy Candler! You just vowed to be thankful for all things, and look at you—bellyaching already."

Decisively, she stood up and took her coffee cup back to the sink in the kitchen.

"It's time to put feet to my prayers," she said. Each word was infused with determination as she closed her Bible and scooped it up from the table. She'd get the name of the man who saved her life and go thank him properly.

After she stood up and tucked the Bible under her arm, she

reached to pick up the phone. A pamphlet fell to the floor.

She stared at the thin piece of paper—trying to remember its significance—until the importance of what she was looking at hit her with a force.

Ah ha! This proved she was in the hotel!

Shakily, she picked up the phone and dialed Brad's number.

A few minutes later, Brad's voice traveled across the phone line on a wave of disappointment. "I'm sorry, Alana. The hotel's not the only business displaying those brochures. Every store in town has a rack full of fliers advertising the waterfalls at Drop-Off Point. They'll just say you picked it up somewhere else."

Alana's sigh blew into the phone. She would love to make it hard enough so Brad would feel the puff of air through the receiver.

"But I didn't pick this one up anywhere else, Brad. I picked it up at the hotel."

"I believe you, Alana. I know you're telling the truth, but we have to have concrete evidence before we go accusing the manager of lying. Please … be patient. If he's involved, we'll find out. Trust me. Okay?"

"All right, Brad. I'll try."

She started to hang up the phone, but suddenly she thought of something else and called back into the phone, "Wait, Brad. Is it okay if I go see Mr. Holbrook? Chet said he'd give me his work address. I'd really like to thank him in person, but … is it safe?"

The phone was silent a moment until Brad answered warily. "I'd feel better if I could go with you, but I've already sent a memo to all the men for a brainstorming session this morning."

She waited while he considered the risks.

"As long as you stay with other people and don't go off by yourself, I think you'll be okay. Don't tell anyone where you're going, and don't stay out in the open very long. And … call me if you see anything suspicious, okay?"

"Okay." Alana hung up the phone and sat back down at the dining room table. Still a little nervous about the trip to Mr.

Holbrook's office, she gathered her courage around her and went to get dressed. No one was going to keep her from living her life. Thanking Mr. Holbrook was the least she could do.

After checking on little Timmy to make sure he was still asleep, Alana changed into a pair of dress pants and a white silk top Lisa loaned her. She was running a brush through her hair when someone knocked on the back door.

Thinking Lisa had forgotten her key, Alana opened the door and stepped back in surprise. Her brows came together in a frown.

"Martin!"

THIRTEEN

ALANA STOOD STARING AT MARTIN Strands—a ghost from her past.

"Hey, Alana baby. How's things goin'?"

She stood staring at his almost too-perfect hair, arrogant stance, and haughty eyes, and anger built up inside of her.

"Martin, what are you doing here?"

The autocratic tilt of his head answered for him. The look on his face said he thought his being there was going to make her day.

"I heard about what happened to you, Alana, and I'm here to take care of you."

"Yeah, right! Like you took care of me when I told you I didn't want to see you anymore?"

"Aw, come on, Alana. You know that was just my pain talking. Breaking the windows out of your house was my way of proving to you I cared."

If it was cold outside, steam would have puffed from her nostrils—she was so angry.

"If you *cared*, you would have accepted responsibility for replacing my windows. Instead, your father handled the interview with the police, and the charges were dropped. I spent all my savings replacing windows. That's some way to show you *cared*."

Martin pulled on the storm door to make his way into the house. "Let's talk about this inside."

"Oh, no, you don't," she said as she jerked the storm door handle and closed it most of the way.

Martin's lower lids tensed and his nostrils flared. He tugged harder on the door handle, forcing her to let go.

Gaining entry into the house would open a Pandora's Box that Alana was scared of opening. She retreated back into the room and moved to slam the wooden door. Suddenly, Martin screamed, "My hand!" and she quickly jerked the door back open.

The color of his face turned blood red, and like a bull after a red cape, he plunged through the door until his larger-than-average body was standing inside the room.

Alana shrank in the wake of his fury and watched her terror change him into someone she didn't recognize. He came at her with both hands raised, and fear turned her blood to water.

He grabbed both of her shoulders and pushed her until she was backed against the wall. Through gritted teeth, he murmured, "I want you back, Alana. I'll get you one way or the other."

He twisted her hair in both hands and forced her head back against the wall. Then he leaned forward to kiss her until he heard the same thing she did—the *toot, toot* of Lisa's van as she honked to let Alana know she was home.

Martin checked his movements and stared at her with disgust.

"You'll be sorry you dumped me, Alana. I'll show you—you can't dump a Strands without suffering the consequences. You better start thinking about taking me back. This ain't over. You'll see."

Stomping to the front door, he pointed his finger at her in defiance and gave her a scathing look before slamming out the screen door. The wooden door stood wide open.

Alana shrank against the wall and tried to breathe. Her air was coming in gulps by the time Lisa finally opened the door and stepped inside the house.

"Alana, honey! What's the matter?"

Alana collapsed into Lisa's arms. The tears she thought had dried up returned once again.

FOURTEEN

THAT NIGHT WHEN BRAD CAME home, Alana was wrapped in a comforter, sitting on the sofa, and staring at the blank TV screen. He sat down beside her and put his arm around her shoulders.

"Are you okay, munchkin?"

"Did you get him?"

Without asking who she meant, he nodded. "We picked him up on the road back to Bishop. He swore he was only trying to make you see he still cares."

A sigh followed a shrug of her shoulders, along with a shiver. "Do you think he's the one … at the hotel?"

"To be honest with you … I'm not sure. He says he has an alibi—that he was at a party with his friends. The friends we contacted backed him up."

"Yeah, they would … wouldn't they."

Brad closed his eyes and lowered his head. Alana could see uncertainty was clouding his judgment. "I can try to keep him in jail overnight for threatening you—to give us enough time to check his story out with people at the party. But, I'll have to let him go in the morning unless you press charges, Alana, and I'm not sure that's the best thing to do. The only thing we can charge him with now is simple assault, and it'll be your word against his, and his father is sure to get involved. We don't have the evidence to make a stiff charge stick, and he'll be mad enough at you without adding fuel to the fire. We'll keep a tail on him for a while after he gets out in the morning. If we find DNA evidence that proves he was at the hotel, we can put him away for a long time."

"I'm sure he's the one behind it, Brad. His eyebrows are thick just like the man at the hotel. If you could have seen his anger ..." She shivered.

He pulled her to him and held her close. "Trust in the Lord, Alana. He's kept you safe this far. I'm sure He's watching over you."

Alana nodded and let Brad's words soak into her heart. The verses she read that morning repeated themselves in her head until she knew being thankful was her only option if she wanted to please God.

Giving thanks always for all things unto God and the Father in the name of our Lord Jesus Christ.

FIFTEEN

THE NEXT MORNING, ALANA SAT in the taxi parked in front of a ten-story building with a yellow piece of paper in her hand. She stared at the address Chet gave her and looked once again at the gold plaque on the side of the entrance to the building.

Ah, 2191. This was it.

The magnificent building sported tall, white pillars and a revolving door edged in gold. Whoever this Jaydn Holbrook was, he certainly worked in an impressive building.

She stepped out of the taxi, glancing at the throng of people passing by, and paid the driver while searching the faces of those around her. Was her attacker close by—maybe watching her from the corner or from another vehicle? After taking a shaky breath, she hurried with resolved steps toward the revolving doors and stepped into the circle.

Inside the building, the butterflies in her stomach increased when she observed the costly furnishings. The inside of the building was even more elegant than the outside. She walked into the foyer and up to a polished desk that sat off to the side of the entrance with "Information" engraved on a plaque across the front.

Smiling at the man behind the desk, she said timidly, "Hello, I'm looking for a Mr. Jaydn Holbrook. I was given this number as an address where I could find him."

The man looked at her as if she was crazy before he recovered his blank expression.

"His office is on the second floor, ma'am, but you can't see him without an appointment. Do you have one?"

"Well ... no, but I just wanted to thank ..."

Her speech was interrupted by the sound of a trolley full of boxes as it rammed into the side of the entrance door. The boxes scattered all across the marble floor, and the man behind the desk jumped to his feet.

"Hey, be careful with those!" He stomped across the foyer with determined steps to issue further instructions.

Alana shrugged her shoulders and headed for the elevator. Once inside, she pushed the button sporting the number "Two" in gold letters and waited while the doors closed.

So she needed an appointment to see Jaydn Holbrook, huh? Must be pretty busy, and in such a beautiful building. She was impressed—mighty impressed!

The butterflies inside her stomach fluttered when she felt the elevator rise to the floor above, but thinking about meeting this hero of hers made them go crazy. By the time the doors opened, her stomach felt queasy and tense. She came very close to pushing the lobby button and running home with her feelings tucked safely inside her.

Then she remembered—this man risked his own life to save hers. He took time from his busy schedule to give her back her life. At the very least, he deserved a personal "thank you."

She tightened her lips in determination and stepped out of the elevator.

The uncomfortable feelings she suppressed in the lobby because of the elaborate furnishings completely evaporated when she observed the inviting atmosphere this floor evoked. It was such a strong contrast to the character of the lobby that it took her breath away. Not only was the office warmly decorated, but it looked as if it consumed the entire area of the whole floor.

A secretary's desk and reception area were centered in the middle of the spacious room. Two solid-paneled doors led to offices on either side of the room, and through the openings, she could see floor to ceiling windows covering the outside walls in each office. Two smaller doors stood behind the desk—perfect replicas of the office doors but smaller. The floor of the entire office was covered with darkly stained wooden planks and was tastefully protected in places with oriental rugs.

A seating area containing leather chairs and a dark coffee table sat in one cozy corner of the room, and a beautiful marble vase of fresh flowers sat on the end table between the two chairs.

Alana stepped into the room and inhaled the smell of its friendliness as it engulfed her. The mahogany desk sitting immediately across the room from the elevator doors was the biggest desk Alana had ever seen. As she walked closer to the workstation surrounding the desk, she sighed with disappointment. The grandeur of the desk was spoiled at once by the clutter spread all over the surface. Papers, books, pencils, mail, and odd pieces of office equipment littered every inch of the desk.

This secretary was the most unorganized person she'd ever seen!

Suddenly, the phone on the desk started buzzing. She tried to ignore the incessant rhythm by looking at the paintings hanging on the wall, but when no one appeared to take the call, she stopped and stared. Should she answer? It really was none of her business, but two years of being an executive secretary compelled her to lean over and pick up the receiver.

"Mr. Holbrook's office."

"Hey, Florence, this is Stanford. Tell Jaydn to get down here right away. I need him in Acquisitions immediately."

"I'm sorry, but this isn't—"

"Look, just tell him, please."

"Excuse me, what did you say your name—"

"Stanford. The vice-president of the company."

"Oh, right. I'll make sure he gets the message, sir."

As soon as the phone went dead, compassion soared through her for Mr. Holbrook. This Stanford man sounded like a demanding boss—something she had dealings with in the past.

Alana picked up a notepad from the jumbled desk to jot the message down, when the elevator doors behind her opened. Swinging around in surprise left her staring up at the irritated face of a tall, dark-haired man.

The first impression Alana sensed when she looked into his scowling face was the blueness of his eyes. She had never seen such vivid color and depth. They seemed to match the handsome features of his face in spite of the annoyed expression filling them now. When the fact he was annoyed finally penetrated her stunned brain, she still could not move. She continued to stare at him as if he might instantly disappear.

His face tightened suddenly, and her temporary surprise only seemed to increase his irritation.

"Are you the replacement?" He growled the words at her.

"I beg your pardon?" Alana stated in shock at his abrasive tone.

The anxiety in his face made his eyes flash a darker shade of blue. "Well, you may as well get started. I expected you earlier."

He withdrew a stack of papers from his briefcase and pushed them toward her. "These must be typed and ready for the mail to be picked up by lunch time. Ask Simmons and Ward if they can meet here in my office in ten minutes. I have a list of phone calls that need to be attended to immediately, and I missed breakfast, so I want a cup of coffee and a pastry on my desk … yesterday."

The last phrase was said as he walked toward one of the darkly stained doors on the left side of the reception area.

"And cancel all my appointments today as well as phone calls. I'll be too busy to talk with anyone."

While he bellowed out his list of commands, Alana stood with her mouth open. He towered over her five foot four inches and awed her into silence.

When he finally paused for a breath and turned back toward her, she could only gawk.

"Do you have any questions?" he asked her impatiently.

When she didn't answer, he took one step toward her.

"What is your name?" he asked testily.

"P-pardon me?"

"What do I call you?"

"Oh, uh … my name is Alana. Alana Candler."

"Well, Mrs. Candler …"

"It's Miss."

"Very well, *Miss* Candler, I'm in a very big hurry. If you have any questions, you can call down to the lobby and ask the building secretary. Now, would you please get that list of things done, and I need those letters typed."

He pivoted quickly and disappeared through the door.

SIXTEEN

AFTER JAYDN LEFT THE RECEPTION area, Alana stood wondering what hit her. She stared at the stack of papers in her hand and tried to remember what he just said.

Martin's angry face flashed before her and was replaced immediately by the features of the irate man who just stomped out of the room.

Then, quite suddenly, she became angry.

Just who did he think he was—ordering her around?

She firmly laid the papers on the desk and marched over to the still open door. When she entered the room, however, the anger that demanded satisfaction had to be checked temporarily.

The aggravating man who had been so rude was now giving orders to someone else on the phone. He restlessly paced in front of a magnificent glass wall that overlooked the city and Lake Morgan. She stood to the side of the door—trying to be patient—and waited for him to finish his phone conversation.

Her eyes drifted around the room in spite of the irritation she was suppressing. When they reached the desk standing in the center of the room, her breath caught in her throat, and she gasped. Her gaze was suddenly glued to the wooden plaque sitting on the desk with a name embossed on a golden plate.

Jaydn Holbrook!

Her whole body turned toward the man standing at the window, and she looked at him with a whole new perspective.

He was nothing like she'd expected. For some reason the name Jaydn Holbrook conjured up a picture of an older, more mature and experienced man. One who took responsibility seriously and let nothing get in his way of doing what was right.

This tall, commanding stranger was the man who risked his life to save her.

Her literal hero.

A new appreciation for his bossy character sprouted in her mind and blossomed into something close to admiration. That intimidating drive and determination was probably what made him jump into the lake in the first place and search for her in the back seat of the car instead of leaving that responsibility to the rescue personnel.

Admiration for his authoritative spirit spilled over into her opinion of his physical features. While he paced back and forth in front of the glass window, she silently observed his profile.

His dark brown hair fell in waves across his forehead. And, in spite of the frown that creased the brows over the top of his sapphire eyes, Alana could hear kindness and patience in his conversation with the person on the phone. Those were rare traits in the men she knew.

Not only was he a hero, highly esteemed in her opinion, but she admitted he was probably the most handsome man she had ever seen.

Shyly, she backed toward the open door. Maybe he hadn't noticed her irritable entrance into his office.

When she once again stood in front of the cluttered desk in the entrance room trying to get her breath, her eyes fell on the papers he threw at her.

He needed those typed. It was the least she could do to thank him for her life—help him out until his regular secretary got here. He probably had a boss somewhere demanding he get these things done.

A quick feeling of animosity toward rich, autocratic bosses flared, and she remembered with disdain a similar experience with Tom, her wealthy first-boss and ex-boyfriend.

Jaydn Holbrook probably cowed to such a boss as well.

Appreciation for his ability to work under a domineering supervisor with such an unorganized secretary gave her heart a nudge.

A single nod of her head when her decision was made prodded her into the task of straightening the desk. There was no way she could complete all those tasks if the desk was in a mess. Several large, empty drawers were the perfect place to hide things out of sight until she had time to sort them later. When the desk was empty of clutter, she sat calmly and tried to remember the list of things he asked her to do.

The coffee!

Quickly she got up and peeked through a small door at the back of the reception room.

Ah ha! A kitchen!

She looked around inside the tall cabinet doors until she located a twelve-cup coffee maker and a container marked "Coffee." After filling the coffee maker with water and coffee grounds, she flipped on the power switch.

Now ... pastries. Where would they be?

A quick glance around the room revealed a small refrigerator hidden behind a white wooden door. She gasped when she opened the door. It revealed pastries of every kind. Carefully, she picked up a small croissant and a chocolate doughnut and arranged them on a saucer from the cabinet beside the sink. Just as she was pressing the buttons on the microwave to warm the pastries, the phone at the reception desk began ringing. Quickly she stepped up to the desk and picked up the receiver.

"Uh, Mr. Jaydn Holbrook's office. May I help you?"

"Yes, this is the Evercrest Employment Agency. I wanted to let Mr. Holbrook know the replacement secretary we scheduled for him this morning had an unexpected death in the family and won't be able to work today. We don't have another secretary available to work with the qualifications he requires, but if he has to have one today, I'll try to find him someone with less experience. I know Mr. Holbrook likes someone with a good deal of secretarial expertise. Hopefully, the lady we planned to send today will be able to return tomorrow."

Alana's tongue covered her top lip while trying to decide what to tell her.

"Hello. Are you there?" The voice on the phone drummed into her ear.

Alana finally spoke into the receiver.

"Yes. Uh … Mr. Holbrook has someone for the day, but if the other lady can come tomorrow, that would be fine."

She hung up the phone and inhaled a cowardly breath. She wasn't sure if she could keep up this hurried pace for a whole day, but she knew she needed to do something for the man who gave her the most precious gift a human being could give another.

Her life.

SEVENTEEN

CHET PULLED THE MAIL FROM his box and stood flipping through the bills and ad fliers. His neighbor, Pops, slammed out of the house and yelled into the air, then lowered the volume to just above a whisper.

Good grief, he's weird!

Chet shook his head as he walked up the driveway and pulled a party invitation from the stack of mail. He saw Pops racing to the back of the house with his hand up to his ear and realized he was talking on the phone. Chet's curiosity propelled him forward as he crept up the driveway, trying to get close enough to hear the phone conversation.

When Pops' voice became excited, Chet shuffled a little closer to a camellia bush and strained to hear the excited whispers. Several words carried across the wind, and what he heard made his skin crawl.

"…sheet … loot … tonight …"

The blood rushed to Chet's face.

Could they be talking about a sheet murder?

He was sure the sudden excitement filling his body caused the bushes around him to shake.

Be careful, Chet! Don't let Pops know you heard him.

He squatted on the ground and waited until his breathing slowed and the trembles in his body stopped.

Could Pops be involved with the murders they were investigating?

He should call the department!

The snickers and laughing faces of Elliott and his other buddies in the department flashed through his mind after his last arrest—an old lady he arrested for shoplifting. She'd turned out to be the owner of the store.

No! He wouldn't call 'em yet. Not until he had proof.

He clenched his jaw and listened for more information. Pops stomped across the yard, talking to the person on the phone until his voice faded away. Chet gulped as Pops disappeared inside the old shed.

He's going out again. Maybe tonight!

Chet squeezed the mail tightly in his hands and crept low until he reached the end of his porch. Sitting on the bottom step, he watched for movement next door and thought about what he'd heard.

The word *sheet* made him quiver. The scene of the last murder haunted his thoughts. The intruders disarmed the security system, broke a downstairs window to gain entrance to the home, killed the owner, and ransacked the place. His face felt cold when he remembered the pools of blood and the body wrapped mummy style.

Of course, the word *sheet* didn't always mean bed linen. It could be a sheet of paper or even sheet metal, for all he knew. He had to be careful not to make a mistake.

He needed to find out if Pops was involved in any way with the murders!

The word *tonight* sent fire through Chet's veins and infused urgency into the situation.

Maybe he'd call Kent. Kent never made fun of him—even when he messed up. Kent would tell him what to do. He crept into the house and dialed Kent's number on his cell phone.

The phone rang several times but went to voice-mail. Chet hung up. Tapping his foot impatiently, he tried to piece together the facts he knew. The seven murders the department was investigating occurred about two weeks apart. Pops went on his midnight runs about two weeks apart, and they were suspiciously close to the same dates the murders had occurred. Pops moved to Landeville a little before these murders began.

The timing is perfect. The events have to be connected. This can't be coincidence! Brad thinks the murders might even be linked to Alana's kidnapping. If I solve both cases, I'll be a hero.

Excitement rushed through Chet's veins as he pictured himself being praised by his chief for single-handedly solving not only the murder cases but Alana's kidnapping as well. He might finally earn the respect and admiration of his fellow officers.

Elliott's sarcastic smile surfaced in his thoughts and ruined the mental picture.

What if all of it *was* coincidence? Maybe Pops really *was* delivering cargo—like Elliott said.

He punched in Kent's number again and listened to the voice telling him to leave a message. With a determined grunt, Chet laid his phone on the bedside table and searched for a pair of dark pants and a shirt. Tonight he was going stalking—he'd gather irrefutable proof before he revealed his suspicions to the department.

EIGHTEEN

ALANA HUNG UP THE PHONE, took a deep breath, and glanced at the clock above the elevator doors. Five more minutes, and she would be done for the day. She closed her eyes and rubbed her forehead, trying to ease the tension that had settled around her eyes.

What a day!

After the phone call she received from the employment agency, the day completely fell apart.

The pastries she was warming were as hard as bricks by the time she rescued them from the microwave, and the coffee was as weak and thin as dishwater. Not only had Mr. Holbrook reprimanded her severely for not having his coffee on his desk, but he also raked her over the coals for forgetting to ask Simmons and Ward to meet with him in his office.

The phone rang off the wall all day—one person after another asking to speak to "Mr. Holbrook, please."

There was no paper for the computer printer anywhere in the desk or the large closet that contained supplies, and when she called the building secretary to inquire about the paper, he said it had not yet been delivered. After borrowing enough paper to get the letters typed, she'd missed her lunch in order to get them finished and ready for the mail before the mailman came to pick them up.

As the mailman stood waiting for the letters, she searched in vain for stamps. Finally, when he waited as long as he could and left, she found them in the envelope box in the bottom drawer.

Angry at no one in particular, she hurried down the elevators to the bottom floor— barely catching the mailman as he walked out the front door— only to return and find three people waiting in the office to see Mr. Holbrook. All three of the fretful visitors were angry about Mr. Holbrook's instructions for not receiving visitors and furious that they weren't informed of his decision prior to "coming all this way" to see him. They released on her the brunt of their anger.

As she sat back in her chair, she reminded herself of her strong resolve the day before to be thankful for all things. Looking back over the events of the day, she had to admit there was only one thing she felt like being thankful for this day: Jaydn Holbrook stepped out of his office at the precise moment she finally had a minute to catch her breath and take a one-minute break in the small kitchen. She was too embarrassed to eat one of the pastries in the refrigerator, even though she missed lunch, and her mouth was watering just thinking about the bountiful supply. She closed her eyes trying to ignore her rumbling stomach, when Mr. Holbrook walked into the room.

Obviously, he was surprised to see her *resting*, quietly drinking a glass of water instead of furiously working at her desk. He demanded, without using kind words, to be shown the letters she spent all morning typing. When she told him they were already stamped and mailed, the surprised look on his face was quickly replaced with satisfaction, and he nodded his approval.

Yes! That one positive, emotional response was something to be thankful for on this day.

She closed her eyes and tried not to think of the one thing she was looking forward to—a hot bath. Her arms ached from spending the whole day at the computer typing, and her head felt like it would burst open any second.

"Well, Miss Candler. If you think I'm going to pay you for a full day's work when you've spent half of it sitting around taking naps, you're mistaken."

Alana jumped up in her seat and stared at him just as the phone rang.

Anger flashed in her eyes as she picked up the receiver.

"Mr. Jaydn Holbrook's office. May I help you?" she said over-sweetly. She pasted a fake smile on her lips for Mr. Holbrook's benefit.

"Alana? Is that you?"

"Brandy! What in the world are you doing calling me here?" Alana turned so her back was facing the irritated man standing in the doorway.

"Lisa gave me the phone number where I could reach you. What in the world are you doing working as a secretary? I thought you gave that up years ago."

"It's a long story, Brandy." She glanced over her shoulder to see if the dark-haired man was still watching her. He was. "Uh, Brandy, did you need something?"

"Oh, yeah! I have some really bad news. I just went by your apartment to pack you a couple of outfits, and ... well ... the place has been totally trashed. Someone really made a mess of everything."

"What?" whispered Alana.

"Books were all over the floor, and the cabinet drawers were dumped everywhere and smashed. Even your bedroom was trashed, at least what I could see from the living room; I didn't stay to look around. It's a mess, Alana. I'm sorry. I wasn't sure what to do, but should I have called the police?"

"Miss Candler. Would you please make personal phone calls on your own time and not on mine?" an annoyed male voice broke into her conversation.

Alana could bear his insults no longer. The emotional strain of being drowned three days before combined with two nights worth of nightmares and the stressful day she just experienced made her reaction to his words stronger than she ever intended them to be.

She told Brandy through clenched teeth not to worry—that she'd call the police after she checked out the apartment herself. Then she hung up the phone and stepped angrily toward the arrogant man glaring at her with his arms folded across his chest.

"I'll tell you what I'm going to do, Mr. Holbrook. I'm going to gather my personal belongings, and I'm going to walk out that door, and I sincerely hope I *never* have to meet such an arrogant, egotistical, overbearing slave driver like you *ever* again. You are the most obnoxious man I've ever had the misfortune to work with, and I don't care if you *did* save my life, I hope I never have to set eyes on you again for the rest of my life!"

Tears filled her eyes long before she finished the last sentence, and when the final word was spoken, she lost the battle controlling her emotions. The strain of trying to repay his kindness in the midst of his demanding personality as well as the rotten day she experienced finally broke through her wall of defenses. Hiding her sobbing face with one hand, she began gathering her things with the other.

Jaydn stood gawking at her. She could sense his confusion by the uncertain way he stood beside her. She could almost see the wheels churning in his brain—trying to piece it all together. The drive home. The submerged car. The woman he'd pulled out of the lake. The same woman who looked like a complete fool blubbering in front of him.

She gave him a sidelong glance. When the blood drained from his face, she knew he'd figured it out. His fists clenched and unclenched in uncertainty. She hoped he was cringing at the commands he'd barked at her all day. He deserved to be brought down a notch.

He took a step closer.

"Please, Miss Candler … I'm sorry. I didn't mean to upset you. Please …"

Alana sniffed at the pleading sound of the apology and fought to control a new onset of tears, but the gentle touch of his hand on her arm only increased her discomfort, and her eyes welled up again.

Jaydn reached one arm around her shaking shoulders and pulled her toward him in an awkward squeeze.

"I'm sorry, Miss Candler. I know I can be a bear sometimes. Especially when I'm swamped with work and can't see the light at the end of the tunnel. My secretary called in sick with the flu three days ago, and it's been a nightmare around here ever since."

He leaned his head forward so she could see his half-smile. "I guess you're *not* from the temporary employment agency, are you?"

Alana took a deep, controlled breath and shook her head. "They c-called this m-morning and said they had no one to s-send you," she stuttered without looking at him.

For a second, Jaydn turned his head to stare through his office door. He took a deep breath and turned to her—a renewed sense of humility filling his eyes.

"Look, why don't we start all over? Let's pretend this day hasn't happened, why don't we?"

Alana nodded and tried to make her swollen lips sound normal as she wiped her eyes with a tissue from the desk.

"I'm sorry, Mr. Holbrook. I didn't mean to fall apart. I really just came here this morning to say thank you for saving my life."

She looked deep into his eyes for the first time and lost her breath at the rich blue color shining on the surface. His gaze reached out to her and probed deep into her soul.

Uncontrollably, her gaze strayed to his lips—lips that touched hers at the lake while he breathed life-saving air into her lungs. The lump in her throat blocked the air and made her breathing raspy. She remembered nothing of the CPR he had performed on her, but the unexpected thought of his full lips touching hers made her blink in surprise.

Jaydn seemed stunned as well. The depth in his eyes seemed to swallow her whole, and she cleared her throat nervously. The sound brought his attention to his arm still around her shoulders, and he dropped his hand as if the touch burned his skin. He took a step back.

His eyes strayed to her lips, and she wondered if he too remembered their contact at the lake. He licked his lips and hurried to comment on her last statement.

"Uh … it was my pleasure, Miss Candler."

He must have realized how ridiculous that sounded because he quickly changed the wording. "I mean, it wasn't my pleasure that you needed rescuing of course, but … well … I'm glad I happened to be there."

Too moved to speak, she just nodded.

"Please, let me buy you supper," he said. "I need to make a trip to Ross tonight, but I have to get a bite to eat before leaving. I'd feel better about today if you'd let me repay your kindness with a meal."

Alana finally found her voice. "No ... no, thank you. I have to get home. I just found out my apartment in Ross was robbed. I need to get back and see what's missing."

Jaydn's face turned one shade lighter.

"You've had a rough couple of days, haven't you? First you end up in the lake, and now this."

"Yeah. Not to mention working for you today." Alana's voice was quiet but held a touch of humor.

Jaydn winced and looked at the floor. "I'm sorry about today, Miss Candler." A sheepish grin played at his lips.

She smiled shyly and ducked her head, a bright spot highlighting her cheeks. "At least I don't have to come back tomorrow." Her attempt at humor made him laugh. Tears still lingered on her cheek, and he lifted his hand as if to wipe them away, but Alana quickly brushed them away herself.

Jaydn dropped his hand. "I really am sorry. Do you think ..."

Once again, Alana found herself mesmerized by the blueness of his eyes, and that feeling smothered out the sound of his words. She could see through his emotions into his very soul, and what she saw made her pulse quicken. Somewhere buried deep beneath that tough exterior beat the heart of a responsive, loving man. A man who could capture any woman's heart. A man who would make a woman do anything for his attention.

She would do anything for his attention.

Stop! She jerked her thoughts into an upright position and tried to focus on what he was saying.

"...so, let's forget today, okay? At least let me take you home. You don't have a car yet, do you?"

She shook her head. "No, I had a taxi bring me this morning. I was going to catch the bus to the police station after ... after I thanked you for saving me."

"The police station?"

"My brother Brad is the police chief."

"Brad Candler's your brother? You're kidding! We went to high school together. At least, we were in several classes together. I'm a year or two older than him, but we were still thrown together quite a bit. I didn't make the connection when I heard your last name. So, you're Brad's little sister." Jaydn scrutinized her face with a smile playing around his lips. "You're not the skinny kid in pig-tails and braces that used to hang around on the chain link fence taunting us while we practiced football, are you?"

Alana had the grace to look embarrassed. "I'm afraid so."

"I guess it *is* a small world." Jaydn seemed to have a brainstorm. "Hey! Let me take you by the station or at least by Brad's house. Maybe I'll get a chance to say hello. I'd love to see him after all these years."

He stepped into his office and came out with his briefcase, then ushered her toward the elevator.

He relayed some of the trouble he and Brad got into during high school, and Alana laughed with him as they stepped into the elevator. Even though the evening air was dark and still damp from recent showers, Alana felt somehow as if her world was suddenly much brighter.

NINETEEN

B RAD WATCHED MARTIN STRANDS PLAYING pool through the window of a corner room in the pool hall—the afternoon sun cast eerie shadows across the pool table as Martin leaned over and made his shot. Suspicion about Martin's being involved with Alana's kidnapping was still rambling around in his head—despite the two friends who gave him partial alibis.

Brad walked over to the front desk and watched the attendant finish his phone call. With spiked purple hair, three nose rings, and a lip ring, the kid in his late teens looked like some of their "customers" in the city jail. When he hung up the receiver, the kid turned to Brad and raised his eyebrows.

"I need to speak to …" Brad checked the list of "friends" Martin gave him who were supposed to have attended the pool party the night Alana was attacked. "Scott Tinley."

"He's not here, dude. Can I help you?"

"What's your name, *dude?*"

"Who wants to know?" The cocky headset irritated Brad. He leaned on the counter, stopping right in the kid's face.

"Brad Candler. Landeville City Police Department." Without changing his position or shifting his eyes away from the kid's eyes, he pulled his badge out of his pocket and flipped it on the counter.

All the brashness of the young man disappeared. His body softened like a wet noodle.

"Hey, man. I didn't do nothing wrong. I'm just minding my own business."

"What's your name?" The tone of his voice got louder and more pronounced.

"Jeff Lund."

His name was at the bottom of the guest list.

"It says here you were at the party Mr. Tinley gave last week at his home on Bickford Road. Is that true?"

Jeff quickly glanced around. Brad could smell the fear in his attitude.

"Yeah, I was there."

"Do you know a man named Martin Strands?"

Jeff glanced fearfully at the pool room door. Moisture appeared above his lip. "He owns this place."

"Was he at the party?"

"Why do you need to know? Is he in trouble or something?"

"Answer the question."

"Yeah, he was there."

"Did he stay for the whole party, or did he leave early?"

"How am I supposed to know, man? I'm not his keeper."

"What time did you see him there?"

"I got there right after basketball practice, about seven o'clock. He was there then. Didn't see him again for an hour or so, then I saw him playing cards with several of the guys. After that, I can't remember. But I wasn't paying much attention. He could have been there the whole time, and I just missed him."

"What kind of car does he drive?"

"Some kind of SUV. Green, maybe."

Brad stared at him, trying to determine whether he was telling the truth or if he knew more than he was admitting, then leaned back and threw one of his cards on the counter. "If you remember anything else about him being at the party, call me."

The kid nodded and looked at the card on the counter.

Brad slipped over to the pool room window and watched Martin leaning against the pool table, laughing with one of his friends. The hotel was only twenty minutes from Tinley's house. Martin could have grabbed Alana, pushed her car in the lake, and returned to the party for an alibi.

Unfortunately, there was no way to prove it.

Breathing out a frustrated sigh, he left the bowling alley and headed back to the station to add Martin's name to a suspect list. The list of suspects was a short list of one, and the list of clues were even shorter—none.

TWENTY

Jaydn stood patiently behind Alana as she rang the doorbell again.

"I can't believe this. I know they're supposed to be home," she said, spreading her arms out helplessly. "Brad told me Lisa would be home all day. I can't imagine where they are."

She took a key from her purse and stuck it into the lock.

Jaydn stepped into the small but comfortable living area and glanced around the room. "This is nice." It smelled clean, cozy, and inviting. He took another deep breath and said with a satisfied nod, "It smells like home."

Loneliness once again gripped his heart when he remembered the stark desolation of his house in Landeville. Closing his eyes helped him enjoy the pleasing smell of the friendly, inviting atmosphere.

"Thank you again for bringing me here, Mr. Holbrook," Alana said. "I'm going to call Brad and make sure Lisa's okay. Would you like a Coke or something before heading out?"

The invitation was given with genuine friendliness, but Jaydn noticed a slight hesitation in the tone of her voice. The fact she refused to look him in the eyes since their eyes linked at the office made him want to explore further.

"Maybe just a quick drink. It's a ways to the apartment in Ross. And, please … call me Jaydn."

Alana nodded shyly. "Okay, if you'll call me Alana."

"That's a pretty name. I never heard your name that night at the hospital. Otherwise, I might have been able to connect the dots at the office before jumping to the wrong conclusion."

Alana led the way through the dining room into the spacious kitchen and picked up the phone to dial Brad's number. "I miss having a cell phone. Water damage ruined my old one."

After waiting for the call to connect, she hung up the phone with a frown. "It went to voice-mail. I'll try again later." She shrugged and put her hand on the back of a dining chair. "Sit here and I'll get you a drink. Is Coke okay?"

"That'd be great."

A strong smell of cinnamon and sugar was in the air. Jaydn sat down at the table and picked up a small piece of paper propped against the flowers used as a centerpiece.

"Hey, you have a note here," he said and handed Alana the white piece of paper with her name scribbled across the top.

Alana read the note and frowned.

"Problems?"

"My sister-in-law's mother had an asthma attack. She went to Waring and won't be back until later."

"Didn't you need to get back to Ross tonight?"

Alana shrugged. "I suppose I'll have to wait. My brother's handling all the paper work for my car, and I haven't gotten the okay for a rental yet."

"How about if I take you?"

A whole host of emotions traveled across Alana's face: surprise, refusal, and ... was that fear?

"No, I don't think so," she said with a quick shake of her head.

"Why not? It's the perfect solution. I have some business in Ross for a couple of days, anyway. Why not let me drop you off at the same time?"

Alana sat down at the table and seemed to melt into the chair. "I just don't think it's a good idea. I mean ... I already owe you so much. I can't impose again. I wouldn't feel right."

Jaydn rubbed his jaw thoughtfully. "Look, if the roles were reversed that night at the lake, wouldn't you have done the same for me?"

When she smiled, he realized his words evoked a mental picture of her pulling his tall frame out the door of a small car in the lake and hauling him to safety.

"I guess that would have been impossible, wouldn't it?"

She nodded.

"Seriously, I mean it though. Let me take you home. I have access to a small apartment in Ross where I'll be staying for a couple of nights until I finish the business for my company. Then when I'm ready to leave, if you need a ride back here to see about your car, I'll bring you back."

Jaydn could tell she was torn—she needed to get to Ross to see about her apartment, but for some reason she held back. Finally, she relented. "Well … I guess so. I really need to get home as soon as I can, and my brother must still be at work. I'm not sure when he'd be able to take me."

"Great! Let me run home and grab some clothes. I'll be back here to pick you up in about an hour. That sound okay?"

She searched his expression—trying to see deep into his intentions. "Okay. I'll try to get in touch with Brad and let him know where I am."

TWENTY-ONE

EXACTLY AN HOUR AFTER JAYDN left Alana at Brad's house, he picked her up and carried her bag to the back of the car to stow it in the trunk.

Alana leaned back on the tan leather seat and tried to relax. Spending four hours in a tight space with a handsome hero whose eyes were a beautiful shade of cobalt blue was not something she looked forward to.

"Did you get Brad on the phone?" he asked as he got back into the car.

"No." She chewed her bottom lip. "It went straight to voice-mail again. Maybe he went with Lisa to take care of the kids and had to turn his phone off in the hospital. I left him a message telling him that I caught a ride to Ross and I'd talk to him tomorrow."

She leaned back in the plush leather seats and glanced at the luxury features.

"Nice car."

"Thanks. It belongs to my company, but it's available to any employee making trips for company business."

"I see." The silence grew until Alana felt uncomfortable. A long sigh told her Jaydn must have felt the tension as well, and finally he started the conversation. "So, how long have you been a secretary?"

"Well, actually, I'm not. I worked as a secretary for three years but hated it."

"Because of what happened today?"

She cast a sidelong glance at him. His face wore an innocent expression. His eyes were on the road. Alana surmised there was no hidden meaning in his words. She was glad to know he wasn't trying to make her feel inadequate as a secretary—just trying to make conversation.

"No. Not really. I got tired of taking orders from wealthy stuffed shirts who had nothing better to do than bark orders at a poor secretary all day and expect everyone who didn't have as much money as they did to indulge their every whim."

He had the audacity to laugh. She glared at him in surprise but then blushed as she realized how pointed her tirade sounded. At least he didn't seem to have taken it personally. "Sorry. I guess old bones resurface sometimes. It's just that in my experience, I've found most rich men are arrogant and demanding—nothing but tyrants in suits."

Jaydn was quiet for a while after her statement. Alana wondered why he seemed disappointed. Maybe he was thinking the same thing about his boss. When he put his thoughts aside and turned to her with a smile, the tone of his voice emphasized the words he spoke.

"You really are a good secretary, you know. The mistakes you made today were because you're not familiar with the way I do things—not because you were incompetent. Your skills as a secretary were remarkable."

She glanced at him to make sure he wasn't pulling her leg, and when she was convinced he was sincere, she smiled.

"High praise, indeed!" she said with feeling.

Relaxing a little more, she sat back in the seat and took a deep breath.

"So what do you do now?" he asked to keep the conversation going.

She laughed. "Well, after I left the secretarial field, I worked for a while as a crime scene photographer for the Bishop City Police Department."

"Crime scenes, huh? Did you enjoy it, or was it just a job?"

"It was a little boring, but I enjoyed it most of the time. It was mainly taking pictures of minor crimes … burglary … vandalism.

Not many murders in the small town of Bishop. I think they only had one in ten years, and that was before my time."

"It does sound a little mundane."

She shrugged. "It was a job. And, I was able to do what I loved—taking pictures. I've taken several courses in advanced photography and used to develop all my own film … until everything went digital."

"That's interesting. So, why'd you leave that job?"

"It was time to leave." The inflections in her voice did not change, but something in her voice must have given away her reasons for quitting because his next question was right on the money.

"I bet you gave it up because of another 'wealthy, stuffed shirt,' didn't you?"

"How'd you guess?"

He raised his eyebrows and smiled. "Something in your voice."

His uncanny ability to read her mind and emotions was jolting. She was always able to keep her thoughts private and not share them with a soul unless she felt it necessary. This man sitting beside her could read her thoughts through the inflections of her voice, and it unnerved her.

She sat back in the seat, determined to give nothing else away. She wasn't ready to share with him the violent way her courtship with one of the officers at Bishop had ended. Neither was she ready to explain her other broken relationship—especially when it revealed her weakness for making poor choices. The words that came out of her controlled lips were light and unfeeling.

"Yeah, I decided I didn't like dating someone in the law enforcement field in the first place—too stressful."

The silence that filled the car told her he surmised more than she wanted him to about the situation, but he let the matter drop.

"A photographer, huh? Are you any good?"

"I won second place in the National Geographic Contest last year."

He whistled. "Wow! That's impressive!"

"Thanks. Only now, I've lost the only camera I had that was worth anything. It was ruined in the car when it sank in the lake. I kept it with me all the time. Taking pictures is calming and some-how keeps me from being lonely."

Jaydn glanced at her. "You should think about settling down. That's a good prescription for loneliness."

That statement surprised her so much that she forgot to main-tain the curtain she pulled down over her emotions. "Have you ever been married?"

Even as the words slipped out, Alana tensed. What had made her ask him that?

Jaydn flashed a mocking grin. "The pot calling the kettle black?"

"Not exactly, but the same could apply for you as well. Your loneliness was shining through your independence when you com-mented on how homey Brad's house was. It might be good for you to settle down too."

Jaydn rubbed the back of his neck and then blew out a resigned breath of air.

"Actually, I've thought about it. It's a nice idea, to go home to someone who loves you in spite of your faults, someone to share your life with." He shrugged. "I guess I haven't found the right woman yet."

Alana nodded as if she understood and waited for him to change the subject, as she suspected he would.

"So, are you still working as a photographer?"

Her soft sigh of thankfulness to be pursuing a more general topic could be heard over the gentle hum of the engine, and she was afraid he might be laughing at her in the twilight.

"Yes, but mostly freelance now. I do magazine photos for a couple of clothing wholesalers and some local department stores. Sometimes I send in candid shots to magazines, just enough to keep food on the table. But, at least I can work where, when, and how long I want to work without having to answer to someone else."

"I know the feeling."

She looked at him and remembered the pressure he'd been under that day as well. *I guess you do,* she thought to herself, but asked aloud, "Do you like your job?"

"I guess so. It just seems oppressive at times—like the whole weight of the company rests on my shoulders. Know what I mean?"

Alana nodded. She felt that way today when she was trying hard to show appreciation for his kindness and everything fell apart.

"What do you do?"

Before he could answer, they rounded a curve and the lights of the hotel where she was attacked lit up the night sky. Alana shivered.

"Whatever you do, don't stay at that hotel," she said softly, still watching the building as if it could reach out and grab her.

The panic she felt was replaced by a serene quiet when she remembered God allowed everything in her life, and He would take care of her. Jaydn leaned forward in the seat and gave her a pointed look.

"A penny for your thoughts."

"I was thinking about all the things that have happened to me in the last four days."

"And, *that* put the calm expression on your face?" he asked with a surprised question on his face.

She smiled. "Not exactly, but it's made me thankful for the things I do have. If you hadn't come along at that particular time, I might not be here. God was taking care of me."

Jaydn's eyebrows lifted in amusement. "Well, it wasn't God who pulled you out of the lake. How do you figure He's the one who took care of you?"

"I believe He sent you to help me." She sat watching his creased brow and the downward turn to his lips. "You don't believe in God?" she asked simply.

Answering that question must have been hard, because he took forever. Then he glanced at her, and the look he gave her seemed to say, "She's one of those,"—as if he could read the word "believer" stamped across her forehead.

"My dad claimed to believe in God. He informed us there was a loving God the whole time he drank ... and swore ... and beat my mom and my brother." He blew out a pained breath.

"…and me. He carried the Bible around with him everywhere and preached at us continually. In public, he was this perfect Christian, but at home …"

Compassion for little-boy-Jaydn hit Alana in the pit of her stomach.

He paused, and she watched him force some of the anger and frustration out of his voice.

"It took me years to realize his brand of religion wasn't the real version. His idea of religion was just a bunch of hot air and lies. By that time, I didn't know what I really believed. I had friends in high school and college who tried to get me to go to church, but I wasn't ready to accept any brand of religion that had my dad's name on it."

Alana sat saddened. Believing in God was such a part of her life. Even growing up, she always went to church.

She turned in the seat and looked at the firm set of his jaw. "You said it took years to realize your father's brand of religion wasn't the real thing. What made you change your mind?"

"I guess it was the lives of my friends in college. They *lived* their religion. Many people *say* they believe in God, but live as if they don't. You know what I mean?"

Alana nodded. She knew exactly what he meant. Sometimes she chided herself for making her beliefs a social religion instead of a personal relationship with her Father. "In other words, they talk the talk, but don't walk the walk."

"Exactly!" He sounded surprised that she would understand.

Alana tried to word her next sentence carefully, but she knew she had to speak from her heart. "In every group, there are those who don't conform to what the rest of the group believes, but that doesn't mean what the group stands for is wrong. Just because your dad *said* he was a Christian doesn't mean he reflected what God is or what He stands for."

Alana turned to look at him thoughtfully and knew she must ask the question. "What do you believe about God now?" she asked quietly.

"I don't really know. I guess I haven't thought about it. I stay too busy to wonder about such things."

"Do you believe that God loves you?"

He raised an eyebrow as he glanced at her. "I'm not sure I believe there is a God."

Her next comment was cut short as they pulled into Ross. She concentrated on giving directions to her apartment, but she felt a numbing sadness for someone who lived his life without knowing God. The Bible was clear— there is only *one* way to heaven— through Jesus Christ and His death on the cross. A person had to believe in God, repent of his sins, and accept Jesus as his Savior.

When they pulled into the parking lot of her apartment building, she sat back in her seat and listened to the motor hum.

"Are you sure you want to do this tonight?" he asked.

Alana nodded. "I want to get it over with, and get things back in order."

"Okay. Let's go."

TWENTY-TWO

J AYDN AND ALANA STOOD STARING at the front door of her apartment.

"Are you all right?" Jaydn asked as she hesitated at the door.

"I guess. I was hoping it was all a mistake, but …" She touched the marks around the door showing signs of forced entry. "… these marks confirm someone was here."

The hairs on the back of Jaydn's neck prickled when he inspected the gashes in the door frame.

Alana fumbled to open the door with trembling hands until Jaydn gently took the key from her. After pushing the key into the lock, he cautiously looked around inside before he let her enter.

"The air conditioning must be off," Alana said as she entered the oppressively hot room.

Jaydn nodded and loosened his collar. He almost tripped over her when she bent to pick up pieces of a broken marble vase.

Tears welled up in her eyes as she laid the large pieces on the table beside the door. "Brad and Lisa gave me this for a house warming present when I moved in."

When she glanced around, reality hit her, and her frame drooped. Obviously, Brandy's phone call hadn't prepared her for the devastation she would find.

A shiver shook her body. A stranger had rifled through her things—that would make anyone feel violated. She slowly walked around the demolished room. When she saw a selection of cameras pulled out of the video cabinet and smashed into thousands of pieces, she sank down on the ripped sofa cushions and rubbed her forehead.

"Why did they do this? What in the world would make someone—"

Suddenly, she stopped and glanced out the window—her thoughts far away. She closed her eyes briefly.

Jaydn waited patiently for her to regain control of her emotions as he looked at the confusion around him. He was appalled at what someone would do to another person's property. The hairs on the back of his neck tingled again. Were they being watched? He glanced uncomfortably out the three-story window. No wonder Alana was upset. She must feel invaded and pursued. A protective instinct wrapped around his heart, and he turned—sensitive to her moves. When he saw her sink onto the sofa and hug the pillow, he could tell immediately she was praying. She was turning to her faith in a time of complete devastation and insecurity.

He watched her carefully as her lips moved, and when she raised her head, he asked if she had been praying.

She nodded. "God wants us to be a thankful people—even in this mess. It could have been a lot worse—I could have been home when they broke in."

He looked at the darkness of her eyes and realized immediately she was completely sincere. There was no pretentious attitude or showy display of emotion. She was truly honest and outspoken with praise for her God.

His appreciation for her loyalty rose high on his scale of estimation, and a powerful sense of wistfulness bounced around in his brain. It would be nice to have such assurance of a Higher Being watching out for you, even in the middle of trials.

He watched as she stood and walked around the room. There were no signs of tears now, just peace smoothing out the wrinkles in her face and a gentle resignation.

"I don't see anything missing in here, just broken, as far as I can tell," she said finally after she inspected the three spaces in the large room.

Her lips quivered when she saw a framed photograph torn into shreds. It was a picture of a bee in mid-flight. She picked it up off the floor. "This is the photo that won second place in the National Geographic Contest."

White dust speckled the surface of the picture. Alana frowned. "Wonder what this white stuff is." She ran a finger through it and looked at her fingertip.

Jaydn took a look. Glancing around, he saw that more white dust was scattered on the carpet outside the bedroom door. His brow furrowed as he brought his gaze up and saw a thin rope hanging from the partially opened door. His senses snapped to attention— once again on full alert.

"What's this?" He stood and turned his head to the side, trying to peek above the partially open door. A wooden platform, barely visible, was attached to the top of the doorframe, and some type of box teetered on the edge.

Alana put out a hand to touch the door, unable to see what Jaydn saw. He grabbed her arm to stop her.

"What do you see?" she asked fearfully.

Jaydn shook his head. As he leaned forward to get a better look, he bumped the door. The box tilted slightly, and the platform shifted. A sudden burst of adrenaline propelled him to action. He jerked Alana back into the living room with one giant sweep of his hands, and she let out a frightened squeal. The pair tripped over a torn couch cushion as Jaydn tried to protect Alana from what he was sure was coming.

Everything seemed to happen in slow motion. As they fell, Jaydn saw the bedroom door jerk open from the weight of the box, and the box fell from the platform. Jaydn turned his head away as an explosion rocked the whole apartment. He fell to the floor with Alana and struggled to shield her from the force of the blast and flying debris.

TWENTY-THREE

W HEN CHET HURRIED TO THE garage where he kept his grandfather's 1988 Toyota, the stars were beginning to peek out in the dark sky overhead. He thought he'd never use the old, beat-up Camry he received when his grandfather died the year before, but now he was thankful for a car his neighbor had never seen. If Pops happened to suspect he was being followed, he'd never guess it was Chet in the old car.

Chet climbed in the Camry, pulled it around to the side of the house hidden from his neighbor's view, and waited. The beat-up car smelled of gasoline and brake fluid, but he didn't care—as long as it ran.

Doubts about his plan crowded his mind when he remembered Brad's words in the department debriefing that morning. "Don't *ever* go into a dangerous situation without backup—no matter how good a cop you think you are."

In the quiet solitude, those two sentences repeated over and over in his mind like a broken CD in a loop.

Is this a dangerous situation?

Maybe.

Maybe not.

Brad might be mad. But, if his neighbor's behavior could be explained simply because he was idiosyncratic, there'd be no harm done. His buddies would have nothing to ridicule him about. However, if these periodic night runs were linked to some crime, especially the sheet murders, it would be worth the risk to find out.

When he had definite proof, then he'd let the department in on it.

Long into the sleepy morning hours, Chet's eyelids drooped. Maybe he would close his eyes—just for a minute. The barking of a neighborhood dog snapped his head up straight again—suddenly, he was wide awake. He blinked and saw a tall shadow move across the yard next door and enter the old shed behind Pop's house. Chet sat up tall in the seat—his hands were clammy—and listened. A motor growled as it came to life, and Pops slowly pulled his white truck out of the driveway.

Sweat rolled down Chet's face and stung his eyes as he pulled his car into the road. A nagging uneasiness urged him to call Kent. He wouldn't be at the station this early, but he could call his cell number—just to be safe. He reached to grab his cell phone, but it wasn't in the holder. He'd left it beside his bed. The call would have to wait.

Chet watched the truck turn onto the next street over and compelled the temperamental Camry down the quiet street.

When Pops reached the lower part of the city and parked outside a run-down mom-and-pop store selling antiques, Chet turned off his lights and coasted to a stop on the corner several blocks away. A short, frizzy haired man rushed out of the building and joined Pops in the truck. Pops popped the clutch and the truck lurched away from the curb.

Chet cranked his car. At the same time, a slow-moving, delivery truck pulled out in front of him. Helplessly, Chet watched Pops make a quick left hand turn at the next light and struggled to keep his neighbor in sight. When the red light caught the truck in front of him, Chet felt disappointment course through his heart. He was going to lose them! Banging his hand on the steering wheel made him feel better, but it did nothing to stop Pops from disappearing down the side street. When the light turned green, the offending delivery truck ambled on down the street.

When Chet continued his left hand turn, Pops and the truck were nowhere in sight.

What rotten luck!

After searching the rows of plush condominiums in the area, Chet headed to the warehouses situated on the waterfront. Turning off his lights, he searched by moonlight—row after row. A couple of hours later, he finally spotted a white blur in the distance parked at the loading dock of a large warehouse. Chet pulled his car over to the side of the alley, and got out slowly. The smell of sulfur and dead fish was strong as he drew in a breath of uncertainty.

Brad was a patient man, but Chet knew patience wouldn't stop the chief from raking him over the coals when he found out what he was about to do—without backup. Following a vehicle alone was less hazardous than entering the suspected hideout of thieves… and murderers. If his suspicions were true, that's exactly what he was about to do.

TWENTY-FOUR

T HOUGH HIDDEN FROM THE BLAST, Alana could feel and hear debris pelting Jaydn's body as he tried to protect her. The force of the explosion sent objects careening through the air toward their unprotected position on the floor. Jaydn grunted as a large object landed full on his back, and Alana whimpered at the impact. Pieces of wood, plaster, and insulation continued to fall around them, and even after the roaring stopped, they could hear crackling and popping noises in the middle of the chaos as it settled in the room.

Alana felt smothered. "I can't breathe," she whispered.

She felt his muscles tense and bulge as he heaved with all his might to move the bedroom door and other rubbish lying on his shoulders. When the door moved a few inches, he shifted his weight, and Alana crawled out from under him.

With all her strength, she struggled to help him move the heavy door and pieces of sheetrock and insulation. Spots of fire popped up around them and grew, licking at the carpet and furniture.

"Call the fire department," he yelled hoarsely through the smoke that was filling the room as he began beating the flames with a small rug.

Forcing her legs to obey her brain's command to move, Alana ran the short distance to the kitchen and returned to throw Jaydn a large, red fire extinguisher.

"Here," she yelled as she dialed the phone with her other hand. The smoke burned her lungs and threatened to close her airway as she coughed her instructions to the 9-1-1 operator.

Jaydn grabbed the red cylinder, pulled the pin, and began

spraying the widening patches of fire. Alana crawled to the windows and opened them both. The fresh air irritated her lungs, and she coughed even harder.

When the spewing noise on the extinguisher stopped, the room was full of smoke, but no open flame lingered.

She saw Jaydn drop to the floor in relief. When he turned and saw Alana leaning against the wall beside an open window, he crawled over to her. "Alana, are you hurt?"

Coughing peppered her speech, but panic strengthened her voice. "I'm okay, are you?"

Jaydn sat up slowly and grabbed the back of his legs. Small holes peppered his pants where pieces of wood splintered through.

"I'm okay," he panted as he pulled the bigger pieces out of his leg and brushed off the rest. He touched his shoulder with the other hand and winced. "Maybe a little bruised."

"You saved my life again," she whispered as she stared at him.

Her voice was steeped in fear. Her brown eyes revealed her terror at realizing that someone had tried to kill her.

Again.

Scooting closer, Jaydn put an arm around her. She laid her head on his shoulder and shook. He held her gently until the trembling stopped, then lifted her chin to look into her eyes.

"Are you sure you're okay?"

She nodded but turned her head to look around her. There was no wall to her bedroom anymore, and half of the ceiling was lying on her bed. The rest was covered in black sooty smoke or debris from the fire extinguisher.

"What's going on?" she asked in a daze.

"Alana, someone's trying to kill you. Surely you don't believe these are isolated incidences."

She shook her head slowly. "Not anymore. But, I don't understand why. I don't have any enemies." She looked around her again in a wide sweeping circle. "Not one that would do this. Martin was upset with me, but …"

At that moment, they heard a frantic knocking on the door.

"Alana, are you in there? Alana!"

Alana struggled to the door and opened it wide to reveal her neighbor, Cynthia Beal. Cynthia was a good neighbor and a faithful friend. She was eighty-one years old and a little on the plump side, making it hard to maneuver up and down the stairs. It was surprising she'd been able to climb the stairs and arrive at her door so quickly.

"Alana! Oh my!" she exclaimed now as she stared at the destruction behind Alana. "I thought I heard an explosion. What happened? Did you let the pilot light go out on the stove, honey?" She patted Alana's arm. "Are you all right?"

Alana smiled. Cynthia's obsessive fear of fire was the topic of many of their conversations. She was always afraid someone in the building would let their pilot light go out and burn the entire building down. Alana could hear the fear in her voice and hurried to assure her.

"No, Mrs. Beal. It was … just … well, everything's okay now. I'm fine."

"Well, okay, dear. Now the fire department will have to come, won't they?" She glanced fearfully at the smoking, charred room.

"They're already on their way, Mrs. Beal. The fire's out, but we've called them anyway, just to make sure it doesn't start up again. Thank you, for checking on me."

When Mrs. Beal was gone, Alana watched Jaydn pull out his cell phone and flip it open.

"Who are you calling?" Alana asked.

"Your brother. He needs to know I'm taking you to my apartment where you'll be safe, just for tonight. What's the number?"

"Your apartment? Why?"

"Look, Alana. Someone's trying to kill you. You need somewhere to hide—a place this guy doesn't know about. At least at my apartment, you'll be safe for the night."

"But, Jaydn, I can't impose on you. Can't I just wait here for Brad? He'll come as soon as he hears, and I can go back home with him. I should be safe at his house. I mean, he's the police chief, for goodness sake! No one would dare attack me there."

"Yeah, but Brad's not at home all the time, is he? I'm sure he's been working harder than ever on this recent string of murders."

Alana had to agree Brad was spending more time at the station. She hardly saw him at all while she stayed with him and Lisa.

"Besides, whoever's doing all this knows where you live. I'm sure he knows Brad's your brother, *and* where *he* lives. It's also reasonable to assume it wouldn't matter if Brad was there, anyway. One bomb would kill you, no matter who else was there."

Alana's eyes doubled in size when she thought about her niece and nephews and the possibility of their being harmed because of her.

"Now, will you tell me Brad's cell number?"

Alana squeezed her eyes shut in resolved acquiescence and gave him the number.

When Brad answered, Jaydn spent time explaining who he was and why he was calling.

Alana half-listened as Jaydn and Brad discussed what steps she should take now. Just because Jaydn saved her life, he thought he had the right to plan her future. She was hoping Brad would disagree with Jaydn's idea and come up with one of his own, but according to what she was hearing, it wasn't going to happen. Both Brad and Jaydn seemed to be in agreement.

"He wants to talk to you," Jaydn said as he handed her the phone.

"Brad?"

"Hey, honey. Are you all right?"

"Yeah, just a little scared."

"I know. Me too. I wish I could be there, but something's come up here, and Ross is out of my jurisdiction anyway. I'll call a friend on the detective squad there to handle the investigation for now. I'll try to get down there tomorrow."

"Brad, do you really have to come all this way?"

"I'd feel better if I were there in person to check out the evidence the police gather."

She nodded silently.

"In the meantime, I want you to go to Jaydn's apartment tonight."

"But, Brad—"

"No buts! I'm not sure the police department will be convinced you need round-the-clock protection, and I don't want to worry about you tonight. At least spend one night there, okay? Until we get something else arranged?"

Alana didn't speak.

"Lane? Please?"

"Okay, Brad, but—" She turned to see where Jaydn was. He was poking through some of the rubbish in the bedroom where he couldn't hear. Convinced he wouldn't overhear her, she asked, "Don't you think it looks funny for me to go to Jaydn's apartment?" she whispered. "I mean it's—"

"Listen, sweetie. Jaydn says the apartment belongs to his company, and they have a live-in housekeeper who stays in a room at the back of the apartment. It'll be okay. You don't really have much of a choice. Trust me. I've known Jaydn for a long time. You can trust him too."

"Okay, Brad. I'll do what you want me to. But, just for one night. Then, tomorrow, we'll think of something else. Promise?"

"I promise, honey. Go with Jaydn tonight, and we'll talk tomorrow."

Jaydn walked back into the room, and Alana handed him the phone.

"Now, get enough clothes to wear for a few days, and we'll …"

"What do you mean for a few days?" she interrupted. "I thought we said *one* night."

Jaydn let out a frustrated breath of air. "Do you have to argue about *everything*? Do you really want to return and stay in this apartment?" He waved his hands around, accenting his argument. "Even if you came back here tomorrow, you couldn't stay. Look at your bed! It's smashed to the floor, and your mattress is torn to shreds. Not to mention the ceiling is scattered all over the apartment. And, whoever did this might be back."

Alana shivered. "All right," she whispered—completely petrified.

The lines in his face relaxed, and he touched her trembling arm.

"Look, I know you're upset. Just take it one day at a time, okay?"

She nodded.

"Great! Now, try not to do anything that might disturb the investigation, but find clothes for a couple of days while I call the police here in Ross."

TWENTY-FIVE

THE APARTMENT COMPLEX WAS RUN down and in one of the lower class neighborhoods, but Martin cruised into the parking spot in front of the first floor apartment as if he had been there before. He jerked his truck door open and hurried to the door marked with the number 15B. The name Sandra Temple was on the metal mailbox mounted on the crumbling bricks. Banging on the door, he glanced around the area—worried he might be seen.

When the door opened and the woman let him inside, Martin strode to the center of the room.

"Sandra, you owe me."

Standing beside the door she had just closed, she raised her hand to her hip defiantly. "For what?"

"For my father keeping your dad out of prison when he robbed that gas station last year. You said you'd return the favor one day, so ... I need a favor."

He waited while she tilted her bleached-blond head to the side and looked at him from the corner of her eye. He could see the *I-have-you-where-I-want-you* look in her eyes and scowled when she crossed her arms and answered.

"Say 'pretty please.'"

How he hated groveling!

"I need an alibi for last Friday night," he said—ignoring her command. "I went to a party at Sidney's house, but I didn't stay the whole night. Now the cops are asking a bunch of questions about a kidnapping that happened that night; they think I was in on it. My dad could fix it, but he's vacationing in Europe with his wife. So, I need you to tell them we came back to your house for a beer or something." He gave her the sternest look he could muster. "Will you?"

Sandra approached him and slowly placed her hands on her hips, then teased him with a smile. "Well, *were* you in on it?"

"Of course not! I just can't prove it. Will you just say we spent the evening together?"

"Marty, darlin', you're sorta over a barrel now, ain't ya?"

Martin heard the blackmail tone in her voice. He shouldn't have come here.

"Look, will you do it or not?"

She wanted to see him squirm, but he wouldn't. She could stare at him all day, but he wouldn't give in.

Finally she spoke. "Can't you think up somethin' better than we spent the evening together drinking a beer?" Her eyes flashed, and her lips curled—a sultry lilt colored her voice. "I could say you spent the night." She leaned into him and wrapped her arms around his neck, bringing her overly made-up face close to his.

Martin pulled at her arms and thrust them to her. "Cut it out, Sandra. I told you that won't work between us. Now, you owe me. Will you do it, or does your *daddy* go to prison next time?"

She stomped across the floor and threw herself onto the couch.

"What's in it for me?"

Martin slung his arm around in frustration and tightened his features. "All right. If you do this right, I'll throw in those tickets to Hawaii you wanted for your vacation this summer. Just say we spent the rest of the evening together and you were with me the whole time. I'll get one of boys to tell the police you crashed the party late, and you and I left together. Is it a deal?"

Sandra slumped against the back of the sofa and crossed her arms. "I guess so, Martin. But, don't come around here again. We're even now."

Martin nodded curtly. Then, he left the apartment and got

quickly into his car. After leaving the area, he finally breathed a relieved sigh. Now maybe the cops would stay off his back.

TWENTY-SIX

W HEN THE POLICE AND THE fire department came to Alana's apartment, there were a million questions for her to answer. Not only did Jaydn call the Ross police department, but Brad also called his detective friend who asked several questions of his own.

No, she wasn't aware of having any enemies.

No, she'd never been on a jury that convicted anyone.

No, she never had anyone threaten her.

No, she didn't know who would want to kill her.

When all the questions were answered and everyone left the apartment, Jaydn turned to her. She tried to hide her harassed look as he put his arms around her shoulders.

"Let's go to my apartment and get some rest, okay?"

She nodded, too confused to even think, much less protest. He gathered the clothes she'd been able to salvage from the mess in what used to be her bedroom, and halted at the door.

"Maybe we should be careful about prying eyes as we leave. Do you have something to wear for a disguise?"

"What?"

"Old clothes? A wig or hat? So no one can tell it's you."

She grunted. "I'll try to find something."

Alana spent the next few minutes sorting through the debris scattered around her bedroom floor trying to find clothes that hadn't been ruined by the explosion, and several more minutes finding the hat Jaydn mentioned.

When she emerged from the bathroom, Jaydn did a double take. "I wouldn't have recognized you, if I didn't know it was you."

Her long blond hair was pulled up in a knot under a large wide-brimmed hat. The jeans she wore were about three sizes too big, and the floppy flannel shirt hung all the way to her knees.

"Brad left these when they came to visit last time. They're a little big, but it hides the real me."

Jaydn smiled. "It certainly does."

Alana blushed.

Jaydn cleared his throat and indicated the door. "Okay, let's get going."

TWENTY-SEVEN

C HET LISTENED FOR SOUNDS OF voices or movement, but all he could hear was water swishing against the buildings. He grabbed his flashlight and a screwdriver out of the glove compartment and got out of the car. Fearfully, he glanced around—making sure no one saw him—and crossed the street to a side door of the warehouse. The lock was old and easily jimmied, so he let himself into the building and gave his eyes time to adjust to the light.

Soft voices rose and fell at the front of the warehouse. Over the top of two brown boxes, Chet saw men talking in a small office located at the front of the building. The words were not audible, but he could barely see through the frosted glass.

Squinting, he tried to convince himself it was *not* a policeman's uniform he saw—maybe a security guard, or a night watchman. He crouched lower and silently surveyed the area around him.

Crowded around the door was old furniture and broken pieces of equipment. He made his way around the pieces in front of him, and what he saw hidden in the back of the warehouse made him gasp. At least ten large, flat-screen televisions stood grouped against the side wall, along with compact computers, laptops, DVD players, and sound systems. A large, wooden display case glittered at him across the way, and he realized it was full of jewelry. His mouth popped open. A yellow diamond ring sparkled on top of the shelf.

That had to be worth thousands of dollars!

The ring was surrounded by several diamond brooches and pins.

This was definitely the proof he needed. He had to get outta here and call Brad!

He glanced around, crept forward, and slipped the yellow diamond ring into his pocket. Now he'd quietly let himself out—then call for backup.

But what if it was a false alarm? What if these items weren't from the apartments of the murdered women? What if it was a legitimate business selling various household items?

What if? What if?

Doubts bombarded his thoughts.

The guys would never let him forget a mistake like this, and Brad would never trust him again.

He couldn't leave yet. He needed more proof.

Listening carefully to keep tabs on the men in the office, he silently made his way around the pieces of furniture, trying to memorize what he was seeing. The reports from the vandalized apartments flashed through his head as he searched through the stash in front of him for something he might recognize as being on the list.

As he turned to check out a rust colored vase, his foot slipped on a cord dangling from a DVD player, and he stumbled. While trying to right himself, he reached toward a leather recliner sitting on his right. Grabbing for anything that would soften his fall, his hand came to rest on the handle that raised and lowered the footrest.

The footrest came rushing up with a loud "pop!"

Panic filled Chet's movements as he righted himself and rushed back toward the door. He had to get out of here! Now!

The voices of the men scrambling through the office door were getting louder. He quickly slipped through the outside door and closed it quietly. Running across the street as fast as his unfit body would let him, he jammed his key into the lock of his car.

Why in the world had he locked his door?

The engine revved up as he turned the key in the ignition, and he slammed out of the side street. The last thing he saw in the rear view mirror was one of the men—standing beside the open door and pointing at his car.

Chet slumped in the seat and slid his car around the corner of an old brick building. He was sure the man hadn't seen him, but he kept the gas pedal to the floor as he sped away.

As Chet turned the curve at the end of the street and went out of sight, Pops came running out of the warehouse. "Who was it, Sam?"

"I don't know. It was the same black Camry we saw following us at the store."

"With no license plate ... and a broken taillight?"

Surprised, Sam turned to him. "Yeah. How'd you know?"

"Charlie saw it in my neighbor's garage ... 'bout a month ago."

"So, you know who it is?"

With a sneer, Pops muttered, "Yeah, I know who it is." The snarl in his face grew darker. "And I know just where to find him."

TWENTY-EIGHT

CHET COULD FEEL HIS HEART pounding a rhythm in his temples as he made a right turn and crept inside a huge warehouse designed to harbor semi-trailers. He backed into the corner shadows and waited to see if anyone was following.

No one passed the bay doors in front of him.

Did that mean he'd lost them? Had the man he saw coming out of the warehouse seen him? He was certain the back of the car was the only thing the man saw. Even if it was Pops, he would never recognize the car and wouldn't know it was him.

What should he do now?

Go straight to the station and compare the ring to the pictures of the stolen jewelry. Excitement built inside of him. What if they matched? He'd be a hero for finding the hideaway of all the stolen items.

The jeers and mocking glances of his friends again busted the hero bubble he'd blown.

What if they didn't match? If this was all a mistake, they'd never let him forget it—especially Elliott. What if it was a legitimate business? After all, he ended up at a warehouse, not a penthouse. He hadn't uncovered a murder in progress. Nothing in the warehouse reminded him of the items stolen from the vandalized homes.

Elliott's words after Chet's last foible burned into his brain. "Another false alarm, *huh*, Chet?"

The pain in his heart talked his head into believing he shouldn't do the logical thing, and his head obeyed what his heart was saying.

No. Not yet. Not until he was sure. First, he'd go back to the station and look at the pictures of the items stolen in the robberies. Then, if he recognized something in the warehouse, he'd tell the guys.

He'd go home now, hide the ring in case it was legitimate. He's put Elliott's name on the box in case something happened to him.

No, not Elliott. Not after the way he'd laughed at him.

Kent, maybe?

Yeah. He'd leave Kent's name on the box. Then when he could prove he wasn't jumping to wrong conclusions, he'd tell the whole department. Maybe he'd talk it over with Kent first. Kent would know what to do. As long as none of the men at the warehouse had seen him, he was home free.

He cautiously pulled his car out of the warehouse and searched the area. By the light of the rising sun's rays, he saw no one. He was clean. Now he could head home—then to the station to check out the pictures of the stolen items. Sometime soon, he was sure Pops would make another trip with the box truck, and he'd be there to catch him red-handed. He might even call backup this time.

TWENTY-NINE

On his way home from the warehouse, Chet planned how he would handle his investigation. Since he was sure no one saw him at the warehouse, he'd have plenty of time to uncover what Pops was involved in. He might even get the names of all of the gang and be able to recover the stolen articles.

He saw no reason to include the rest of the department in the glory if he could solve the murders by himself *and* hand over names to his chief. Why, he might even get a promotion. A smile spread across his face as he envisioned his buddies being forced to admit he was better at investigating than everyone, including the chief.

He might even be recognized by the mayor for single-handedly solving these horrible murder cases.

As he pulled the car into his side garage and yanked the door shut, his ego formed the whole plan in his mind.

He locked the garage door and quickly strode through the house to his den. There, he sat down at his desk and jerked open the bottom drawer. Inside was a half-empty box of paper clips. He dumped them on the desk and pulled the yellow diamond ring out of his pocket. After wrapping the ring in a wad of tissue paper, he placed it carefully in the box and taped it shut. In bold capital letters, he wrote "KENT McDANIELS" on the outside of the box and put it in the back of the drawer. He closed that drawer and opened the top drawer to pull out a yellow pad of paper. He sat for a minute considering the information he'd gleaned about the warehouse.

Carefully, he worded the note he'd leave with the ring explaining how—without anyone's help—he found the warehouse and its contents.

Kent,

I think I've found the hideout for the sheet murder suspects as well as the stolen items. There's a tall gray warehouse located on the eleventh row at the waterfront—the fifth building on the side closest to the water. Stored there are numerous articles I suspect are related to the burglaries we've been investigating. If anything happens to me before I'm able to finish my investigation, check out my neighbor, Pops. He's involved. I found this

The pen froze in the air above the next word when Chet heard something in the doorway that made his heart pound in his chest—the hammer of a gun being cocked.

A voice, low and raspy, spoke from the doorway. "Raise your hands, Chet ... really slow."

Dropping the pen and slowly lifting his hands, Chet looked up to see the face attached to the voice.

Pops!

The blood drained from his face, and he felt a cold wave fill his veins.

"You didn't think we'd let you get away with that little visit you paid us this morning, did you?" Pops said with a growl.

Chet made a feeble attempt at ignorance. "Wh-what do you mean? I've b-been here all morning."

Pops made no comment, just sneered and yelled over his shoulder to someone behind him. "Charlie! Get in here."

The short, frizzy haired man Chet saw that morning bounded into the room.

"Get his gun and hand me that paper. Let's see what my neighbor's been up to."

Chet's upper lip glistened as Charlie pulled the Glock revolver from Chet's side holster with a gloved hand and snatched the yellow paper from the desk.

Pops took the gun, handed his own gun to Charlie, who stuffed it down into the waist of his pants, and read what Chet wrote on the paper.

The darkness of Pops' soul turned the color of his eyes black. He turned toward Chet and pointed the revolver toward his chest. Through gritted teeth, he snarled, "Since I'm the one you call *Pops*, you just bought yourself a ticket to see your dead relatives."

Chet stared into the black eyes and knew there was nothing he could do. His heart pounded in his chest, and he could feel the pulse beating in his temples.

"Watch him, Charlie."

Charlie moved to the front of the desk and pointed his gun at Chet's head.

With his free hand, Pops pulled a phone out of his shirt pocket and dialed a number.

"We got him, boss."

A wave of panic stung Chet's face when he heard the mumbled voice on the other end of the line. He'd heard that voice before.

Pops nodded and said into the phone. "I'll take care of it."

Pops hung up the phone and keeping his gaze on Chet's face, he pointed the gun at Chet's head.

"All right now, neighbor, where is it?"

Chet swallowed. "Wh-what do you mean?"

"That little gift you gave yourself that doesn't belong to you. The boss knows you took it. Now where is it?"

Anger built inside Chet's temples. His jaw tightened, and his lips pressed tighter together. He couldn't cave. He *wouldn't*.

Pops shrugged. "It doesn't matter. No one can connect us with it. We'll find it *after* you're gone." Then, he turned to Charlie.

"Tear another sheet out of that pad, Charlie. Chet's gonna sign another note for us."

Charlie reached toward the desk and grabbed the yellow pad. He tore out the next sheet and set it front of Chet with a pen.

"Now, *neighbor*, you either sign this paper at the bottom, or you've just picked a hard way to die."

Chet's spine went limp, and he sank down into the chair. Sweat rolled into his eyes, and the paper blurred before him.

"You won't get away with this, Pops. The guys at the department'll figure it all out. Then you'll add the murder of a policeman to your list of crimes. That'll guarantee you a death sentence."

Rather than answer, Pops came around to the side of the desk and pointed the gun toward Chet's knees.

"Sign it, or we'll start the shooting with your kneecaps."

Chet stared at the yellow shape in front of him until Charlie reached across the desk and raised his hand to hit him.

"Wait!" shouted Pops. "The boss said not to leave a mark on him. They have to think he did this on his own."

Chet's mind blurred with crazy thoughts of jumping up and grabbing the gun, but he knew they would shoot him anyway. He didn't have a chance. The only way he could make his death worth something was to leave some kind of clue. He reached over and put the pen down on the bottom of the paper and with shaking hands, signed: Chetworth Edom Fabian.

As Chet laid the pen back on the desk, Pops grabbed the paper and handed it to Charlie.

"Print it."

Charlie took the paper and fit it into the printer on the side of the desk. He reached across the desk, pulled the keyboard from in front of Chet, and pounded on the keys.

Chet's mind was racing furiously, trying to figure a way out.

"Look, Pops. If you let me go, maybe we can work out something." His face lit up. "Hey! I can run interference for you at the station. You know—let you in on the evidence they find. Come on, Pops. You know killing a cop's a death sentence for sure."

Pops said nothing—his expression dark and menacing. After the printer stopped, Charlie handed him the paper.

Pops read what Charlie wrote and laid the paper on the edge of the desk. Leaning toward Chet, he looked him in the eye. "I tell you how you can help us, Chet—like this—" He turned the gun toward Chet's head and pulled the trigger. Chet's body slumped to the desk.

"Get the car, Charlie."

As Charlie scrambled from the room, Pops walked around the chair, wiped the gun clean, and put it into Chet's hand. The last thing he did before leaving the room was to touch the point of the gun to Chet's head and put Chet's finger on the trigger.

THIRTY

ALANA STRETCHED HER LIMBS AND sighed contentedly before she opened her eyes. When she realized where she was
and where she'd spent the night, the events of the last few days
hit her like a blow to the chest.

It was 2:30 in the morning when they crashed at the plush
corner apartment, and she had been too exhausted to pay attention to her surroundings. After a five-minute shower, she
dressed in her gown and crawled into bed. She was asleep in
seconds but woke up shaking—convinced the bed was exploding. Exhaustion kept her awake—lying in the jet black room for
what seemed like hours before she finally dozed off.

Now, she glanced at the clock beside the bed and saw it was
already past eight o'clock. Pushing the covers back, she perched
on the edge of the bed and looked around her. The room was
devoid of any personal touches whatsoever. It looked more like
a hotel room than an apartment—containing only five pieces of
furniture in the stark room.

The bed was boxy but comfortable and was covered with
matching sheets, a quilt, and a comforter with a pink swirly
rose pattern. Across from the bed was an entertainment center
that held a television and DVD player, and two average-size
windows balanced the wall on either side. There was a pink
floral arrangement perched on the smooth surface of the dresser
on the right side of the room, with a large mirror attached.

In the corner beside the closet, a rose-colored recliner sat
forlornly.

She remembered taking her shower in the adjoining bathroom to the left of the room. On the wall beside the bathroom door was a chest of drawers standing by itself.

Except for those large pieces of furniture, there was nothing else in the room—nothing to offer a cheery "Welcome." It was a lot like a hotel room.

The black wallpaper was unusual. Silver stripes, laced with tiny rosebuds in the center of each silver band, touched a chord of melancholy in her soul. The shiny black drapes hanging lifelessly from the straight rods above the windows were covered with the same silver color and matching rose patterns.

Alana shivered when she studied the depressingly cold setting and wondered if sadness influenced the decorator's decision.

Beggars can't be choosers, Alana!

It wasn't exactly her style, but last night when she piled into the spongy bed, she was thankful she had a place to sleep without fearing for her life. She shook slightly, remembering what happened to her the last time she stayed in a strange bedroom— at the hotel.

Questions filled her head.

What did this maniac want? Why did he trash her apartment? There was nothing she owned that was that important— worth her life. None of it made sense.

Don't think of that now, Alana! Just one day at a time, remember?

Deliberately, she climbed off the queen-size bed and walked across the plush carpet to the bathroom, where she frowned at herself in the mirror. Strands of hairs hung around her face— limp and forlorn—and there were stress lines under her eyes.

She looked like something the cat dragged in!

A light tap on the door startled her.

"Miss Candler?" A woman's voice sounded hushed through the painted door.

"Just a minute," she called. Slipping into her robe on the end of the bed, she hurried to the door and pulled it open slightly.

An older woman in a white uniform with a pale blue apron

stood in the hallway outside the room.

"Hello, Miss Candler. I'm Naomi Nelson, the housekeeper. Mr. Holbrook asked me to let you know that breakfast will be served in the kitchen area whenever you're ready." The slight Irish accent was almost non-detectable but somehow comforting. The smile on the older woman's face was genuine; her eyes issued a confirmed welcome. Her short, gray hair bobbed up and down as she relayed Jaydn's message—as if it were the most important thing she had to do today.

"I can be down in about fifteen minutes," Alana told Naomi with a returning smile.

"The kitchen is down the stairs and to the right. You can't miss it."

"Thank you."

Alana picked through her small assortment of clothes before putting on the first blouse she could find that didn't need ironing. It was golden brown with small brass buttons and a thin square collar. The only shorts she could salvage from her apartment were blue jean walking shorts that didn't need ironing, so she slipped them on also.

After giving her hair a few quick strokes with the flower-lined hairbrush on the bathroom counter, she opened the door and peered cautiously into the hall. Taking a deep breath, she walked out the door.

As she started down the wide set of stairs, Jaydn's voice boomed from a downstairs room next to the foot of the stairs. She hesitated on the top step, trying to decide whether to join him or find the kitchen on her own. His voice sounded irritated and the volume was loud enough she could hear every word.

"I said I'm sorry! What more can I say? I was detained last night and couldn't pick you up ... I know I should have called, but ... no, I didn't ... look, Patricia, can we talk about this another time? This is a bad time. Patricia ... no ... I don't have time for this now. I have to go. We'll talk later."

Alana was surprised at his angry tone. Even from this distance, she could feel his anger as he abruptly hung up the phone.

Tiptoeing silently back up the stairs she slumped against the corner wall, hidden from the downstairs hallway. He missed something—a date?—because of her. Strange, the way he treated the caller like more of a nuisance than a romantic interest. Her heart skipped a little, but she knew his helping her was only a duty—nothing more. His personality demanded he step in and take charge—it wasn't personal. Even at the lake, he attended to her needs before he knew her personally. He gave that attention willingly but only out of an admirable sense of duty. It would be silly to imagine anything more.

Alana crouched in the shadows of the paneled wall and waited, giving Jaydn time to calm down. She dreaded the thought of confronting his anger. He'd be embarrassed if he knew she overheard his conversation.

Tones on the phone sounded as he called another number and spoke again—his voice flat and controlled this time.

"This is Jaydn. Is Florence back?" He blew out a frustrated breath. "Tell the new secretary I won't be in the office today. I'm taking care of some business in Ross. Tell her to cancel all my appointments and record all my conference calls. I'll have to check with her at lunchtime to see if anything new has come up. If she has any questions, tell her to ask you or Ward. I'll probably be back tomorrow or the next day."

Alana waited until she heard him place the receiver back on the phone, much quieter this time before she carefully rounded the corner and headed down the stairs.

When he walked out of the narrow door to the left of the stairs, she was half way down the winding staircase. A small black bag was nestled in the crook of his arm as he waited for her to descend.

"Good morning," she smiled tentatively.

"Morning," he said.

She bit her lip deliberately to keep from asking questions that were none of her business and glanced down shyly. He raised his head and smoothed out the features of his face.

"Did you sleep well?"

"Yes, thank you. The bed was very comfortable." Something in her tone halted his next remark, and instead he searched her eyes for the truth.

"In other words, you had nightmares."

"Well, to be honest, I did wake up a couple of times with the cold sweats."

Sympathy darkened his eyes. "I thought you might. You should have called me."

The pictures his words conjured up in her mind were startling. She felt the pull of their hearts, and he seemed hesitant to break the connection.

Jaydn took a step back and spoke quickly. "I mean, I could have asked Mrs. Nelson to find something to help you sleep." He looked down at the bag in his hands. "I have something for you. I bought it years ago but then lost interest. You may as well have it and enjoy using it."

He handed her the black bag.

Alana took the bag and raised a brow. "What is it?"

"Open it and see." Jaydn was giving nothing away, so she opened the bag. Inside was a Canon EOS 5D Mark II digital camera with a zoom lens.

She sucked in a gulp of air, and her mouth hung open.

"I ... I can't accept this." She stared at the camera in the bag.

"Look, it's not being used. I have a smaller one I use when I'm in the mood. This one's just being wasted. Since yours was ruined, why can't I let you have this one?"

Alana hesitated, but she knew there was a new sparkle in her eyes. Jaydn would be able to see the excitement even if she tried to hide her delight.

"Go on. Take it, please."

"Well, okay. I guess I could borrow it a while, if you're sure," she said with a lilt in her voice.

Jaydn acted as if he hadn't heard the "borrow" comment and watched her pull out the camera and turn it on. Immediately she held it up and snapped a picture of Jaydn's surprised face.

He grinned at her. "I can already tell you're gonna be trouble. By the way, there's another memory card stored in that bag somewhere if you need it. Feel free to use it. It won't fit my other camera."

He held his arm toward the kitchen. "Are you hungry?"

"A little."

"How about some coffee and muffins? Or do you prefer eggs and toast?"

"Anything will do. I'll eat anything."

Jaydn led her into a large kitchen with a small bay area and a dining table situated at the end of the room. Bright yellow curtains hung in layers around a window seat directly behind the table. Naomi was busy laying out shiny blue plates full of strawberry muffins, slices of coffee cake, and several different types of fruit.

Her stomach growled when she saw the food in front of her. It had been too long since she last ate. She walked to the table, glanced out the window, and suddenly gasped in delight. Outside the window, birds were everywhere. They all gathered around several feeders located head high on the manicured lawn. There were red birds, blue jays, and a mockingbird or two interspersed among a whole group of sparrows, and all of them were feeding from the same feeders.

Alana pulled out the camera and started snapping pictures of the birds as they fluttered to the ground and all around the feeder.

She sensed Jaydn watching her and smiled at him. "This must be Naomi's hobby. I can't imagine it being yours."

Naomi stood back. Her eyes glittered with pleasure. "I love watching them. It reminds me that if God can take care of the sparrow, I know He'll take care of me."

Alana dropped the camera back on the strap around her neck. "'But the very hairs of your head are all numbered,'" she quoted softly as she thoughtfully played with the strap of the camera. "'Fear not, therefore; ye are of more value than many sparrows.'"

"That's right." Naomi looked at Alana with surprise. "That's from Matthew, isn't it?"

Alana nodded but noticed Jaydn's frown from the corner of her eye. She said nothing more but watched the confident manner of the housekeeper as she placed two cups of steaming coffee on the table along with a ceramic cream and sugar set.

"Would you like something else for breakfast, Miss Candler?" she asked. "We have eggs and bacon, if you'd rather have more."

"This'll be fine. Thank you, Naomi." Alana smiled.

Jaydn pulled out one of the chairs and indicated she sit down.

He handed her the sugar and cream, but she waved them away. "I drink mine as black as I can get it. The stronger the caffeine in the morning, the better."

He said nothing, but she noticed he pushed away the sugar and cream from his coffee as well.

She supposed their individual thoughts kept them quiet during the meal, but eventually there was nothing for them to do but speak to each other.

"I talked to Brad this morning." Jaydn broke the silence. "He's coming to Ross this evening."

Alana nodded. "He said he'd come. He's such a worrywart."

"I'm sure he loves you very much."

The scratchy way he said *loves* made them both uncomfortable. Jaydn was the first to look away. He cleared his throat. "I have business in Ross today, but I have a friend who's a sketch artist. Brad and I thought maybe you could talk to him and see if he can help you remember anything about the man you saw in the SUV at the hotel, or the guy in the black hood."

Alana closed her eyes and blew out a troubled breath. "I told Brad, and I'll tell you, I didn't really see either of them."

"We know that, Alana. We're just trying to cover all the bases. Ralph is good at what he does, and sometimes he helps victims remember more than they think they can. Just try, okay?" Jaydn reached over and touched her hand on the table.

The touch of his hand sent sparks through her body, and she wondered if he felt the same. Instead of pulling back, his hand covered hers with a deeper motion. Her chest rose in tiny movements—it was all she could manage.

When Naomi walked into the room, Alana pulled her hand away and leaned back in the chair, closing her heart to the brief moment of regret she imagined she saw in his blue eyes.

Jaydn stood up slowly and took his plate and cup to the sink. "I think I better go."

Alana couldn't tell if their brief contact affected him the same way it had her, but she told herself that it wasn't likely.

"There's a computer and printer in the den if you'd like to download your pictures and print them out." He said, turning around. "There's also a good selection of books and some DVD's in the cabinet under the television in the living room. Hopefully, that'll keep you occupied while I'm gone. I'm leaving the car with Naomi if you need anything. Will you be all right here with her until I get back?"

"I'll be fine, Jaydn, but … are you sure your company won't mind me staying here? You won't get fired or anything for letting me stay, will you?"

Jaydn laughed and glanced at Naomi, who seemed silently amused as well.

"No, I'll be fine. I told you, the company doesn't mind anyone that has business in Ross using this apartment. Now, stop worrying. I probably won't be back until later tonight. Make yourself at home, and I'll see you then."

Alana watched as he picked up his briefcase and left through the back door. The birds outside the window scattered and flew in all directions as he passed by them on the walk. She sighed as they all landed immediately back in their same positions and began once again eating from the feeder.

"That's the way we are as humans too." Naomi's voice was quiet. "We scatter at the least little thing that comes into our lives, and then afterwards, go back to doing just what we were doing before. We don't learn a thing. It's sort of sad, isn't it?"

Alana was silent but watched the birds, a thoughtful expression on her face.

THIRTY-ONE

Pops sat on the unmade bed in his tiny brick house with the TV blaring in his ear and a can of beer balanced between his knees. With one hand, he punched the mute button on the remote while he stared at the phone in his other hand—dreading the private call he had to make. He opened his phone and waited for his cell phone to gain service, then punched in the number "1" on speed dial.

"Is it done?" The voice on the other end of the line barked.

"Yeah. It's all taken care of."

"Are you sure you did it right this time? He didn't talk to any-body else?"

"Nope. He didn't have his cell phone on him, and one of the boys followed him in. There's no way."

A relieved puff of air sounded through the phone. "What about the ring?"

"We couldn't find it, boss. He must have stashed it somewhere."

The silence on the other end of the line was deafening. When Pops could stand the silence no longer, he blurted out, "Well, what do you want me to do now, boss?" His voice sounded desperate as he watched the silent reality TV show flash across the screen.

"I wanted that ring back, but it's not a fatal mistake. They'll never connect it to us. Tell Sam to lay low until we get ready for him again."

"Okay, boss. Anything else?"

"There's just one more problem, but I'll take care of that myself. Just stay near the phone."

Pops pushed the end button on the phone and started dialing again. That "one more problem" the boss referred to made him nervous. The boss didn't like "problems," and lately, there seemed to be an awful lot of them. Sweat broke out on his temples. He sure hoped he wasn't one of those "problems."

THIRTY-TWO

BRAD PUSHED THE DOORBELL BUTTON once more—with a little more force this time. A banging noise finally sounded from inside the rattrap of an apartment, and a raspy voice yelled. "I'm comin'! I'm comin'!"

Brad and Vernon shared an impatient glance. When the woman finally opened the door, she looked like she'd just gotten out of bed—even though it was almost noon. Her greasy brown hair hung in clumps, and her cotton gown was wrinkled and dirty. When she saw the uniforms, her eyebrows shot up. An orange tabby cat escaped out the door and through Vernon's legs before the woman could grab the screen door and pull it closed.

Brad and Vernon turned back to the woman.

"Sandra Temple?"

"Yeah."

"I'm Brad Candler from the Landeville City Police Department, and this is Officer Vernon Smith. We'd like to ask you a few questions. Would you mind if we come in?"

"Yeah, I mind. What's this all about, anyway?"

Brad stared at her through the screen. "Do you know a man named Martin Strands?"

Sandra's eyes twitched and she looked down at the floor. "Yeah."

Brad shared a glance with Vernon.

"When's the last time you saw him, ma'am?"

Sandra shifted from foot to foot, and the whites of her eyes increased in size. "Oh, 'bout a week ago. We sort of met at a party, and then we came by here for a beer … I mean a Coke … I mean, I had a beer and he had a Coke. He had to drive home, you see, so he didn't want to drink and drive." She laughed a hoarse laugh. "You guys might pull him over, right? Anyway, we were just talking, you know? I don't really know him very well, but he's a nice enough guy … not too crazy about cats, though. I have a cat, and they didn't get along too well …"

Brad and Vernon listened to her rambling for several minutes until Brad finally interrupted her. "How long did he stay with you drinking his *Coke*?"

She paused for a minute and panic filled her expression. "Uh … I … really don't remember. I think it was several hours. I guess I had too much beer. I don't know for sure."

Brad looked at Vernon, who rolled his eyes.

"Can you tell me where you work, Ms. Temple?"

"At the Roadster Café. Every weekend."

"Does that mean Friday nights too?"

"Yep."

"What about last Friday night?"

"Look, I told you, I work every weekend. That includes Friday, don't it?"

"If you work every Friday night, then how could you be working at the Roadster Café when you were supposed to be at a party meeting Martin Strands?"

Sandra trembled, and the pupils of her eyes dilated. Brad could practically see the wheels in her head churning, trying to backtrack and make up a lie to cover the one she'd already told.

"Oh … was that on a Friday night? I'm sorry … I forgot. I called in sick that night so I could go to the party. I wasn't really supposed to be there, but a friend invited me just that day, and we went late. Then I met Martin at the party, an' he asked if he could come over for a little while for a beer … I mean a Coke … and …" Her voice died away as she became agitated and reached to close the door. "I have to go now. I have to get ready for work."

"Thank you, Ms. Temple. We might be back to ask you a few more questions."

She nodded and shut the door in their faces.

They grinned and walked down the rickety steps.

"She was lying through her teeth." Vernon declared through tight lips.

"Yep. So, what does that tell us?"

"Martin Strands needed an alibi, so he found one. That means he's probably swimming in guilt up to his eyebrows."

Brad shook his head. "He's too hotheaded to pull off Alana's kidnapping without leaving some kind of clue. I don't believe he's the one in charge, but he might still be involved. Let's check with Sandra's boss at the Roadster Café and come back after we've shot her story full of holes."

An hour later, they sat in the Roadster Café and watched Sandra waiting on tables. She had waited on them with shaky hands and short, clipped sentences.

Vernon pushed the salt and pepper shakers around in circles on the table. "She knows we caught her lying. When are we gonna confront her with it?"

"That's her last customer. When he leaves, then we'll have a little talk."

Ten minutes later, the white haired man left a tip on the table and walked out the door. Brad raised his hand to Sandra and motioned her to their table.

When she inched up next to the table, Brad glared at her.

"We know you worked last Friday, Sandra. Your boss said you were here, and we talked to several of the regulars who said you waited on them that night. Now, how about telling us the truth?"

Sandra's countenance fell, and she slumped down in the seat. Brad could tell from her face—she knew this was going to be a long night.

THIRTY-THREE

B RAD SAT AT HIS DESK and blew out a troubled breath as he listened to the voice on the other end of the phone. The police chief in Ross was not being cooperative. He couldn't—or wouldn't—believe the attempts on Alana's life were connected. Brad leaned back in his chair, the chair creaking as its worn springs protested under his weight. He hadn't gained weight, but the chair had seen better days.

"I know, Chief Carlson, but this is my sister we're talking about. Wouldn't you want protection for *your* sister? Yeah, yeah, I know all about budgets and overspending. I understand. I still have men on sick leave too." He frowned at the clock across the room. "Okay, sir. Let me know if you find out anything else, and I'll try to see if I can come up with a clear connection."

Bo walked into Brad's office and threw down a stack of papers. "I need these okay'd before the bookkeeper will give me a payment voucher." He stared at Brad's face.

Brad stared back. "What're you looking at?"

Bo leaned forward and spread his fingers on the smooth metal desk. "Those dark circles under your eyes. Man, you look like you could use a shave and a shower. Something else happen?" Curiosity resonated from every syllable.

"I can't get the Ross police to understand that Alana's life might be in danger."

Bo straightened up slowly and looked alert. "What do you mean?"

"I mean someone tried to kill her again last night with a bomb in her apartment, and the police in Ross think it was planted to cover up evidence of a *burglary*—only there was nothing stolen. They won't consider giving Alana protection."

Bo went pale. "Is she okay?"

"Yeah, she's fine. Jaydn was there, and he shielded her from most of it."

"Jaydn?"

"Jaydn Holbrook."

"Are we talking about *the* Jaydn Holbrook?"

"What do you mean?"

"Is he the same Jaydn Holbrook that runs International Enterprises down on Fifth Street?"

Brad shook his head. "No way! That's Ross Holbrook. I've met the man. He's a good thirty years older than Jaydn. This Jaydn Holbrook and I went to school together. I haven't seen him in years, but we used to be pretty good friends. I'm just glad he was with Lane when the bomb exploded."

"Where's Alana now?" Bo asked.

"She's with Jaydn at his company apartment in Ross until we can get her some kind of protection. At least whoever's doing this won't have a clue she's there. Listen, Bo. I can't be with Alana every minute, and I was hoping maybe you could help me keep an eye on her."

"Sure, Brad. Just let me know when. I'll mention it to Kent. We'd be happy to take a turn."

Brad walked over to the filing cabinet in his office and took out a handful of files. He placed them in a cardboard box on the floor and picked up the box.

"I'm headed to Ross to make sure Alana's okay. I'm gonna take these with me and see if I can find some kind of connection between all these murders. Let me know if anything comes up."

"Sure, Brad. Will do."

"By the way, what about Martin Strands? How did his other *alibis* check out?"

"Most everyone saw him at the party, but no one could say for certain he was there the whole time. I still have to get in touch with a couple more people. There were some last-minute party crashers he mentioned, but I haven't been to see them yet. If he's bribed another patsy, no one's come forward. He lied once. It's a cinch he'll do it again."

"Let me know what you come up with," Brad said.

As Brad walked through the door carrying the heavy box, the phone on his desk rang.

"Get that for me, will you, Bo?"

"Chief Candler's office. Bo Watson speaking."

Bo straightened up quickly and looked over his shoulder at Brad. "What?" Bo squinted in disbelief as he listened to the person on the line. "Okay, Vernon. We'll be right over."

Bo hung up the phone and turned to Brad.

"Dispatch got a 9-1-1 call. Someone reported hearing a couple of gunshots over in the Morning Side subdivision. When the officers got there, it was Chet's house."

Brad sat the box on a chair, dread filling his throat, making it hard to breathe.

Bo lowered his head and closed his eyes. "It's Chet, Brad. He's dead. That was Vernon. He said Chet left a suicide note."

Brad slumped against the door. "No way! Chet wouldn't take his own life. How?"

"Vernon said gunshot to the head. I told him we'd be right over."

Brad nodded. His hands felt clumsy and numb, but he took the files out of the box and locked them back into the filing cabinet. Then he headed out the door, right behind Bo—an empty feeling in the pit of his stomach.

THIRTY-FOUR

B RAD STOOD IN THE MIDDLE of Chet's den and stared at the scene, hands hanging limply at his sides. He couldn't turn away from Chet's body, slumped over the desk—blood staining the desk calendar and the wooden floor.

Footsteps behind Brad came to a sudden stop. Bo now stood in the room with him.

The police photographer, standing just inside the door, looked a little green. Brad knew it had to be hard—photographing a murder scene as personal as this one.

"When you're ready, sir, I'll start in here, and then get pictures of the rest of the house," the photographer said quietly.

Brad nodded. "Thanks, Adam." Brad motioned to the responding officers who stood waiting for Brad's orders. Huddled beside the small bay window, they were quiet and somber.

"Who did this?" Brad's voice came out just above a whisper as he stared at Chet's body.

His men, understanding that it was a rhetorical question, shifted on uncertain feet and waited.

"…because, I don't believe for a minute it was a suicide."

In order for his brain to accept a fallen friend under his watch, Brad wrapped his feelings around his determination. He *would* get to the bottom of Chet's death.

"Go ahead and get started, Adam. Sam, let's secure the scene. Put tapes across the doors and don't let anyone in without my permission. Vernon, set up the grids and start checking for fingerprints, DNA … any kind of clue. Assign all the grids and record the assignments. We're *not* taking for granted this was a suicide. I don't believe Chet would take his own life, and I don't think any of you do, either. Let's find out who made it look like he did."

The men in the room jumped to follow Brad's orders, and he took a couple of steps toward the desk where he could read the note on yellow paper lying in front of Chet's body.

I'm sorry. I can't take the pressure anymore. This is the end.

Chetmore Edom Fabian

Brad straightened and spoke to Bo. "I thought his middle name was Parker."

Bo shook his head and shifted his weight from one foot to the other. "I don't remember."

"Find out, Bo, and label and bag this note. Tell the lab to check for fingerprints, and get a handwriting expert to make sure this is Chet's signature. There should be a copy in his personnel file."

Bo stood staring at Chet's body. The camera lens clicked as Adam took pictures around the area. Brad rubbed the back of his head. Bo looked a little distracted. He must have been closer to Chet than he imagined.

"Bo?" His voice prodded quietly.

Bo shook his head and then took out a bag from the police backpack he had hanging on his shoulder. He tugged on a pair of rubber gloves and picked up the paper by the tip of the corner—careful not to disturb any fingerprints that might be left. After stuffing the paper into the evidence bag, he also bagged Chet's glasses and the pen sitting on the desk.

The medical examiner came into the room, and Brad moved away from the body to give him access.

When Brad heard a commotion at the front door, he strode out there to see Sam holding Elliott back at the door.

"I don't think you should go in, Elliott. If you do, you'll always remember him like this."

"Let me go, Sam." Elliot's voice was low and controlled, but Brad knew the growl meant business. Brad nodded, and Sam dropped his arm to let Elliott pass.

Brad met Elliot's eyes. "Are you sure you want to do this, man?"

Elliott swallowed hard then nodded and turned into Chet's den. His hands were thrust deep into his pockets and his breath came in short falls of his chest. When he saw Chet's body, Brad saw emotions flash in waves through his eyes. "Who would do this?"

The anguished cry broke Brad's heart, but he didn't try to answer. There was nothing he could say.

Vernon came over to Brad with a yellow pad in his hands. "Sorry to interrupt, Chief, but I think you oughta see this. I found it in the top drawer of the desk." He handed the pad to Brad then pointed to the torn surface. "It looks like the suicide note was pulled from this pad."

"Suicide!" Elliott's normally reserved voice fractured the serious mood of the room into a million little pieces, and everyone turned to stare.

"No way, man! No way! Chet did *not* commit suicide!"

Brad turned to lock onto Elliott's gaze. "I agree, Elliott. Now help us prove it."

In his anguish, Elliott faced Brad, and the air rushed out of his lungs. "I have to get some air."

Brad waved at one of the other officers as Elliott stumbled out the door. "Go with him."

Vernon stood with Brad as he pulled on rubber gloves and examined the yellow pad on the desk. Scratched indentions across the surface of the paper caught Brad's attention. Picking it up carefully, he held it up to the light and had a thought. "Check it for prints, Vernon, then rub a pencil across the top of the page and see if you can bring out any words Chet might have written."

"Yes, sir."

Brad checked the front and back doors for evidence of a break-in. Both doors were intact, but when he checked the door leading to the garage, he saw brown gash marks.

"Hey, Bo. Check this out."

When Bo saw the marks, he shook his head.

"It could be furniture marks. Chet was always selling his furniture and buying antiques. Remember, his dad was an antique dealer before he died."

"Yeah, I suppose you're right. Make sure Adam gets pictures of it anyway, okay?"

Brad walked back into the den as Vernon raised his head excitedly.

"Chief, look at this."

Leaning over Vernon's shoulder, Brad saw only three words revealed by the pencil rubbed across the high areas of the paper.

"murders ... waterfront ... Pops ..." Brad read the words thoughtfully.

"Pops?" asked Elliott, standing in the hallway.

Brad turned to Elliott. "You know what that means, Elliott?"

"Yeah. Pops is the guy next door." Elliott motioned toward the east end of the house. "Chet said he was strange. He told me about a box truck Pops keeps in a shed in his backyard and said he took it out all hours of the night. He wanted me to go with him ..." Elliott's voice broke.

"Do you know his neighbor's real name?"

Elliott shook his head and turned to stare skeptically at Chet's body.

Brad motioned to Vernon. "Tell Steve and Marty to go next door. See if Chet's neighbor is home. If he is, I've got some questions for him."

Brad picked up the bag containing the suicide note and showed it to Elliott. "Elliott, take a look at this. Do you think it's Chet's signature?"

Elliott took the bag, his face twisting. "Yeah, I think that's his, but that doesn't sound like something Chet would say at all. And, that's not his middle name—it was Parker, not Edom. I've heard that word before somewhere. Edom ... Edom ..." Elliott shook his head. "I can't remember."

"Think about it, Elliott, and if you remember, let me know. It might be a clue."

Vernon returned to searching the desk and stood up quickly.

"Hey! Look at this. He held up a box with "KENT McDANIELS" written across the top.

Brad nodded. "Open it."

When Vernon opened the box and unwrapped the tissue paper, a ring spilled out onto the desk. He whistled long and loud.

Bo walked back into the room and ambled over to the desk when he heard Vernon's whistle. He leaned over and examined the ring closely. "Probably fake. Chet couldn't afford the real thing. It's got Kent's name on it, though. I guess he meant for Kent to have it, or maybe it belongs to Kent."

Brad reached across Bo and picked up the ring. He examined it closely.

I'll make sure Kent gets it."

Steve and Marty slammed the screen door as they entered the house.

"Chet's neighbor wasn't home, Chief."

"His truck's still there. Run his truck plates and see if you can find out his real name, then put out an APB."

Bo inserted himself into the conversation. "An all points bulletin? Do we have evidence that he might be involved?"

Brad stuffed the yellow pad of paper in an evidence bag and held it, nodding. "Yep. I think we do."

THIRTY-FIVE

SOUNDS OF WATER DRIPPING IN the shower put a frown on Brad's face as he leaned back in and turned the valve tighter.

"That faucet needs fixing one of these days," said Lisa as she pulled on her knit top.

"Yeah, and I can name several other repairs around here that need my attention as well." A sigh followed his words as he dried off with the towel. Disappointment and self-condemnation weren't a good way to start the day, but house projects didn't frame the frustration in his heart. It was Alana … and the murders.

"Don't worry, hon. There's nothing here that can't wait to be seen about. Soon, you'll get a break and put whoever is responsible behind bars. Then life'll settle down again."

The piercing ring of his cell phone on the bedside table broke the silence, and Brad reached to answer.

"Candler."

"It's Elliott, Chief. Thought you'd like to know what we found on Chet's neighbor … the one he called Pops. His name's Gene Hollister. Six feet two inches, around two hundred pounds, white hair, fifty years old. He has several aliases: Jim Hargrove, James Howell, John Hoover—John Hoover's the most active. Under that name, he's wanted in Ohio on four counts of burglary and one assault and battery. He skipped bail and left the state a year ago. Looks like the man he assaulted was an off-duty policeman."

"Hmm, that's interesting. What else?"

"None of the neighbors know much about him, and we can't find a cell phone or vehicle registration listed in either of his aliases.

His truck is registered to a Bill Waverly. There's no background on him whatsoever."

"How'd you find his record without the vehicle registration?"

Brad could hear hesitation in Elliott's answer. "He'd carved initials several times in the wood on the front porch. After that, it was just a matter of finding the right combination of names."

"Way to go, Elliott. Keep up the good work. Has there been any more activity at his house?"

"Nope. We've had a detail stationed in Chet's backyard watching Hollister's house, 24/7, but no show."

"He's on the run. Notify the surrounding counties about the rap sheet and the updated info, and pray we get lucky. Enter his picture and information in the FBI database and send his records to them as well. Anything else, Elliott?"

"Yeah. If he ran, he left without his dog. It's in a pen in the back, and it seems anxious. Oh, and uh … we got a DNA report back from the lab on a single hair found in Alana's car."

Brad stiffened. "Yeah?"

"It's odd, Chief. The lab sent it through the FBI files twice and found a match both times."

"Will you tell me, already? Whose is it?"

"Kent's."

"Kent's? Are they sure?"

"The lab says it's a perfect match. I figured he probably lost it while searching for clues in the car."

"Yeah, that makes sense. Okay, Elliott. Keep at it."

"There's one more thing, boss." The tone of Elliott's voice changed, and his voice dropped two notches. "Chet had been studying a set of Hebrew flashcards so he could read the original Hebrew translation of the Bible. That's where I saw the word 'Edom.' I looked it up, and one of the meanings is 'red.'"

"Red?"

"Yeah, the color. You know, Chief. Like Bo's hair."

"Elliott! You're not suggesting Bo is our perp, are you?"

"Of course not."

"Well, good. Come up with something we can use, will you?"

"Sure thing."

The phone clicked as Brad slid it shut, and the sound pierced his inner thoughts. Chet was murdered, and in his own way, he tried to send them a clue. If they could just figure it out.

THIRTY-SIX

"JUST PUT YOUR FEET UP, lean back, and relax."

Alana sat back in the brown leather recliner and pushed her legs out in front of her. Across from her stood Ralph Evans, the tall, lanky, sketch artist friend of Jaydn's. He tugged a straight-backed chair into the middle of the room and sat down on the chair backwards, propping his sketch pad on the short back of the chair. He pulled a pencil from the wavy, black curls behind his ear.

"Now, close your eyes, Miss Candler, and relax." Mr. Evans sharpened his pencil in a hand-held sharpener and perched his hand above his pad of paper.

Alana closed her eyes and slowly answered his questions as she relived the events of her hotel nightmare. She heard him scribbling notes on everything she said and sketching pictures when appropriate. She described the hotel, the furniture, the stormy weather, and the manager in detail, but when she got to the hooded stranger dressed in black, her mind went blank. There was simply nothing there to remember. The man's face was hidden, and his size was distorted by the oversized black raincoat.

"Describe his eyes," Ralph whispered.

Alana eyes popped open, and she shivered. "Dark. Black. Sinister. You could see the evil seeping out … like the blood cloud of a devilfish."

"Were they set wide apart or close together?"

"Close—with thick eyebrows that met in the middle. I think … he might have a scar … right in the middle of his right eyebrow. And his eyes were small, but evil."

"Good, good! What else?"

The air deflated from her lungs, and she shivered again. "That's all I remember."

While she was talking, his pencil never stopped until he looked at the paper for a minute then let her see his drawing.

Her breath froze in her throat. Only a few feet away were two eyes fixed on hers—staring at her with the same evil intentions.

She shivered involuntarily. "Th-that's him, exactly!" And it wasn't Martin; she realized that right away.

"Good. Now think about the rest of the face."

She shook her head and turned her face away to stare out of the window. "I couldn't see anything else."

After several attempts at trying to help her describe a face she hadn't really seen. Mr. Evans assured her that notes and sketches he'd made might help with the investigation in some way. There was nothing to remember about the shadowy figure in the SUV. It simply wasn't in her to give.

Angry defeat and failure filled the room as she watched him pull his black car out of the apartment building's parking lot. "Criminal Investigator" was imprinted across the side of the shiny black surface.

Alana climbed the stairs back to her room—her head hung low and her shoulders drooping. Naomi had already made the bed, and she sank into the billowing comforter.

Dear Lord, it's so hard to be thankful when I don't have any idea what's going on. I'm scared, Lord. Please help us figure out why this man is trying to kill me. And help me be calm.

She lay back on the bed and closed her eyes. There must be a reason for the two murder attempts on her life. Was there a common factor between the hotel attack and her apartment explosion?

Nothing but her! What had she done to make someone so angry?

The strain of the last few days constricted her muscles until they were at the point of cramping. Her black leather Bible sat on the table beside the bed, so she picked it up and turned to the first page that opened. The pages fell open to the New Testament book of

Second Corinthians. She rested her head on the pillow and tried to relax as she read God's promise to hear our cries and save us.

When she read verse fourteen, she sat up in bed. The words burned their way into her soul.

"Be ye not unequally yoked together with unbelievers; for what fellowship hath righteousness with unrighteousness? And what communion hath light with darkness?"

Jaydn's face popped up in her head. He was an unbeliever. Was he unrighteous?

"No! He's not! He saved my life!"

The heated words spoken aloud gave her the courage to push the Bible away from her on the bed—refusing to accept the ominous forewarning.

"I will not think of that now," she said aloud to the clouds outside the window as if that made everything all right. She lay back down on the soft pillows and took several deep breaths—unwinding each knotted muscle of her body, one at a time. First her feet, then her legs …

Sounds of children laughing outside drifted in and out of her hearing as she concentrated on loosening her tight muscles. Clouds drifted by the window, and in her tired state, she felt herself drift away on top of their billowy softness with troubled thoughts of light and darkness.

THIRTY-SEVEN

JAYDN STOOD BEHIND THE SMALL desk he was using at the satellite office in Ross and spoke into the receiver. "What about the lot you were checking into for the new parking deck around the town square in Bishop?"

"That's all taken care of."

Jaydn's head popped up immediately. "Oh yeah? How'd you manage that?"

"I went over the lease with a fine tooth comb and found a legal loophole. I simply told the group renting the building that it was being condemned, and they'd have to move—preferably by the end of the month."

"Did I hear you say the building was being condemned?"

"Well, it will be when we decide to tear it down, right?"

"I see. Are you sure that's legal?

"Would I lead you astray?"

Jaydn rubbed his chin with his hands. "Okay. Who has it rented now?"

"Some non-profit group."

"Good work, Steve. You're worth the salary I pay you every month."

"Thanks! Maybe it'll be a little higher next month since I'm worth so much?"

Steve's statement in the form of a question made Jaydn laugh. "Whatever you say. Send me the bill and keep me informed, okay?"

He hung up the phone and stood staring out the window of the office, watching a billowing white cloud that looked a lot like

Alana's face.

Why did her face haunt his thoughts? It was hard to concentrate on the important things—like work.

He sat back down at the desk and began pushing his pencil across the page. His mind was several miles away when a loud commotion sounded outside his office.

Patricia flounced into the room followed closely by his secretary. Jaydn scowled. Then, waving his secretary aside, he spoke to Patricia. "What are you doing here?"

"I told you last week I was coming, Jaydn. Don't you remember?"

The look on her peaches and cream face suddenly captured Jaydn's attention and took his daydreams away from a certain blonde staying in his apartment.

"Jaydn, are you listening to me?"

Jaydn, dwarfing the small desk he was using, raised his head to stare at the face of the woman standing in front of him. Her features were so familiar and yet so foreign. The frown that creased her forehead under a blond lock of hair was becoming all too common—a crack in her composure she tried desperately to hide.

"I'm sorry, Patricia." His distracted thoughts got him into trouble. "What did you say?" He tried to keep the irritation out of his voice, but even he could hear the impatience bleeding through.

Patricia owned an apartment in Ross as well as one in Landeville, but she rarely made the trip to Ross unless she was doing a modeling job. To see her waltz into his small office here surprised him, to say the least.

She blew out an exasperated breath. "I said, I've decided to forgive you for standing me up last night. I'm here in Ross for the banquet we're supposed to be attending tonight. Surely you didn't forget I'm receiving an award for Super Model of the Year."

Jaydn stood up and hurried around the edge of the diminutive desk.

"Patricia, I thought that was next week."

"No, I called and left a message at your house that it was changed. When I called your office this morning, they told me you were already here. I thought you must have gotten the message."

Jaydn ran his fingers through his hair with vehemence. "I haven't been staying at the house in Landeville. I've been staying at the company apartment so I could be close to the office."

"That horrible place! Why in the world are you staying there?" She leaned over close to him and crooned into his ear. "I thought I told you to stay in my apartment if you needed to be closer to work."

It was all he could do not to recoil from her touch. How in this world had he let this relationship progress this far?

His thoughts soared to the petite woman back at his apartment. Comparison was inevitable. The difference between the two women made him sick. Patricia was a fun-seeking, selfish, instantaneous type of person, while Alana was level-headed and stable—the word *permanent* kept stabbing at his brain.

When finally he realized Patricia was waiting for an answer, he pulled her hand away from his arm and walked to gaze out the small outside window. "Patricia, I don't know if—"

"Jaydn," she interrupted with a calculated lilt. "You promised to take me. After standing me up last night, I think it's the least you can do. If I've heard you say it once, I've heard you say it a million times, you hate people who don't keep their word."

Jaydn rubbed his jaw ruefully. She was right. He'd have to take her to the banquet.

He'd call Alana and tell her he wouldn't be home for the evening. If he left right after the award presentation, he might not be gone that long.

"All right, Patricia. What time do you want me to pick you up?"

The determination in her eyes softened, and she picked up her purse from his desk, triumphantly swaggering to the door. "About eight o'clock." She turned when she reached the door. "By the way, wear your tux. It's a formal affair." She blew him a kiss and walked out the door.

Suddenly a cloud of gloom descended over his head, and he sank in the office chair—not interested in business any longer. He stared at the phone for a full minute, before picking up the receiver and dialing the police department in Landeville.

"May I please speak with Brad Candler?"

He waited wearily for Brad to pick up the phone. What a marvelous evening to look forward to: a stuffy dinner with ultra-ego personalities concerned about their appearance and nothing more. He tried to shake the downcast feeling that such a hollow evening would leave.

A more exciting evening was what he had been planning. An evening with Brad and Alana would be much more enjoyable. He rubbed his forehead. Why did time with her seem so important?

"This is Brad Candler."

"Brad, this is Jaydn. I just wanted to let you know I won't be at the apartment in Ross this evening until late. I wanted to spend the evening with you and Alana, but I had a previous engagement that was just brought to my attention."

"Don't worry about it, Jaydn. I need to spend some time with my sister, you know? She's going through a lot, and she needs to know I'm watching out for her."

"Listen, why don't you plan on spending the night? We have several spare rooms, and it'll keep you from having to drive back tonight."

Brad's laugh was genuine. "I'll confess, I was hoping you'd ask. It's a long road to drive that late at night. I was planning on staying in a hotel if you hadn't asked. Are you sure your company won't mind us being there?"

"Not at all." Jaydn's conscience pricked a little as he twisted the truth to suit his needs. "I told you, the apartment's here for anyone with business in Ross. It's fine."

"Tell me how to get to the apartment. I haven't been in downtown Ross in years."

Jaydn had a sudden thought. "Hey, since you have to come through here anyway, why don't you stop by my office and follow me there? That will be easier than trying to follow my directions."

"That's a good idea, Jaydn. I'd like to talk to the police chief in Ross anyway and see if he has new information about Alana's apartment. I should be leaving here sometime after lunch. I'll stop and talk to Chief Carlson, and then I'll call when I'm close to your office. That okay?"

"Great. I'll be waiting."

Jaydn hung up the phone, then picked it up again and dialed the apartment number.

Naomi answered with a cheery, "Hello."

"Hey, Naomi, can I speak with Alana for a minute?"

"She's asleep, Jaydn. Do you want me to wake her up?"

"No." Jaydn let out a relieved sigh. "I'll be home a little after seven. Then I have to go out later. Tell Alana … Never mind. I'll tell her myself when I get there. Just keep her happy for the day, okay?"

He hung up the phone and frowned.

You are a chicken, Jaydn Holbrook!

THIRTY-EIGHT

"Are you all right, dearie?"

Alana jumped and opened her eyes, trying to focus.

Naomi's voice was quiet and comforting as she sat on the edge of the bed and touched Alana on the arm.

Alana rolled toward her and gazed up at her compassionate face. "I'm okay." Even Alana could hear how sluggish her speech sounded.

Naomi patted her on the arm. "I'm sorry to wake you, but I was afraid if you slept any longer, you'd be up again tonight like you were last night."

Alana propped herself on her elbows and looked at the kind woman. "How did you know?"

"Most young people your age don't have dark circles under their eyes unless they miss a few nights of sleep."

Alana blew out a troubled breath.

"Trust in the Lord, dearie. He'll take care of you."

Alana considered her with renewed surprise. "You're a Christian, aren't you?"

Naomi smiled her pleasure. "I gave myself to God forty-one years ago, and I haven't had a single moment of regret."

"I've been trying to trust Him, but it's hard when I can't understand why He's allowing all these things to happen. What's the purpose?"

"Does there have to be a purpose?"

Alana thought about that question for a minute before answering.

"I know we're supposed to glorify God in all things, but how can someone trying to take my life glorify God?"

"It's not God's taking away the trouble that glorifies Him—it's our praise of Him even in the midst of trouble. That's what glorifies Him."

Alana stored that thought in the back of her mind for future analysis. The wisdom of this woman made sense. How had Jaydn escaped believing in God's existence when this woman influenced his life daily?

"Jaydn doesn't believe God exists, does he?" Alana asked.

Naomi shook her head sadly. "He had a hard childhood, that one did. His father just about beat all the believing out of him. But, I've seen a change in the last couple of years. He's mellowed some. I don't think it would take too big of a push to get him moving in the right direction." She looked at Alana with a smile on her face.

A deliciously spicy fragrance wafted into the room, and Alana sniffed the air.

Naomi stood up and glanced toward the door. "Are you hungry? I've been keeping lunch warm for you. You can come down anytime you get hungry."

Alana looked at the clock on the wall beside the door. It was two o'clock. No wonder her stomach was doing flips, trying to get her attention.

"I'll be right down, and thank you."

Naomi patted her on the arm and, with a smile, walked out the door.

Alana gazed at the open doorway where Naomi exited and wondered if she would ever be as confident in her faith as the saintly woman who managed to calm her worries.

Thank you, Lord, for that encouragement!

To Alana, the rest of the afternoon seemed to drag. Just a few hours turned into what seemed like days. Too restless to watch a movie or read, she followed Naomi through the house helping with the housework until finally begging Naomi to let her help with supper.

"No, dearie. There's nothing you can do. It's all taken care of."

She looked at Alana's frustrated features. "Now, let's see. Jaydn said to keep you happy, and that means keeping you busy, right? Why don't you go for a swim? There's a pool for the apartment building out back, if you like to swim."

When Naomi saw Alana frown, she quickly added, "Or, you could just watch the kids from the apartment's day care as they swim. The owners bring them out to play in the water every afternoon."

Alana thought for a minute and then smiled. "That might be fun."

As Alana walked toward the pool area, she heard excited voices of children playing and loud splashes of water on cement. Crepe myrtle bushes full of red, pink, and white blooms hugged the chain link fence surrounding the pool.

She strolled through the open gate and found an unoccupied lounge chair. The chair, warmed by the sun, welcomed her, and she stretched out and relaxed. The antics of the children playing in the pool kept her entertained. She laughed aloud when an impish little boy drew both legs up as he jumped into the pool yelling, "Cannonball!" Water splashed up over both his teachers. Both of the ladies screamed and leaped away from the pool's edge.

"Okay, Jimmy Lance, I guess that means you're ready to get out of the pool," said the younger of the two as she wiped her face with a towel.

Moans and groans from all the kids grew until the teachers had all the kids lined up and marching back to the building.

It was so peaceful by the pool that Alana stayed there after the children left. She wondered whether Brad would be arriving soon. Jaydn would surely be arriving before long; it had to be near suppertime.

The sparkling water invited Alana to dip her toes in its warmth. Swimming was something she had no interest in after nearly drowning, but dipping her feet in the clear water would be fun. Alana took off her sandals and sat down on the deep side of the pool, dangling her feet into the water. She smiled.

Sparkles reflected across the clear water—magnifying the

turquoise patterns of the liner and making them sharp and clear.

Clouds overhead were lined with a deep red and orange hue that glittered in the fading sunlight. The sun hovered just above the trees forming a halo of white and yellow around each pine frond. She smiled and sighed with contentment. She was safe here, surrounded by beauty.

Then she looked at the water in the pool. Memories of water filling her lungs at the lake made her shiver.

She closed her eyes and prayed for peace and protection.

Footsteps sounded behind her. A smile began to spread across her face, sure it was Jaydn or her brother coming to greet her. She took her feet out of the water, preparing to stand and turn around. Before she could complete the action, strong hands hit her back and shoved her into the pool.

As she sank beneath the water, Alana fought the panic rising in her chest. Who had pushed her in? Was this some kind of cruel joke?

Struggling back to the surface, Alana could see a dark figure standing at the edge of the pool with a long pole—his face covered with a dark hood.

Horror froze her limbs until she realized she had to get away. Adrenaline gave her the energy she needed to strike out for the opposite end of the pool—to put distance between her and her attacker. If she could get out of the water on the other side of the pool, she could scream for help. Surely someone would hear her. Terror circled her like the fog in the mountains.

When she broke through the surface at a full swim, she felt something close over her head and push her back under water. She reached up to grapple with it, and her hands met metal and netting. Clawing and pushing with her hands, she tried to remove the stiff material from her head, but the person above her was jabbing the net harder onto her head, forcing her to the bottom of the pool. Her lungs begged for air as she fought to free herself. Hysteria rose in her throat and threatened to engulf her.

Lord, help me! Help!

THIRTY-NINE

Jaydn met Brad on the street in front of his office and smiled.

"Hello, my friend," he said as he shook Brad's hand.

"It's been a long time, hasn't it?"

"Too long."

"Yep." Brad nodded. "Talking with you the other night brought back good memories, Jaydn. I really enjoyed the fun we had in school together. How did we let ourselves drift so far apart?"

Jaydn shrugged. "Going to different universities didn't help. Then I guess we both got caught up in our jobs and responsibilities. It happens."

Brad tilted his head and grinned. "Best I remember, you were the best quarterback the school ever had. I sort of figured you'd get a free ride to college on a football scholarship."

"Nope," said Jaydn proudly. "I ended up with a master's degree in business administration." His sheepish grin peeped out of his reddening face. "To be honest, the only reason I played football in high school in the first place was because of the cheerleaders."

Brad laughed. "Yeah, you *were* pretty popular with the ladies."

They both laughed, and Jaydn's eyebrows rose in a teasing sort of way. "I remember a couple of interesting facts about you too— like you being named 'King of the Wrestling Team.' And, I think those toned muscles of yours seemed to draw a few flies of your own." He rubbed his mouth with his hand, and Brad could tell he was hiding a grin.

It was Brad's face that reddened this time. "Touché. I won't mention your past if you won't mention mine."

They both shared a laugh.

"I'll tell you what," Jaydn said suddenly. "Instead of following my car back to the apartment, why don't we just take yours? That will give us more time to catch up."

With that settled, they climbed into Brad's car and pulled away from the office. They shared a few more laughs on the way to the apartment. Laughing was rare for Brad these days, and it felt good. But the humor in his heart quickly morphed into sorrow when Chet's death invaded his memory. Brad stilled.

Jaydn notice the change. "Alana tells me things have been rough for you lately."

A long sigh was Brad's only answer for the space of a minute. Then he said, "Alana doesn't know the half of it. We found one of my men murdered yesterday. Whoever did it tried to make it look like suicide, but we're pretty sure from the evidence we've compiled … he was murdered."

Jaydn sucked in his breath. "Man, I'm sorry. Do you have any idea who did it?"

"We think it might have something to do with the serial murders we've been investigating. The murdered man's partner told us Chet suspected his neighbor, but we haven't been able to find him to question him."

"Do you have any leads in any of the murders?"

Brad shook his head. Defeat polluted the air like a cloud of gas. "Nothing."

He banged his fist on the steering wheel. "You would think after seven murders, they'd leave something! A cigarette butt, fingerprints, or a small bit of DNA—something! These people are good. They cover all the bases. We don't have a clue."

"Do you think it's more than one person? I mean … the way you're talking, it might be a gang or something."

Brad shook his head. "We don't know for sure. It would be hard for one man to single-handedly do everything we suspect them of doing."

"I'm sorry, Brad. I wish I could help. I know all this with Alana isn't helping either."

"I don't want her to know about this if I can help it. She wasn't *best* friends with Chet, but they were friends. She's upset enough as it is. If she knew I had Chet's murder to worry about as well as everything else, and now this with her ..."

Jaydn waited for Brad to continue.

"The fact is ... I'm worried sick about her. I can't concentrate on this murder investigation for worrying about her safety. You don't know how much I appreciate your letting her stay with you last night. For the first time since all this started, I didn't worry about her. I actually knew she was safe."

"I'm glad, Brad. She can stay as long as you need her to. What about the police here? Have they agreed to give her protection?"

Brad laughed angrily. "*Humph!* That's a laugh! They won't even consider it unless I show some kind of motive. They still think blowing up her apartment was to hide evidence of a burglary."

"But nothing was missing from the apartment."

"Chief Carlson said they probably got scared off before they were able to take anything."

"What about the business at the hotel and the lake?"

"We can't prove it even happened—except for Alana's word. There's nothing to prove her story, and I'm not even sure they believe her. If they do, they can't see how the two attacks are connected. In their eyes, it's just coincidence." Exasperation bled through his voice.

"Did they gather anything they could use from the bomb in her apartment?"

Brad shook his head. "The only thing we know was that it was wet dynamite."

"Wet dynamite! How does it explode if it's wet?"

"When it gets wet—*really* wet—it's about as bad as nitroglycerine—very volatile. It doesn't even need a detonating device. Any kind of jolt will make it explode. That's why it was put over the bedroom door. It would have exploded on top of her if you hadn't ..." He shuddered then spoke with feeling. "Jaydn, I have to tell you again how much it means—you saving Alana's life at the lake and at her apartment. She means the world to me, and ..." His voice broke, and he rubbed his face to gain control. Turning to his friend, he nodded. "I'll never forget it, man."

Jaydn's cleared his throat and turned away from Brad's gaze. Neither of them spoke again until they pulled into the apartment parking lot.

Brad turned to Jaydn. "Was Alana *sure* nothing was taken from her apartment?"

"Yes. As far as she could tell, everything was there."

"Then what was the point? I can't figure it out. She has nothing of great value. What's this lunatic looking for?"

"Maybe he wasn't looking for something particular. Maybe he's just trying to get to her."

"Then why trash her apartment?"

They sat in silence staring at the three-story apartment building.

"Maybe the bomb was planted later ... after they ransacked the place. Brad, you don't suppose ..." He stopped in mid-sentence. "Hey, look over there!"

Brad turned to look at the end of the parking lot. Beside the pool, he saw a hooded man with a pole in his hand, pushing on something in the pool. Just the hood itself was enough to make his blood turn cold, but to see the angry force he was using made his stomach leap into his throat.

Brad turned as white as a sheet and looked at Jaydn. "Was Alana going swimming today?"

Jaydn didn't answer but jumped out of the car and headed toward the pool at the fastest run he could manage. Even so, Brad still beat him as he pushed through the hedges and ran toward the figure in the pool.

FORTY

JAYDN DASHED ACROSS THE PARKING lot—the terror he felt for Alana pumped a burst of power into his legs. Surreal images of her drowning in a car, exploding in a blast, fighting for air at the bottom of a pool swirled in his mind.

The man in the mask heard Brad's shouts and loosened his hold on the pool net as his head turned to see Brad and Jaydn running toward him.

Alana twisted to the side of the net with a frantic jerk. When the net went slack, she pulled the pole out of the hands of her attacker. Wrenching the net off her head, she kicked away from that side of the pool.

When her head broke through the surface, she gasped a mouthful of air and water and began coughing from deep in her chest. Her wild-eyed gaze swept the poolside area for a glimpse of her attacker, who had pivoted to make his escape. She heard shouts from Brad and Jaydn, and relief flowed through her. Her legs thrashed weakly like spaghetti noodles as she tried to reach safety. Coughing zapped what little strength remained, and she feebly sank back into the water near the opposite side of the pool.

Running around the bushes toward the gate, Jaydn thought they would never reach her in time. Brad ignored the gate. Instead, he took one leap and sailed over the fence, yelling, "Hold on, Alana!" He leaned over the edge of the pool and grabbed the sleeve of her shirt.

Jaydn was right behind him, and Brad motioned for Jaydn to take her arm. Brad pulled out his revolver and chased after the man who bounded over the chain link fence surrounding the pool. Then, he disappeared into the hedges.

With one jerk, Jaydn had Alana sitting on the edge of the pool. Looking up in fright, she recognized him. Realizing she was safe, she covered her face with her hands and sobbed between coughing spells. He wrapped his jacket around her, then pulled her into his arms and let her cry on his shoulder.

"It's okay, Alana. You're okay. We're here. We won't let anyone hurt you."

Her sobs filled the air around the pool and seemed to vibrate off the water.

"W-why is this h-happening?" she sobbed.

"It's okay," Jaydn kept repeating. He tenderly kissed her on the forehead, and held her close.

When finally her sobbing slowed, she leaned back away from his shoulder and whimpered, "I'm g-getting your jacket w-wet."

"It's okay, honey." He leaned back and looked at her wet face. Pushing the wet strands of hair from her eyes, he asked, "Are you hurt?"

Before she could answer, Brad pushed through the hedges close to the swimming pool and trudged through the open gate.

Jaydn looked over Alana's head—a question in his eyes. Brad shook his head—defeat obvious by his stooped shoulders. "Let's go inside," he said with an uneasy look around the apartment grounds.

As Alana stood, her wobbly legs refused to bear her weight. She stumbled and fell forward. Jaydn didn't say a word. He caught her before she hit the ground, and without even a grunt, he picked her up and carried her out of the pool area.

At first, Alana struggled to be set down, but her weak limbs finally gave in. Submissively, she relaxed back in his strong arms and let his warmth radiate through her wet clothes.

Although the weather was still very warm, Alana shivered uncontrollably from shock. A strong sense of protectiveness invaded Jaydn's heart as he felt her light weight in his arms.

Back in the apartment, Jaydn let Naomi fuss over Alana until she was in warm clothes with towel-dried hair and sitting on the couch in the living room wrapped in a warm quilt. She turned on the television to keep Alana occupied, then hurried to the kitchen to make hot chocolate.

Brad was sitting at the kitchen table with a pad of paper in front of him, talking on the phone with Chief Carlson. Standing halfway between the kitchen and the living room, Jaydn watched Alana sitting bundled on the couch, her eyes staring unseeingly at the television. He was watching Alana, but his ears were tuned to Brad's conversation with the Ross police chief.

When Brad put the phone back on the receiver, he turned to Jaydn with a furrowed brow.

"He's sending a cruiser to take our statements. I think he finally realizes Alana's in danger."

Even from a distance, Jaydn could see a pale tint to Alana's lips. He sent a pointed look to Brad then nodded in Alana's direction. "She's pretty upset."

Brad ran his fingers through his hair. "Nothing like this has ever happened to us. She's always been a strong person, but I can tell that she's in trouble if this keeps up. I bet she's not sleeping at all." He hit the table lightly with his fist. "It just doesn't make sense. She doesn't have an enemy in the world. She's a friend to everyone she meets. Alana is one of those people who picks up every stray cat and dog she sees to find them a home and keep them from suffering. I can't figure out why anyone would want her dead."

"Maybe it's something to do with your job. In your line of work, haven't you had people who vowed to get revenge for one reason or another?"

Brad shook his head. "I've only been chief of police for a year. I haven't had time to make serious enemies yet. Before that, I worked for the investigation division. Nothing there to make enemies, either. What really scares me though, is how the perp knew she was here."

Jaydn's head jerked up, and he stared at Brad. "That's right," he said in a low voice. "How *did* he know she was here? She was disguised when we left her apartment. I don't even think you'd have been able to recognize her. I took a back road here in case someone might have followed us, and I even parked in front of the apartments across the road in case someone did find the complex."

"Did anyone see you leave the apartment?"

"There was man washing his car at the end of the building, but he hardly looked our way."

"Did you tell anyone she was here?" Brad studied him carefully.

"No, just Naomi." He turned to look at the housekeeper, a question in his eyes.

"No, sir. I didn't tell a soul," Naomi assured him as she stirred the hot chocolate on the stove.

"What about you, Brad? Have you mentioned it to anyone? Someone who might have mentioned it to a friend?"

"I didn't tell anyone, except for Lisa. She wouldn't mention it to a soul. She knows enough about my work to know better. What about Alana? Has she talked to anyone since you brought her here?"

Jaydn once again looked to Naomi for the answer.

"Not to my knowledge, sir. She spent most of the day with me too."

Jaydn pulled the kitchen chair out farther from the table so he could sit down and still see Alana. His concern for her grew. Her soft smile and familiar presence got under his skin. "You know what this means, don't you?"

"We're going to have to move her again."

"Or get full police protection."

"No good." Brad shook his head. "Chief Carlson says even if he has positive proof she's in danger, he doesn't have the manpower to leave someone with her twenty-four/seven. Three-fourths of his men are out with the flu. He suggested finding a safe-house that no one knows about."

Suddenly, Jaydn tapped his head with the palm of his hand. "I have the perfect solution. I bought a house in the mountains about six months ago to spend time there on my days off—which I haven't had yet." He grimaced. "No one knows about it but my lawyer. It's on an island surrounded by Lake Monty and one hundred acres of dense wooded mountains. There's only one access to the house—across a bridge that spans the lake. And, the house has a full security system."

Brad sighed with relieved caution. "That sounds perfect. What about access from the lake?"

Jaydn shook his head. "There's a swimming beach about a mile from the lake, but it's secluded, and there's no boat entrance."

Brad tapped his chin and nodded. "That sounds perfect."

Jaydn reached for the phone. "I'll call for the company helicopter and take her up there myself until you get this figured out."

Brad leveled a thoughtful gaze at Jaydn. "One of my men said … that is … what company do you work for? Is it International Enterprises?"

Jaydn closed his eyes and pinched the bridge of his nose. After a moment, he nodded.

"Are you related to the Ross Holbrook who owns International Enterprises?"

After a glance at Alana, Jaydn responded in a low voice. "He was my father, but he died about two years ago. I run the company now."

Brad whistled. "Man! The kids in school were right when they voted you 'Most Likely to Succeed.' I can't believe it."

Jaydn felt Brad staring at his lowered head. Discomfort grew in the pit of his stomach.

Brad finally spoke. "Does my knowing bother you?"

Jaydn hung up the phone and looked again into the living room where Alana was flipping channels. He shook his head. "People treat me like I'm from outer space when they find out I own the biggest company in the state. So, I don't mention it. People tend to think wealthy men are … well …" He shrugged, and his focus strayed to the blonde sitting on the couch, "arrogant and demanding tyrants."

The conversation with Alana had stung—her exact words opening a raw wound. For the first time in his life, he felt his money was a liability. Jaydn watched Alana. He could tell from the look Brad gave him that Brad understood more than Jaydn wanted him to. He was sure Brad knew of Alana's views about people with money—especially bosses and company owners.

"Jaydn, I think you're a great guy. Rich ... poor ... owner of a company or not. I've always thought you were. I'm sure when Alana gets to know the real you, she'll think so too. But, if it means that much, I'll keep your secret."

Jaydn's spirits soared in the light of Brad's honest praise and promise. "Thanks, Brad. You don't know how much I appreciate that."

"Let's get back to this house you're talking about. How far is it from here, anyway?"

"Almost two hours—probably thirty minutes with the helicopter."

"Is anyone up there now?"

"I have permanent staff that live on the property. A man and his wife keep up the grounds and the housekeeping. Naomi will probably come later. She usually goes with me when I travel."

"Bo will really flip when I tell him he was right about you," Brad said as he shook his head.

"Who's Bo?"

"One of our detectives. He was asking me the other day ..." Suddenly, Brad froze in mid-sentence.

"What's the matter?"

"I told Bo where Alana was staying," he announced quietly.

"Do you think he might have leaked it?"

"I don't know, but I intend to find out."

Brad picked up the phone receiver again. His dialing was interrupted by Jaydn's exclamation.

"Brad! The news!"

Brad turned to see what had captured Jaydn's attention. Spread across the TV screen in front of Alana was a picture of Chet Fabian, and the newscaster was repeating the facts of his death.

Alana stood up shakily, still wrapped in the quilt. Her face—
bleached a frosty white—turned from the television screen to
meet her brother's gaze with a dazed look. "Brad ..." she whispered. Then, she grabbed for the back of the chair before the
world around her collapsed and she slid to the floor.

FORTY-ONE

A WET WASHCLOTH WAS PRESSED TO Alana's forehead. Her head felt as if it had been pounded with a meat tenderizer. She lifted a shaky hand and touched her numb lips. "Can I please have some water?" she whispered.

Naomi appeared suddenly with a glass of ice and water. "Here you go, dearie. I put a straw in the glass."

Alana sipped the water and looked around at the three concerned faces hovering above her head.

"What happened?"

"You fainted, munchkin."

Brad's face was strained as he knelt beside her—his hand patting her own.

"Brad, the news! Why didn't you tell me about Chet?"

"You didn't need something else to deal with right now, Lane."

"But, they said he committed suicide. That can't be true, can it?"

"They said 'apparent' suicide, Lane, and you're right—it wasn't suicide." He left the rest unsaid.

"Oh, Brad! Poor Chet."

Jaydn turned to Naomi.

"Would you mind getting Alana's things together? We're moving her tonight."

Naomi nodded in complete agreement as she started up the stairs. "I'll only be a minute."

Brad sat down beside Alana on the couch and picked up her hands. "Alana, whoever tried to kill you tonight knows you're here, so we're moving you to another location."

She lowered her head to hide the tears as she shivered with a ripple of fear. "Brad, I'm scared."

"Hey," Jaydn chided softly as he perched on the end of the couch, "What about that God of yours? Didn't you say He was protecting you? He brought Brad and me here tonight at just the right time, didn't He?"

Shame circulated through Alana's body. Some testimony she was showing. She nodded her head. "Where are we going?" she asked meekly.

Brad rubbed her back in a soothing motion. "Jaydn has a house in the mountains. It's off by itself, away from other houses, and no one knows about it but us."

Alana looked up into Jaydn's eyes. "Does it belong to your company too?"

Something inside him turned his eyes a deep shade of blue as he glanced at Brad and said, "It belongs to me, Alana. And, you're welcome to stay there as long as you need a safe place. There's a nice couple who stays there and keeps the house and grounds. Naomi will fly over later." His eyebrows were raised—waiting for her approval.

They sat staring at each other for what seemed like an eternity. Finally, Alana nodded in assent.

Jaydn stood up abruptly. "I'll take Alana tonight. Naomi will come tomorrow. She'll have to close up everything before she can leave here. Brad, will you go back to Landeville tonight?"

Brad shook his head. "No, I've done what I can there until some of the lab results come in. I'll probably stay here, if that's still okay?"

Jaydn nodded. "Stay as many nights as you like. If you need to come back to Ross for something else, use the apartment, okay?"

"Thanks, Jaydn." He turned a pointed look at Alana. "For everything." Alana blushed and lowered her head. Embarrassment flooded through her. Protecting her was consuming the time and energy of so many people.

Naomi came trudging down the stairs with a small bag in her hands. "This is all I could find. You didn't bring much," she said to

Alana as she handed her the small bag and her worn leather Bible.

Alana took the bag and the Bible and closed her eyes tightly, as if doing so could shut out the frightening circumstances of her life.

"I didn't have much to bring. Most of my clothes were trashed along with my apartment."

She tried to hide the thread of tension in her voice as she sat on the sofa and hugged the Bible close. It was her lifeline.

Jaydn turned to Naomi. "Stay with her, Naomi, until we get all the details worked out."

Jaydn pulled Brad into the kitchen and picked up the phone. "Let me know if there's something I forget."

Jaydn's conversation lasted only minutes. He watched the surprise in Brad's eyes as he forcefully gave instructions to several men on the other end of the line.

When Jaydn hung up the phone, he turned to Brad.

"I think I have all the bases covered. If you see any problems, let me know. The helicopter will land at the Ross airport, about ten minutes from here. Someone might follow us from here, but it's a cinch they won't be prepared to follow a helicopter once we get to the airport. Naomi will follow tomorrow or the next day. You're welcome to ride with her if you want to see Alana, and please feel free to use the apartment for any reason if you have to come back to Ross. I'll let the apartment manager know you might be coming back. He has an extra key. When we get to the cabin, I'll have Alana call you. I'm sure she'd like to hear your voice by then, anyway."

Brad stared at him. "Wow, Jaydn. I'm impressed with the way you've handled everything. Every little detail is taken care of. It seems safe enough. I th—"

The doorbell interrupted his sentence.

"That must be the police." Jaydn guessed.

"Wait!" Brad whispered loudly as Naomi rushed to answer the door. He pulled his gun from his holster and stood in front of the door. Jaydn carefully pushed aside the closed curtains to peek out at the serious face of two Ross policemen. The street lamp illuminated their cruiser parked on the street behind them.

Jaydn nodded to Brad—a wave of relief relaxed his stance. Brad put away his gun and reached to open the door.

Jaydn headed to the stairs. "Okay, then. I'll pack a few things while you fill them in. By the time they leave, the helicopter should be waiting at the airport."

When Jaydn came back into the room, Brad was sitting beside Alana—her hands in his, and she was answering questions the police detectives asked them. She was shaky and weak, but she answered the questions with more calm than Jaydn thought possible. When the detectives had taken all their statements and left, they gathered her belongings and helped settle Alana in Jaydn's car.

It wasn't until after Jaydn packed his bag in the trunk and sat in the car on the way to the airport that he remembered his promise to pick up Patricia two hours before.

FORTY-TWO

THE TRIP ON THE HELICOPTER was a new experience for Alana. After she was buckled in, she sat up straight to see as much as possible. Part of her was excited to undergo her first helicopter ride, but the rest of her felt numb. Long hours of insomnia wrapped her head in a cotton sea of make-believe, and the emotional stress of the last few days seemed like a dream.

The question of who owned the helicopter flashed through her mind but was soon forgotten as she watched the moon reflecting across the tops of the clouds. The airport lights disappeared, and the mountains loomed tall and stately on the horizon.

She felt a sense of satisfaction as her arm touched Jaydn's in the close confines of the small cabin of the aircraft. He turned to her with a smile that made her heart melt like hot wax. It was so amazing that she felt such a peace in the presence of someone she had known for only a few days. Their personalities seemed to fit together like apple pie and ice cream—as if they'd been friends for years.

Jaydn turned his head to glance out the window when the helicopter made a sharp turn to the left. He pointed out the window. "That's where we're going."

Alana looked out the window and gasped. Even in the middle of the night, the lights around the cabin highlighted a massive lake nestled in the middle of four dark mountains.

The log cabin, surrounded by manicured lawns and trees, sat in the middle of an island encircled by an oblong-shaped lake and towering mountains—like a throne in the middle of its loyal subjects.

Floodlights from dozens of utility poles illuminated the area and made the scene as bright as daylight. The dark green of the trees almost enveloped the roof of the picturesque cabin and sent a surge of calm through her veins.

Her exhausted mind hoped and prayed this would be a safe haven. That whoever was hunting her down like a deer in season would never find her in this obscure setting. She sat back and waited for the helicopter to land.

Jaydn opened the door and hustled her down the sturdy steps, pushing her head low to clear the swirling motion of the overhead blades as they walked a short distance away. She turned to watch Jaydn pull their bags through the gaping hole of the helicopter, then observed with awe as the metal bird flew away into the night sky.

Jaydn threw the straps of their bags over one shoulder and held out his other hand, inviting her to walk hand-in-hand with him to the house. Alana turned toward the picturesque setting and thought how nice it would be if this place could erase the trouble in her life, at least temporarily.

The walk to the cabin was short, but each step became labored for Alana. It was well past two a.m., and her legs felt like lead. The pains that shot through to her temples from either side of her head pounded harder with each step she took. By the time she reached the door of the wooden structure, all she wanted was a bath and a bed.

Alana was vaguely aware of a short, round woman, introduced as "Sam," who led her up the stairs to the first bedroom on the right. The kind woman showed her through one of the bedroom doors to a bathroom and a tub filled with warm soothing water. Alana's clothes slipped to the floor, and she reveled in the peaceful warmth of the water as it covered her body.

When she slipped into bed later that night, a blanket of peace covered her completely, and she thought of nothing but peaceful, refreshing sleep.

FORTY-THREE

BRAD AND NAOMI WALKED BACK into the apartment after Jaydn and Alana left, and Brad locked the apartment up tight.

"I'm going to bed now, sir. Make yourself at home. If you need anything, let me know."

"Thanks, Naomi. I'll be fine."

Brad walked into the dining area and listened to the clock ticking on the kitchen wall. The tapping of the second hand moving around the face of the black dial irritated his already taut nerves. He pulled out his cell phone and pushed the number one—his speed dial number for home. Hearing the voice of someone he loved would calm his worried heart.

"Hello."

"Hey, Lisa."

"Hello, sweetheart. Can you hold on a minute? I'm just getting Timmy out of the tub."

"Sure." Brad pulled out one of the black lacquered chairs and sat down. He rolled his head around on his shoulders, trying to relax his tense muscles. Until he heard from Alana and knew she was safe at Jaydn's mountain cabin, he wouldn't be able to relax.

He sat there rolling his head from side to side when the meaning of what Lisa said finally pierced his tired brain. He looked at the clock hands that showed 1:30.

In the tub? At this time of night?

"Brad? Are you there?"

"Yeah, what do you mean, you have Timmy in the tub?"

"Well ... he's got a fever."

"How high?"

"It's 103.2."

Brad could hear Timmy whimpering in the background, and his voice rose a pitch higher. "That high?"

"Remember, Brad, he always has a higher fever than Rob or Jan. Especially when he's got an ear infection."

"How do you know he has an ear infection?"

Lisa's end of the conversation got quiet. "I didn't want to worry you, hon, but I took him to the doctor this afternoon. He's had a fever all day."

Brad blew out a grieved sigh. "I'm sorry, Lisa. I wish I could be there to help you."

"We're making it fine, sweetheart. Just worry about Alana now and your work. The Lord'll take care of us. He always has. How are things going? Did you make it to Ross okay?"

"Yeah, I made it fine."

"You sound like something's wrong."

He should have known Lisa would pick up the troubled tone in his voice.

"Someone tried to drown Alana in the pool tonight."

"Oh no! Is she all right?"

"She's fine. But it's a miracle she wasn't hurt, or worse. Jaydn and I just happened to pull up when the guy was pushing her head under the water with one of the pool nets. When he saw us coming, he dropped the pole and ran. I chased him, but he had a car waiting." He blew out a troubled breath.

"Did you see his face?"

"No. He wore a mask."

"Did you tell the Ross police? Can't they give her protection?"

"They don't have the manpower." Frustration rippled through his tone of voice. "They have the same flu bug we've got in Landeville, only worse." His breath puffed out between his teeth. "I just don't know who's after her, or why. It's eating me alive. If I knew the reason, I'd know how to fight it."

"Honey, you have to trust the Lord. I'm sure God put you there in time, and He'll give you the answers if you trust Him. He's allowing these things to happen for a reason. Maybe He's trying to teach us a lesson about something. Let's trust Him and find out what it is. You know what the Bible says, 'All things work together for good to them that love the Lord.' Trust Him, Brad. He knows what He's doing."

He leaned back and relaxed in his chair. "Now I know why I called you, sweetie. Thanks for the encouragement. I love you, Lisa."

"I love you too, Brad, and I miss you. You aren't driving home tonight tired, are you?"

"No. It's too late. I'm staying at Jaydn's apartment."

"He has an apartment in Ross?"

"Well, it belongs to the company, but I found out tonight that Jaydn inherited the company from his dad."

"The whole company?"

"Lock, stock, and bonds."

"Wow!" was all Lisa could say.

"He doesn't want anyone to know, so don't mention it, okay? Anyway, I'm staying tonight. Tomorrow, I'll probably spend some time with the police chief here and see if he has any ideas or leads. Then, I'll head home."

"Okay, sweetheart. Please don't worry about Timmy. I started him on antibiotics right away, and I can tell he's already feeling better. As a matter of fact, his temperature's down a little from this afternoon. So, don't worry, okay?"

"That's easier said than done, but I'll try."

"Oh … I have two messages for you. Your secretary called to tell you that the CD of pictures Alana dropped off at the station—the ones she took of the last murder scene—got misplaced at the office and were somehow mailed to the lab in Stranton. It took the lab there forever to figure out where they came from. When they finally saw someone familiar in one of the pictures, they knew it came from your office. They said they'd overnight it tomorrow. You should receive them the day after that. Sandee didn't know how they got mixed up. Anyway, she asked me to let you know."

"At this rate, I could have had prints made at the local Wal-Mart.

What's the other message?"

"Let's see, I have it written down. One of your officers called … here it is, let's see … it was Elliott. He said he finished some of the lab work and wants you to call him … at home if you need to."

"Thanks, Lisa. I'll give him a call. I love you, honey. Sleep well."

He hung up the phone and quickly dialed Elliott's home number. When Elliott picked up, Brad could hear fatigue in every syllable.

"Hey. Lisa said you called."

"Yeah. Just thought you'd like to know. No fingerprints on the suicide note or the pen."

"None? As in wiped clean?"

"Yep."

The chair creaked as Brad sat back down. "Well, well. How do you imagine Chet managed that? He writes the note, wipes it *and* the pen clean, then shoots himself? Does that make sense to you, Elliott?"

"Nope."

"We need to label this a homicide, get back into the murder scene, and do some serious digging for clues. Get the boys in there tomorrow and go over Chet's house with a fine-toothed comb. Check out his desk at the station as well. See if he left any clues there."

"Okay, boss."

"Nice work, Elliott. What about the hotel where Alana was attacked? I know they didn't find any prints, but what about DNA evidence?"

"I'm afraid not, Chief. It's strange that there weren't many prints. You'd have thought the maids would have left something. Actually, it looked like a brand new room to me … new carpet, new furniture. Even the walls looked freshly painted. There was a slight odor that might have been aired out paint fumes."

Brad blew out a frustrated breath of air.

"What about Bo and Kent's report? Was there anything suspicious in either report?"

"Haven't seen either report."

"Well, I have a feeling the hotel manager is in this up to his eyeballs. Okay, Elliott. There's one more thing I want you to do. Alana met with Jaydn's sketch artist to see if she could remember anything about the man who attacked her at the hotel. They came up with a sketch of the man's eyes. I'd like you to take a look at it and see if it looks anything like our man, Hollister."

"Okay, Chief, but I didn't get a good look at the guy, and the mug shot we have is several years old."

"See if you recognize anything at all."

"Okay, Chief. There's one more thing. The other day when I took Chet home from playing tennis, he was ridiculing his neighbor's 'icky *red* house.' Remember the word he used for a middle name means red? Chet might have been trying to point a finger at his neighbor as being his killer and maybe involved in the sheet murders."

Brad rubbed his face with his hand and mourned for his friend. "It probably wouldn't hold up in court, but you might be right, Elliott. Good work. Keep digging. I'll be back sometime tomorrow afternoon."

Brad sat back wearily in the chair and closed his eyes.

Lord, Lisa's right. I know I have to trust you. Please help me find the answers. Somewhere, there are the pieces I need to solve this puzzle. Will you please help us find them?

Feeling restless, Brad left the dining room and strode into the darkened living room, where he sank into the recliner and sat with his head held in his hands for a while—praying to God—hoping answers would be revealed magically. He knew God didn't work that way, but he could use a miracle right about now.

When the telephone started an insistent ringing, he jumped up and walked back into the kitchen.

"Brad Candler."

Jaydn's voice came over the line, making his report. "Alana was dead on her feet when we got here, so I sent her to bed. I told her I'd call and let you know we got here without problems. I don't believe anyone even followed us to the airport."

"Thanks, Jaydn. I'll call Alana in the morning."

"When you call, use the house number. Sometimes the cell

service out here is sketchy. I left the number on a pad beside the phone. We're locked in, and the security system's on over the whole grounds. No one could get in here tonight without sounding enough alarms to make us all go deaf."

Brad let out a relieved laugh. "Thanks, Jaydn. I'll rest easier, knowing my sister's safe."

"I thought you'd also like to know security guards from the office are here too, stationed all around the property—especially around the lake perimeter. They're off duty until next week, so they're prepared to stay for as long as we need them."

Brad was speechless. If it wasn't for Jaydn, Alana would be dead. How could he convey his thanks for something as significant as that? When he spoke, his voice was quiet and husky. "Thanks, Jaydn. I don't know what I'd do without you, my friend."

The silence was deafening. It had been an emotional day for them all.

"Just get a good night's sleep, buddy. I'll talk to you in the morning." Jaydn's voice was hoarse.

"Good night."

Brad hung up the phone and climbed the stairs. His legs felt thick and heavy, but he made it up the stairs to his room and fell into bed. His weary eyelids closed, and he prayed for wisdom. Tomorrow would be another day, full of more questions. Hopefully, with God's help, they'd find answers.

FORTY-FOUR

THE NEXT MORNING, JAYDN JOGGED around a short path where the daily walks of Evan and Sam had worn down the grass and packed the dirt into a level running field. He waved at one of the security guards as he passed his position and slowed down to a fast walk. The sweat running down his forehead had more to do with the mental turmoil he was fighting than the physical exertion. His reaction to Alana's entrance into his life stunned him. Just being in the same room with her made his pulse rate increase. And the desire to hear her tantalizing laughter and breathe in her flowery scent was overwhelming.

As he passed the second story window where she was sleeping, he thought about the thing that made her special to him—her strong faith in a Supreme Being—something he wished he could share. Her loyalty to God stirred the pot of hidden emotions swirling within his tormented soul.

Alana was nothing like his father's brand of Christian. She was *real*. And, yet, he wondered if he could find that closeness to God and actually *live* what he believed. It wasn't just *important* to him, it was *essential*.

A longing crept over his heart like kudzu, squeezing out his independence—making him long for a Higher Authority he could trust in and lean on. It was a longing that would not go away. He craved a decision about God—one way or the other—and soon.

Patricia's face suddenly appeared before him.

Was she a "real" Christian? She went to church every week, but she never talked about her faith—or her God—as Alana did. She never displayed affection or trust in a Supreme Being. Her relationship with God, if there was one, differed so much from Alana's trust and friendship with her God.

Other comparisons between Alana and Patricia suddenly plowed their way into his thoughts. Alana made his heart glow with radiance and life, whereas Patricia just made his heart feel dead and lifeless. And to think he actually considered giving her a ring.

"Thank you Lord, for saving me from making that mistake!"

Suddenly, he stopped dead in his tracks. He just spoke to a God he vowed didn't exist—until now. That was a prayer, wasn't it? He stood in stunned silence as the sweat ran down his face and burned his eyes.

Distractedly, he wiped away the burning from his eyes and pinched the bridge of his nose. To mumble a prayer meant he believed a God existed, or he wouldn't have spoken. *Did* he believe there was an omnipotent being?

Yes!

He realized with a start that his whole view of God and Christianity changed in an instant. And, why? All because of a brown-eyed believer who put her faith where her heart was supposed to be. She *lived* her faith, and through her life, he saw how important God could be in a person's life. In *his* life. He longed for a relationship with a God that loved him unconditionally and wanted the best for him in spite of his faults.

He plopped down on the stretch of plush green lawn. Dread filled his heart. How unfit he must be in God's sight. He recalled the admonitions of his Christian friends in college. Everyone must die, and after death comes judgment. All men must give account for every sin.

He must give account for *his* sin.

But according to Bible verses his friends had quoted, Jesus Christ satisfied God's requirement for a pure sacrifice for sin when He died on the cross. Anyone could have a relationship with God if he believed in that sacrifice.

Jaydn looked up into the sky, trying to find the courage to talk to God.

God, I know I've broken Your commandments. I know it was because of my sins You died on the cross to save me from an eternity in hell. I ask forgiveness for my sins on the basis of what Jesus has done. Please accept me as Your child, and help me learn to trust in You, God. Help me learn to make You real in my life, like Alana does. Thank you, God.

Suddenly, Jaydn felt a load lift from his chest. It felt as if his heart suddenly developed wings. The many years of ridiculing his father and watching in disgust as he ranted and raved his religion seemed to float away on the clouds. The pain and uncertainty of a life full of doubt was washed away like the sands on the seashore in a storm. The storm clouds lifted from his heart, and he was genuinely happy.

He wanted so much to tell Alana, but his newfound faith felt so wobbly. What if he failed? What if he ended up like his father? Doubt clouded his decision. He didn't want to tell her until he was positive his faith would stand up to any test. God would show him. God would let him know when the time was right to tell Alana.

FORTY-FIVE

WHEN ALANA ROLLED OVER IN bed and stretched, her muscles screamed at her—*be still, and go back to sleep*! A tiny sliver of light penetrated the thick curtains, informing her the day was here. A thin ray of sunlight fell across the camera sitting on the nightstand. *That* made her want to jump into the day with both feet.

She sat up in bed and drank in her first impression of the room around her. Warm and harmonious, the colors of the decor blended to radiate an air of coziness and welcome. A faint smell of apples gave her the definite impression of scented candles or potpourri.

The huge four-poster bed was enveloped in a maroon and hunter green comforter with touches of color splashed over the silken surface. The carpet, dark green in color, was thick and plush with vacuum marks dispersed across the floor in random patterns. Dark maroon curtains on windows across from the bed reached from ceiling to floor with the smallest amount of sunlight peeking around the edges of the thick fabric.

Alana crawled out of bed and pulled the string on the right side of the windows to slide the curtains open. What she saw took her breath away. A short distance across the meticulously trimmed lawn was the lake she had seen from the sky—shimmering like a diamond in the morning sun.

She grabbed the camera, opened the sliding glass doors, and stepped out onto the wooden balcony. The brisk morning air tickled her senses and smelled of lake water and magnolia blossoms. Between the lake and the house were twenty or thirty white geese roaming around in circles, squawking and fluffing their wings.

Snapping pictures quickly, she took several shots of the geese flapping their wings and then photographed the geese in front of the light shimmering across the lake.

Two of the geese waddled off by themselves and rubbed necks together. Alana held her breath. She'd heard that geese mated for life—like humans. The camera shutter once again broke the silence as she photographed the pair that was oblivious of everything else but each other.

A wave of envy stole over her body. Would she ever find the perfect mate that God planned for her? A vision of Jaydn rose in her mind's eye, and she wrapped her arms around her waist, contentment flowing through her veins.

As she sat down on the bench seat on the right of the balcony, she watched the white, billowy clouds overhead.

"Thank you, Lord for this beautiful day. This is definitely something to be thankful for. Thank you, also, for Jaydn—that he's willing to let me come here. Please help me be the right kind of testimony to him. Help him feel Your love ..."

Help him feel *my* love ...

The Bible verses she'd read the day before pricked her memory like a bee sting.

She walked into the room and reached for the Bible on the nightstand. After sitting down on the edge of the bed, she turned to the verse she'd read the day before and found those convicting words.

"Be ye not unequally yoked with unbelievers."

That means Jaydn, doesn't it, Lord? Are you trying to tell me we can only be friends?

Alana's heart felt wrenched in two. The attraction she felt for Jaydn had inched up on her when she wasn't looking. To control the feelings she felt for him was going to be hard, if not impossible. When she looked into his eyes, her heart simply melted.

However, her relationship with the Lord was growing into something she depended on more each day. Now, when things were frightening and confusing, trusting God was more important than ever—more important even than a relationship with Jaydn or her desire for a husband. She wanted the Lord's blessing on every-thing she did, and she needed to know He was watching over her. Becoming attached to Jaydn, an unbeliever, would not have the Lord's blessing.

"Please, help me, Lord. Keep me from forming a strong attach-ment to Jaydn. Help me keep our relationship friendly, and please take away the strong …"

Her prayer was interrupted by a quiet knock on the door.

"Alana, are you awake?"

Alana grabbed her robe and opened the door enough to see Jaydn's face.

"Good morning." A smile radiated from his face.

The smile she gave him hung loosely on her face as if it could be snatched away at a moment's notice. "Good morning."

"Are you feeling okay?"

Alana had seen the ashy color of her face in the mirror and was sure that's what prompted the worry in his tone.

"I'm fine. Just a little tired."

Jaydn would understand her being tired, but he'd never under-stand the look of aloofness in her eyes.

"Sam's making some eggs and toast, if you'd like to eat something."

"I'll be down soon. Thank you."

She closed the door but frowned at the look on his face. He would question her withdrawal, but her decision to follow God's will in her life mattered too much. She had to hold on to the fact that God was in charge, or she'd go crazy.

Help me balance both the relationship I have with Jaydn and Your will, Father.

She dressed quickly, grabbed the camera, then opened the door and ventured into the wide, open hallway. The hall of the upstairs section of the house was just as plush and tastefully decorated as her bedroom, and she turned toward the stairs while inspecting the décor around her.

The top half of the hall walls were painted with a sky blue color and ended with a hand-painted ivy border around the top of the wall next to the ceiling. The bottom section of the wall was painted in a dark green, the same color as the shadows in the ivy border that ran across the top of the wall. Another border of ivy ran around the bottom of the wall, just above the trim molding. The carpet was a tan color with flakes of gray mingled here and there to match the gray lines of the border.

When her foot touched the first step on the winding staircase, a cell phone downstairs on the hall table rang and continued its ringing until she reached the bottom.

It might be Brad. Should she answer?

Alana expected the housekeeper or Jaydn to hear the incessant ringing, but when no one appeared, she picked up the phone.

"Hello."

"Who is this?" The shrill voice on the other end of the line caused Alana to step back.

"This is … uh, who are you trying to call?" The reason she was hiding in this house hit her between the eyes again, and she was afraid to give her name.

"I'm trying to get in touch with Jaydn Holbrook. Do I have the right number or not?" The irritation evident in the angry voice grated on Alana's already frazzled nerves.

"Yes, you have the right number, but he doesn't seem to be around at the moment. Could I take a message?"

"No, you *cannot* take a message. I insist on talking to him at once."

"Well …" Alana glanced around. Uncertainty flowed through her like a chill from a frosty wind. "I told you, I'm not sure where he is at the moment, and—"

"Are you one of the help?"

"I beg your pardon?"

"I said are you one of the maids, or the housekeeper or something?"

"Um … no. Not exactly." She fought to make her voice sound pleasing and unemotional. "Could I take a number and have him call you when he returns?"

Her question was met with silence. Alana could feel the tension traveling across the phone line, and she shivered.

"If you're not one of his employees, then what are you doing with Jaydn's phone? Who are you?"

Alana's mouth felt like cotton. She didn't know what to say. Maybe she should just hang up. Her gaze fell on the wooden planks in the hallway as she wrestled with handling that explosive question.

Jaydn appeared in a back doorway. He took one look at her face and the phone in her hands, and his lips parted in a question.

Alana didn't say a word, just shook her head and handed him the phone.

"Hello?"

"Jaydn? Is that you?"

Patricia!

FORTY-SIX

Now Jaydn knew why Alana's face was so pale. Patricia must have unleashed an angry tirade on her.

"Jaydn, I'm furious! Do you know what you've done? Since you didn't have the *decency* to call and say you weren't coming to pick me up last night, I was forced to catch a ride with Johnson. I was *late!* I had to accept my award after most of the crowd was already *gone.* Do you know how *embarrassing* that was?"

Jaydn frowned at the rage in her tone. He glanced up to see Alana disappearing through the living room doorway.

"Patricia, I'm sorry. It couldn't be helped." He spoke quietly so that Alana would not overhear.

"You're sorry! You're sorry!? You've got to be kidding! Is that all you can say? I must say, Jaydn, I expected more than that. After what you did to me, you could at lea—"

"Patricia, please. I can't explain right now."

"I will *not* wait for an explanation. You will give me one right now, or you'll be sorry."

Jaydn turned quickly stepped into the powder room. Anger seething in the back of his mind pushed its way to the surface, and he spoke with authority.

"Patricia, if you want an explanation, you're going to have to wait. If you can't trust me enough to believe that I have a good explanation, then maybe we shouldn't see each other again. Relationships are built on trust, not accusations."

Silence.

"All right, Jaydn. I'll wait, but not for long. You know I have other friends who are willing to step in and take your place if I so desire to let them."

That threat didn't dent Jaydn's resolve. He spoke quietly. "Goodbye, Patricia. I'll call you later."

He headed for the living room, where he found Alana standing beside the window. What should he tell her? She sensed Patricia was someone who was more than a friend. Should he explain? Should he treat the whole thing lightly? For some reason, he didn't want Alana to know about Patricia. His indecision made him pause long enough for Alana to cut the silence with the first words.

"I'm sorry, Jaydn. I guess I shouldn't have answered the phone."

"No, that's all right. There was no reason why you shouldn't."

Alana's gaze wavered between the floor and his face.

Jaydn could read indecision there, and shame. He decided to change the subject. "Are you ready to eat? I'm starving."

She blew out a relieved breath and nodded.

Jaydn summoned the biggest smile he could manage, bowed, and waved toward a door at the end of the hallway beside the stairs. "Your breakfast awaits, my lady."

She managed a shaky smile and preceded him through the doorway.

Jaydn fell into step behind her, consumed with a sense of failure. She might make his heart flip-flop when she was near, but being open and honest with her about his relationship with Patricia only made his heart heavier than a two-ton weight.

FORTY-SEVEN

ALANA SAT ON THE CONCRETE bench under the drooping weeping willow in peaceful silence, gazing out over the lake. A slight breeze caused ripples on the water's surface. Her hair tickled her nose as the wind blew strands around her face.

Waves slapping against two motorboats tied to a long pier in the water calmed her tense nerves and relaxed her tight muscles.

She kept replaying the phone conversation over in her mind. The woman, Patricia, must be more than Jaydn's friend.

Once again, she felt the heavy burden she had placed on Jaydn's shoulders by allowing him to bring her here. It was obvious he felt obligated to protect her, and it was costing him. It was damaging his relationship with the woman on the phone, and if he missed more days at work, it might cost him his job.

"What am I going to do, Lord? I want your will in my life. Maybe Jaydn's not a part of it, but right now, I need his help. If it weren't for him, I wouldn't have this place to hide. Please help his friend understand."

Her heart felt lighter after talking to her Lord, but she still had no solution to the problem.

She had avoided Jaydn all morning—trying to keep her heart from chasing something she knew wasn't right. The first few hours of the day were spent dodging him as he worked in and out of the office of the big house. When lunchtime finally arrived, she was no more at ease in his presence than she had been during breakfast.

Brad would call tonight and let them know how the investigation was going. This morning, he'd told her what he learned so far—nothing—at least not enough to put all the pieces together. She was hoping he might have better news tonight.

She watched the gentle breeze blow the long sweeping branches of the willow tree as it kissed the tops of the clipped grass in the yard.

When she heard Jaydn calling her name, she turned to see him standing at the door of the house, searching the yard. Her position beneath the willow tree, among the bushes and flowering plants of the garden, hid her from his view.

She stood and waved.

When he saw her, the relief settled on his face as he waved and headed in her direction.

"I was beginning to worry. Neither Evan nor Sam saw you leave, and my imagination ran wild."

Alana felt heat rise on her face. "I'm sorry. I'm not used to people watching my every move. I needed some time to myself."

Her gaze strayed to the three security guards walking around the lake's edge. "Bodyguards remind me that I'm in danger, you know?"

He moved to stand behind her and began massaging her shoulders. "Just relax a few minutes and don't worry. You said God has taken care of you up to this point. Surely you don't believe He'll quit watching out for you after all the protection He's given so far."

Her muscles softened in response to the deep pressure. The stiffness in her shoulders gradually faded away.

"Jaydn, I'm really sorry about this morning." She said as he moved to sit beside her on the outdoor bench. "I guess it was hard for your friend to understand why another woman was answering your phone."

Misery burned in the back of her throat—misery for the situation she was in, misery for the position she forced upon Jaydn, but most of all, misery that Jaydn had a girlfriend who had the right to be angry when a strange woman answered his phone.

Jaydn turned his body toward hers and raised her chin with one finger.

"Alana, I don't want you to worry about the woman you talked to this morning. Believe me when I tell you that the … relationship … I had with Patricia is over."

The next words stuck to her tongue, but she forced them out.

"Because of me?"

"Absolutely not! We already fought every time we saw each other. Our values, our goals, even our plans for the future were going in two different directions. A break-up was inevitable. I guess I've known it was over for a long time. I just didn't want to admit it."

Alana saw the yearning in his face—heard it in his voice—that desire to love and be loved. She softened her gaze and placed an understanding smile on her face. Surprise flashed in his eyes, and his gaze held hers captive. Her breath caught in her throat. She could get lost in the dark blue pools and want never to be found.

Be ye not unequally yoked!

Please help me, Lord.

She turned to pick a daisy from the bush next to her seat on the bench—trying to plant her feet back on firmer ground.

A ragged breath escaped Jaydn's lips, and he stood to his feet.

"I have to go. I mean … I need to see about some things at work. If it's okay with you, I'm going back to Landeville for a little while this afternoon. If there's something you need me to pick up for you, let me know."

"No. There's nothing." Then, she had a sudden thought—almost a wish for something familiar in the midst of chaos. "Hey, wait! Would you … oh, never mind. It's silly."

"Come on, what?"

"I just thought it'd be nice to do something normal for a change— maybe watch a movie and make a bowl of caramel popcorn?"

"What?"

Alana heard the surprise in his voice and noticed the tension that tightened his jaw. Shocked at his reaction to her request, she replied hesitantly. "Well, I noticed you have a couple of *Indiana Jones* movies in your stash. I just thought … it's not any fun to watch movies without caramel popcorn."

Jaydn stiffened. Almost as if a shutter closed over his eyes, his emotions slammed shut in her face.

Alana felt his withdrawal like a slap in the face. She was confused and lifted her head in puzzlement. One minute he acted like he cared, and the next minute he withdrew—physically and emotionally. Over a simple request of popcorn and a movie.

Fine! If that's the way he wanted to be, she could be aloof as well. She didn't want the caramel popcorn, anyway.

"Never mind. It was just a thought. Thanks anyway."

Jaydn stood there—looking pained. "I'll post extra guards while I'm gone, and I think it'd be a good idea if you stayed inside … at least until I get back. If you need anything, ask Marty. He's in charge while I'm gone."

Her mouth was too dry to answer, so she just nodded. She watched him as he turned and walked into the house, wondering what in the world just happened.

FORTY-EIGHT

AFTER LEAVING ALANA SO ABRUPTLY, Jaydn mentally kicked himself all the way back to the house. He stopped outside the cabin and paced back and forth in front of the double-glass doors.

What in the world was he thinking?

He was spending too much time with a certain young lady. She was becoming attached. He could see it in her eyes— the uncertainty, the anticipation, the longing. He knew she felt the same pull of attraction he did, but when she found out he lied …

He remembered her words: "Rich men are arrogant and demanding. They're nothing but tyrants in suits."

For some reason, her words churned up a whirlwind of disappointment he didn't want to contemplate just then. After the way he acted at the office, he knew she would lump him into the pile of "tyrants" she had known. And she would be right.

Getting too close to Alana meant having to reveal his secret— he was a selfish, arrogant fool.

So what else was new?

Why should what she thought of him matter so much? He was letting her thoughts and beliefs influence what he thought about himself—just like it was in the beginning with Patricia. Patricia had used the fact that he had money for her own advantage, but with Alana, it would be the opposite. She hated money, and she hated power.

And what was that about caramel popcorn? Had Naomi told her that caramel popcorn was his favorite snack? Did Alana intuitively know that he longed to have someone to share it with?

Suddenly, his thoughts choked him, and he couldn't breathe.

What was he doing? He needed to get away from here!

He took a long minute convincing his heart this was the thing to do and then turned on his heels and headed into the house.

Saying he felt a strong attraction to Alana was an understatement. She filled his whole world with hope for the future.

Their future.

Could they have one together?

He wished they could.

He needed to feel they could.

But she had made her feelings perfectly clear about people with money, and she would never forgive him for deceiving her about his fortune.

FORTY-NINE

BRAD'S PRECINCT BUILDING WAS LOCATED in downtown Landeville—about three miles from Jaydn's office building. Comfortable clothes made it easy for Jaydn to jog the short distance, and his troubled thoughts kept him company as he ran. By the time he pushed through the front doors of the building, clouds billowing overhead matched his mood perfectly. Maybe spending some time with Brad would offer insight into how to come clean with Alana.

"Jaydn! Man, you're the last person I expected to see here!" Brad's voice suddenly turned to panic. "What are you doing here? Where's Alana?"

Sweat popped out on his forehead, but Jaydn answered assuredly, "She's fine, Brad. She's still at the cabin. Security's on code red, and the alarm system's set on the highest setting." He paused to let Brad's heart rate return to normal. "I needed to see about some things at work, and …"

Brad's countenance changed, and he took a calming breath of air. "I'm sorry, Jaydn. I didn't mean to imply—"

"It's okay. I understand. Anyway, I'm headed back in about an hour, but first I thought I'd come by and talk to you."

"Come on in the office, buddy. I have a few minutes to give you."

Jaydn stood beside Brad's cluttered desk and held his breath when he saw what covered the surface. Grizzly photos of a body wrapped in sheets, along with a ransacked apartment and topsy-turvy rooms.

"Man, how do you do this every day?"

Brad scooped up the photos and put them inside a file folder. "It's hard sometimes, but I'm ashamed to say it all becomes routine after a while. It's hard to have empathy with a grieving family when every case melds together into one big unsolved responsibility."

"Were those the pictures Alana took?"

"No, for some reason, those got mailed to the Stranton lab. They'll get here tomorrow, I hope. I haven't even had a chance to look at them yet. Have a seat there, Jaydn, and tell me what's up."

Jaydn sat down on the lumpy cushion.

"If you really want to know … it's Alana. She's been … sort of keyed up, but, I'm afraid it's not just from this business." He pointed at the file folder. "This morning she intercepted a phone conversation that was meant for me. I'm afraid the woman I've been dating wasn't happy to hear another woman's voice answer my cell phone. Not to mention the fact that I was supposed to pick her up last night, and with all the trouble, I completely forgot."

Brad winced. "Man, I forgot you told me you had an appointment last night. I'm really sorry."

Jaydn raised his hands. "It's okay, really. I've been trying to find a way to break off my relationship with Patricia, but it's not an easy thing. Maybe it was for the best. If she gets mad at me and breaks it off herself, then it'll save her pride. I'm just sorry Alana had to bear the brunt of her anger this morning."

"You know, Jaydn, I think Alana likes you. I've never seen her as open and responsive with anyone else in my whole life. She's usually more reserved."

"Maybe it's only the strain she's been under."

Brad shook his head slowly. "No, I don't think so. She's always been reserved and private. But with you?" He nodded his head decisively. "I think she cares a lot about you. And, I don't think it's because you saved her life, either."

Jaydn looked out the window at the traffic stopping for the red light. "I like her too, Brad. But, do you know what I like the most about Alana—the thing that draws me to her?"

Brad tilted his head and waited.

"It's the sincere way she lives her religion and the closeness she has with her God. Well, with *my* God now." He flashed Brad a half-smile and waited for his response.

Brad raised his brows and Jaydn squared his shoulders as Brad probed further.

"What exactly do you mean by '*my* God,' Jaydn?"

"I finally accepted God as my Savior."

Brad came around the desk and pumped Jaydn's hand enthusiastically with a big smile on his face. "That's great, Jaydn! When did this happen?"

"Just yesterday. You know, I think I really believed there was a God all my life, but I wasn't ready to put my faith in Him until now. It just sort of happened."

"Does Alana know?"

Jaydn shook his head. "No, I haven't mentioned it to her yet."

Brad sat on the edge of the desk and patted Jaydn on the back. "Well, Jaydn, I won't deny that I was worried about Alana. I could see she cared about you, and I worried she was becoming too attached. The Bible asks the question 'How can two walk together unless they be agreed?' I knew it would cause problems for you both down the road unless you were on the same page about your beliefs. I'm happy for you, man."

"You know, I thought being a Christian would feel like being in somebody's army, but it just feels peaceful and serene. There's something calming about giving a loving, powerful being complete control of your life."

Brad laughed at his description. "Yep, you got it all right. Ain't it grand?"

Jaydn just laughed and nodded. "Better than anything I could have imagined."

A knock on the door interrupted their conversation.

"Come in."

Bo stuck his head in the door. "We just got a call from Elliott. A body washed up on the shore of Lake Morgan. He said you need to see this one."

Brad jumped to his feet. "Drowning?"

Bo shook his head. "Nope. He has a bullet hole right in the

middle of his forehead."

Jaydn, thankful he had not gone into police work, watched Brad grab his gun and holster from the coat rack beside the door.

Brad turned to Jaydn. "I gotta run. Tell Alana I'll call her tonight."

"Will do," Jaydn said as he preceded Brad out the door.

Brad locked his office and strode down the hall with Bo. Jaydn leaned against the wall and looked up at the ceiling in defeat. He hadn't had a chance to ask Brad how to handle telling Alana the truth. Blowing out a frustrated breath, he trudged back to his office to get to the helicopter, fly to the cabin, and face Alana.

FIFTY

ALANA SAT DROOPING IN THE armchair in front of the television. She sighed, telling her heart to stop wondering what Jaydn was doing. Sitting around the house was rarely something she enjoyed, and for some reason Jaydn's face kept invading her mind, distracting her from the movie she was trying to watch. The DVD collection stored in the den contained a wide assortment, but even the *Indiana Jones* movies almost seemed tame compared to the life she was living at the moment.

She flipped off the TV and stood up decisively. Maybe Sam would let her cook supper since she'd been busy doing laundry all afternoon.

The laundry room was located at the back of the house and smelled like cotton candy—or was it lavender? Alana sniffed appreciatively and smiled at Sam, who was carefully ironing a man's shirt.

"Hey, Sam. Would you mind if I cooked supper tonight?"

Sam smiled at her thankfully. "That would be great, Alana. I was just thinking I needed to stop soon and get some kind of meal started. These men are all a hungry bunch. I guess guard work makes for big appetites." She laughed. "I'll be glad when Naomi gets here. She's better at cooking than I am. I'm not used to cooking for so many."

Alana laughed. "Well, I'll take care of it this time. I'm used to cooking for a passel of kids at the orphanage, so it'll be fun."

Sam sighed. "Thanks, Alana. There's plenty of food in the pantry. A couple of the security team went and bought groceries this morning, and I think they bought out the entire store. There should be ingredients for just about anything you might wanna cook."

"I'll find it. Thanks, Sam."

Sam smiled at her warmly and went back to ironing.

Adding up the number of security men she could remember, she formulated a mental note of how many servings she'd need. Then, she opened the pantry and checked to see if the ingredients were on hand for chicken parmesan.

Everything was there except for the bread crumbs—a batter with flour would do just as well.

The first thing she'd make would be a chocolate cake. The kids loved her white icing made with Crisco, flour, milk, and just a little bit of sugar. Not too sweet—but just enough to taste like dessert.

When she had the cake baking in the oven, she pulled out the ingredients for the main course.

Carefully, she lowered spaghetti noodles into boiling water to let them cook while she sautéed onion, garlic, and bay leaves in a little olive oil. Then she carefully added basil and tomatoes and cooked it slowly until the mixture thickened. Setting that aside, she beat the strips of chicken until they were a consistent thickness and dredged them in a mixture of flour, salt, and pepper. After coating them completely in the flour mixture, she dipped them into eggs beaten with water until they were frothy, then back into the flour mixture for the final coating. When they were completely coated with the seasoned mixture, she laid them carefully into a pan with a thin covering of hot olive oil and cooked them until they were tender.

While the chicken cooked in the pan, she found several jars of home canned vegetables and poured them into pans to heat. Then she whipped up a batch of butter biscuits. They were just coming out of the oven when she heard the helicopter.

A helicopter meant only one thing—Jaydn was home. Her stomach did flips, and her heart turned over in her chest.

Behave! She scolded herself as she dumped the biscuits into a basket lined with a towel, and stirred the cake icing vigorously, try-ing to let out some of her bottled-up emotions.

"Mmmm, something smells good. I'm starved."

Even though she knew he was coming, she still jumped at the sound of his voice from the doorway. She turned around and smiled at Jaydn's bemused expression.

"I thought it was Sam in the kitchen when I smelled dinner cooking," he said. "Where is she?"

"She's busy doing laundry, so I offered."

"It smells delicious. What is it?" He lifted the lid off the pan on the stove containing the chicken and gave an appreciative sniff.

"Chicken parmesan."

When she turned her back, he pinched off a tiny piece of chicken and popped it into his mouth. "Mmm. This is great!"

"Hey! Stay out of my food, you buzzard." Her shaky smile took the sting out of her words as she slapped at him with the dishtowel.

"Where'd you learn to cook?"

"My mom." The sadness in her heart lasted two seconds before she turned back to icing the cake. "I cook quite a bit for the orphanage. It's fun, and I enjoy seeing the kids. Of course, the kids are easier to please than a whole group of men. To be honest, I'm a little nervous." She glanced up and smiled.

"They'll love it, believe me. Should I call the first shift in?" He snitched a corner off one of the biscuits as he walked out the door to ring the dinner bell hanging on the iron railing.

Alana laughed and turned to drain the noodles in a colander and mix them with the tomatoes and spices. Then she spooned it onto each piece of the browned chicken and sprinkled them all with mozzarella cheese and a touch of parmesan. When everything was ready, she set all the food on the island—buffet style—and pulled out plates and silverware.

Jaydn walked in the door ahead of the security team. "I think I'll work in my office until all the men have eaten." He turned before he reached the door and handed her a bag he'd been carrying around. "Oh, by the way, I brought you something."

The strange look he gave her as he left the room made her place the bag carefully on the counter. When she looked inside, a warm blush covered her face.

Caramel popcorn!

The back door slammed as the first group of men came in, and she stayed busy dishing out food for the hungry men who were keeping her safe.

After all the security detail ate and gave a cheerful thanks for the delicious meal, Alana took a plate out of the cabinet and filled it with her meal while Sam was washing up the dishes. She covered the serving bowls and left the rest of the food on the bar for Jaydn. A large picnic table sat on the wooden patio outside, so she picked up her plate and sat down on the bench seat contentedly. In such a peaceful setting, she could almost forget why she was here.

Halfway through her meal, she heard shouting from the lake. One of the guards yelled up the yard toward her. "Get down, Miss Candler! Get back in the house!"

Alana looked where he was pointing and saw a motor boat slicing through the water, approaching the dock. Terror turned her legs to water, and she couldn't move.

Jaydn pushed open the back door and grabbed her, pulling her back into the kitchen. An alarm was sounding from somewhere above her and made her insides vibrate.

"Get down, Alana, and stay here with Sam." He pushed Alana to the floor next to where Sam was sitting away from the windows and door. Then he jerked the basement door open. Inside was a tall rack that held four or five rifles. After loading one with bullets from the shelf, he turned to glance down at Alana's pale, stunned face.

"In the basement, there's a secret lever hidden under the bottom shelf of the bookshelves. Sam can show you where. Pull that lever, and a hidden closet will open. A lever inside the closet closes the door. If I tell you to, get in that closet and stay there until I come get you. Understand?"

She nodded, but the alarm in his eyes flamed a feeling of helplessness. She wrapped her arms around her waist and looked up at him. "Please, don't leave me, Jaydn," she said as he carefully peeked out the door window.

"It'll be okay, Alana. The guards are good at what they do." He smiled at her and took a stance just inside the back door.

Sam took Alana's hands in hers and smiled at her reassuringly. Alana leaned out and peered around the corner cabinet into the backyard. She saw two of the guards approach the boat that was now parked at his dock—guns drawn and tense in their stance. She saw them talking to the man and woman aboard the boat and breathed a sigh of relief when the couple started the engine and pulled back out onto the lake. She turned back to Sam and whispered, "The boat's leaving."

Marty, the head of his security team, ran back to the house and entered the back door.

"False alarm. They were looking for the concession stand at the swimmer's beach. I told them there wasn't a place to park their boat there, so they headed back the way they came."

"Where *did* they come from? I thought there was no access to the lake on this side of the mountains."

"There's a private campground on the other side, but it's not usually that busy. It's a long boat ride around the mountain—most people don't come all the way around."

"Are you sure they were telling the truth?"

Marty looked at him pointedly. "I'd stake my life on it."

Alana remembered Jaydn saying Marty had been with him for several years and knew Jaydn trusted his instincts.

"Tell the men to be on the look-out for more boats. Thanks for being alert, Marty." Jaydn patted him on the back as Marty turned to leave. Marty nodded then headed back to his security team.

Alana was sure they would be on extra alert for the next few hours.

After Sam gave her a hug, Alana turned from her with trepidation in her heart. Going outside to eat was a stupid thing to do. Being out in the open was dangerous.

Her appetite gone, she headed upstairs to spend time in her Bible. Only God knew why these things were happening. She needed to spend time with Him and let Him deal with everything.

FIFTY-ONE

The next morning, Jaydn ushered Alana outside into the sunshine.

"Where are we going?" Her voice held a touch of trepidation.

"What you need is something to help take your mind off the last few days and relax a little."

Alana was a little nervous to be outside where anyone could be lurking in the dense stand of trees surrounding the lake, but when Jaydn led her to a small pathway surrounded by reed cane, she began to relax. He stopped in a small clearing under several old oak trees and dug something out of his pocket.

"My buddies and I played this game when I was little. We called it Washers—for obvious reasons." He opened his hand and showed her a pile of the largest washers she'd ever seen. "Have you ever played a game like this?"

The surprise on her face made him laugh. "I'll take that as a *no*. It's a lot of fun when you get the hang of it. Let me show you."

Alana saw three round holes dug in the ground exactly the same distance apart. The bare dirt around the three holes was packed, and she could tell this game was played often. About twenty feet away, there were three more holes dug in the same way.

"It's a lot like horseshoes, but a little different. You stand behind the hole closest to you like this." He gently pushed her until she stood behind the small round hole closest to her.

"Then you take a washer and throw it to the other set of holes.

You have to land the washer completely in the hole for the points to count. If you get your washer in the first hole, it's five points. The second hole is ten points, and the hole farthest away is fifteen points.

"The object of the game is to get exactly sixty points. If you have fifty-five points and you get more than five with the next throw, you start all over with the extra amount. Let's say you had fifty-five points, and in the next throw, your washer landed in the fifteen-point hole. That is ten points over sixty, so now your score would be only ten. Do you understand?"

Alana nodded and took the washers he held in his hands. "I've never seen such large washers. Where did you get these things?"

"Believe it or not, I bought them at the local hardware store. They're cheap, and this is a fun game. Evan and Sam play it a lot during their hours off."

"Do they stay here at the house all the time?" she asked as she took the first washer in her hand and looked toward the three holes at the other end.

"Most of the time. At the other house—" He suddenly stopped and started again. "At the other … job where they worked, they had much more to do. But, they're getting older and wanted to slow down a little. So, when I bought this place, they asked to move in here and take over as caretakers. They take a vacation twice a year, and usually spend time in a hotel at the ocean. But, most of the time, they stay here."

Alana stood for a minute, surveying the distance to the holes, and then tossed her first washer. It landed firmly in the fifteen-point hole.

"Hey! That's great for the first throw."

The next washer veered off to the left and rolled to the base of the tree.

"How many points do I get for hitting the tree?" Alana joked.

"None, I'm afraid."

She threw her third washer, which landed on its side in the bottom of the hole. She looked at Jaydn, and he smiled. "Yes.

That one counts. As long as it's all the way in the hole and touching the bottom of the hole."

After throwing her other two washers, she ended up with twenty-five points. Then it was Jaydn's turn. Alana could tell that Evan and Sam weren't the only ones who played this game often. After his five pitches, he had fifty points.

Alana stepped up next to Jaydn to throw her second set of washers. When he didn't move, she raised her head slowly. He smelled of musk, woods, and mountain air, and her senses went on a journey to a peaceful, homey place where she wanted to stay for a while. With their faces only inches apart, she stared into his wistful, deep blue eyes wondering what it would feel like to get lost in their depths.

When Jaydn's gaze strayed to her lips, longing reached around her heart and squeezed. His lips were full and strong. His head leaned closer, giving her time to pull away. Instead, she leaned toward him and raised her face to his, inviting his closeness.

The kiss was soft and full of promise. Her arm curled around his neck and pulled his head closer. The feel of their lips together overpowered her senses.

Alana was lost in a world of bliss until something in the distance pulled her back to earth. Evan, standing at the door of the cabin, was yelling into the yard. "Mr. Holbrook? Are you there?"

Slowly, Jaydn pulled away from her. When he leaned back, he let out a ragged sigh. He walked to the end of the reed cane and waved at Evan.

Alana heard the troubled sigh, and reasoning overcame the elation filling her heart. Jaydn was sorry he kissed her—she felt it with her whole being. He was a handsome man, and he must have dated lots of girls. His sigh proved he was afraid kissing her might give her the wrong impression.

She'd just made a terrible mistake. Not only did she practically throw herself at Jaydn, but she shouldn't have kissed him in the first place. Hadn't she vowed to keep their relationship on a friendship basis?

Lord, I'm so sorry. It's hard to stay away from someone who makes me feel so complete. Please, help me, God.

She watched Jaydn walk to the house, not looking back. She was glad. If he looked back, she was afraid she might see regret in his eyes.

FIFTY-TWO

JAYDN WALKED TOWARD THE HOUSE, shaking his head.

What have I done? What was I thinking?

Her soft scent and sparkling eyes drowned out his good sense. And those lips—soft and tempting. He'd missed too much in life if this was what it meant to be happy. He could see them together for a lifetime—a happy-ever-after ending.

His heart plummeted when he remembered there could be no future for them. Alana hated the type person he couldn't help being.

He slipped back into sadness and resignation. She hadn't yet figured out he had money, but when she did, she would have nothing more to do with him.

He took the phone from Evan.

"Hello? Yes, I'll speak to him."

He watched Alana approaching the cabin slowly. Her head hung low, and her eyes were lowered—trying not to seem interested in his phone call. Either she was still nervous about her morning conversation with Patricia, or she regretted the kiss. Why did he have the horrible insight to believe the latter was the case?

Alana followed Jaydn to the cabin, scolding herself for what she allowed to happen. Listening carefully, she heard Jaydn say hello to Brad. She moved to stand beside him and listen to the conversation.

"Hey, Brad. What's going on? … You're kidding! Do you know why? … Yeah, she's right here. I'll let you talk to her."

Jaydn handed Alana the phone. "Brad says their office was burglarized last night, and several files were stolen."

Alana took the phone, her mind churning for a connection. "Hey, Spot."

"Hey, munchkin! Are you feeling better?"

"Much. But, what's this about files being stolen?"

"When Bo came into the office this morning, he found the contents of all the file cabinet drawers scattered all over the floor. It'll take all day to put everything back in order, but so far, the ones we know for sure are missing are the files of the murder at the Remington Complex."

Alana sucked in her breath. "That's the one I took pictures of."

"I know. The whole set of files are gone. Late last night, the Federal Express man brought the CD that Stranton mailed, and I filed it before I went home for a quick bite. Now the CD and the notes you made are gone. Please tell me you made duplicates."

"Sure, Brad. You know I always do. I e-mailed myself a copy of the notes and mailed a duplicate CD to my apartment in Ross. But, what's this about Stranton mailing you a CD?"

"It's a long story. Do you still have the same e-mail account?"

She nodded. "Yeah, but I don't have a computer here. I'll give you the password, and you can print the notes from there, can't you?"

"I'll get Kent to do it. The Chief of Police in Ross can get someone out to your apartment to get the CD."

"Wait a minute, Brad. When my apartment got trashed, I had all my mail sent to the post office box I keep for my photography business. The CD should be there."

"Oh. Do you have the key for the P.O. box?"

Alana slapped a hand to her forehead. "It's at the apartment—in the middle kitchen drawer right next to the refrigerator. At least, I guess it's still there."

She paused for a moment, and her brow tightened up as she frowned. "Brad, do you think this has a connection with someone trying to kill me?"

Brad let out a troubled breath. "I'm not sure. We'll have to take a look at the pictures and see what we can find. That's the only set of files missing so far, but the picture CD's of the stolen items from each of the burglaries are missing as well. Somebody's scared of something we might discover in those files. Maybe there's a connection somewhere. Jaydn said I could come out to the cabin in the helicopter with Naomi this evening, so we can put our heads together and brainstorm then. I'll make an extra set of the pictures and bring them with me, along with the notes."

"Okay. And, Brad … please be careful."

"I will, Lane. Don't worry, okay?"

Alana punched the end button on the phone and handed it to Jaydn.

"Whoever vandalized Brad's office stole the file of a murder scene that I photographed, along with all the photos of the stolen items from the sheet murders."

She stood staring at the clouds moving in the distance, her mind miles away in a jumbled apartment, seeing again the horrible scene—the room in turmoil, stripped of its beauty, and a woman dead—rolled in a bloody sheet.

Something she saw must be the key. What was she missing? Why couldn't she figure it out?

Jaydn put his hands on her shoulders. "Alana? Are you okay?"

She jumped and shook her head. "It's the pictures. It has to be. Something in the pictures he doesn't want me to remember." She put her head in her hands.

"Are you sure it's a *he*?"

She stared at him then shook her head. "I don't know."

"Can I ask you a question? Why do you call Brad *Spot*, and why does he call you *munchkin*?"

The sudden change of subject surprised her for a second, until she realized he was attempting to divert her thoughts from the murders.

For a moment, she struggled to re-direct her train of thought. Then, humor chased the apprehension from her thoughts, and she answered.

"When we were little, it was Brad's job to make us snacks after school. He thought I was weird because I only liked crunchy snacks. So, he started calling me munchkin. Then one day after school, when I was about ten, Brad was teasing me about making a snack I couldn't munch—instant pudding. He was making it in the blender, and he forgot to put the top on before he turned it on. Pudding went everywhere. It splattered all over the cabinet, the walls, and all over Brad. We laughed so hard, we cried. I told him he looked like Spot, our dog. Spot was tan with dark brown spots. After that, every time he called me munchkin, I'd call him Spot. The names sort of stuck. It makes us feel closer, somehow."

A gentle smile on her lips relaxed her face until it blossomed into a full-blown smile, and Jaydn held his breath. He was afraid breathing would cover up the rays of the sun that just lit up Alana's face.

FIFTY-THREE

T HAT EVENING, JAYDN WATCHED AS Alana ran down the wide front steps of the cabin and waited for the rotor blades on the helicopter to make a complete stop. When Brad stepped onto the ground, she threw her arms around his neck.

"Spot! Oh, it's good to see you again."

"It's only been a few days, munchkin."

"I know, but it seems like forever."

She gave him an affectionate kiss on the cheek and turned to Naomi who stood beside him.

The older woman looked a little green around the gills. Jaydn hid a smile.

"Are you all right, Naomi?" Alana asked.

"Naomi doesn't like flying," said Jaydn, coming up behind her.

"Never did like it," said Naomi as she shook her head vigorously. "I'll be okay, though, now that me feet are planted firmly on the ground."

Jaydn smiled at the Irish accent, made stronger by the obviously distasteful experience of flying, and took the heavy bag from her shoulders.

Brad returned Alana's hug and handed her a bag.

"I brought two things for you. First of all, Lisa sent you more clothes. She said they were sent for the mission barrel at church and are supposed to be your size."

Alana's eyes suddenly grew moist.

"Thanks, Brad. Thank Lisa for me too. What was the second thing?"

"A computer." He hand her the second bag. "It's an old laptop I had before the station pitched in and bought me a new one. It's not too fast, but you can at least check your e-mail and edit your photos."

She linked her arm through Brad's and took the second bag with a smile. "Thanks, Brad. I don't care how slow it is. Just having a computer is wonderful! Did you bring the crime scene pictures?"

"Right here." He patted a small overnight bag he was carrying on his shoulder. "I also called several of the insurance companies covering the burglaries and asked them for pictures of the items reported stolen. I haven't had a chance to go through any of them yet, but maybe we'll finally get a break and find something to connect some of the dots."

Alana bit her bottom lip, and Jaydn saw hope in her expression—hope that Brad could finally solve these terrible murders, hope that she could stop fearing for her life, but most of all, hope for an end to this nightmare.

"Don't worry, Lane. We'll figure it out. God will help us somehow."

Brad nodded toward Jaydn, and Jaydn could tell in a glance Brad had more to say. Jaydn glanced at Alana then nodded his understanding as they headed into the house.

After the evening meal, Alana sat at the kitchen table with Brad's old computer and opened her e-mail inbox. A strange e-mail address came up on the screen.

"Huh. I wonder who ms12345 is. Maybe it's someone looking for a photographer."

She opened the file and started reading.

Hey Baby. Just letting you know I'm not giving up. You better be thinking about us again, or else you'll be sorry, and you know it. See you later, Baby. I'm never far away. I'm keeping my eyes on you.

"Brad!"

Brad filled the doorway. "What?"

She gestured to the computer screen. Brad leaned over and read the message written in bold letters. Then he rocked back on his heels. "It's just bluster, Alana. Martin's not proving to be very bright. There's no way he can find you here. I'll get Bo to pick him up. Then he'll have some explaining to do. If we have to, we'll get a restraining order." He touched her on the arm and smiled reassuringly. "Just forget it. Why don't you start sorting through those pictures I brought? I'm counting on at least one of them giving us a clue about why these things are happening."

Alana nodded and opened the box containing all the pictures.

After an hour, she still sat in the same spot, meticulously scrutinizing the pictures of the crime scene at the Remington Complex—a cup of coffee in one hand and a pencil in the other.

Brad spent most of the evening on the phone talking to his men and the dispatch office. Jaydn alternated between watching Alana scrutinize pictures and listening to Brad in the next room talking on the phone. Finally, Brad pulled Jaydn aside into the den with a nervous glance in Alana's direction. "We had another victim yesterday," he half-whispered.

Jaydn shook his head. His heart hurt for the victim. The flicker of hope he saw in Brad surprised him. He waited for more.

"We think we have a clue that might give us a lead. One of the investigators found a black hair hung in a ring the victim was wearing. Her hair was gray, she's not married, and her only pet, a cat, is yellow. If this belongs to the murderer, we can possibly get a DNA match from the FBI data files."

He actually looked happy.

"It's our first real break. At least, we hope it is."

"Don't you want to tell her?" Jaydn nodded toward Alana, bent over the pictures.

"No. The murder would upset her. Plus, the strand of hair might get her hopes up and then turn out to be nothing. I have to go back first thing in the morning, but I'll leave the pictures with you and Alana. See if you can find anything odd. Maybe we'll get lucky."

Later, Alana walked back into the room where Jaydn was talking to Brad as he ate a late-night dinner.

Alana shuddered and rubbed her head in frustration.

"I just don't see anything out of the ordinary in all these pictures. Everyone on the investigative team saw everything I did, but no one else is being targeted."

Brad pushed back his chair. "Lane, think a minute. Can you remember anything you might have seen that you didn't photograph? Sometimes even the smallest detail seems unimportant, but it breaks the whole case."

Alana shook her head. "Brad, I got everything in the room down in pictures. You know how I am. I take a sweeping shot of everything. There's nothing in that room that wouldn't have been in these photographs."

Brad let out a defeated sigh. "I know. That's why I asked for your help this time. We weren't getting anywhere in the murder investigations. I was hoping your set of pictures might be more thorough—maybe pick up something the other photographers were missing."

"Besides," Jaydn interjected, "why would the pictures have been stolen if Alana saw something but didn't photograph it?"

"Maybe the thief thought she got it down in pictures as well."

Alana shook her head in confusion. "But, if that's the case, then everyone on the team would be in danger."

She blinked several times at the light overhead as she dropped her head back and rolled her neck around. Jaydn saw telltale signs of a headache coming on.

"I just can't look at them anymore tonight." She stood up and turned toward Brad.

"I have to go to bed, Brad. I'll see you in the morning."

She turned to Jaydn and spoke. Her voice sounded soft and rote. "Thanks again, Jaydn, for letting me stay. Goodnight."

The blank expression on her face worried Jaydn. He exchanged a concerned look with Brad as they watched her retreating figure.

Brad leaned back in his seat and let out a tired sigh. "She's taking this better than I expected, but she's awfully strung out."

Jaydn watched Alana trudge up the stairs and nodded.

Brad picked up the files containing the pictures and placed them on the sideboard. "Maybe you or Alana can find something in these. I'll have to look through them later. I have another hour's worth of work to do, then I'll be ready for bed too. I'm beat, old man. I've been up for twenty hours straight."

Jaydn grinned at him sheepishly. "The way I feel, I won't be able to sleep tonight at all. I think I'll dig Dad's old Bible out of the cobwebs and read for a while. I bet I get something different out of it than he did."

Brad grinned and nodded. "Good idea. Good night."

FIFTY-FOUR

THE NEXT MORNING, ALANA WAS the first one downstairs—her mind on a conversation she was planning to have with Brad. He would be firm and say no, she was sure, but she was determined not to back down.

The smell of freshly brewed coffee teased her and called her into the large family-style kitchen. Naomi was pulling a fresh batch of blueberry muffins out of the oven.

"Mmmm. Those smell great, Naomi. No wonder Jaydn takes you everywhere he goes. I would get spoiled on your cooking."

Naomi beamed with pleasure. "Oh, go on with you now. Sit down here and eat your breakfast before it gets cold. I guess the boys will be here shortly. I heard Jaydn up early this morning, but I've seen neither hide nor hair of him yet. He's probably having his morning run."

Naomi pushed the basket of hot muffins toward Alana and hurried to pour her a cup of hot, steaming coffee.

"Does Jaydn run every morning?" Alana envied his freedom to run. Her morning runs had been neglected since the kidnapping. Running in open areas would be like inviting another attack on her life.

"Just about."

Alana said no more but finished her muffin and leaned back to enjoy her coffee. She watched the gentle mountain breeze blow the treetops on the mountain outside the window. Such a peaceful scene.

Standing, she walked to the thick glass door to drink in the sunshine shimmering on the morning dewdrops. Her gaze fell on the cement bench she enjoyed the day before. Jaydn's still form was seated there, huddled over what looked like a book. He wasn't running now. He was reading—and quite absorbed in what he was reading, if his still, bent-over form meant anything.

As she watched him, he closed the book and walked up the stone walkway to the house. She groaned. He would be here to voice his own objections to the bombshell she was about to drop on Brad. Brad's opposition was enough to tackle at one time. She sat back down and braced herself for a battle.

"Good morning!" Jaydn said as he walked through the sliding glass doors. Jaydn's cheerful tone and glowing countenance made Alana steal a second glance.

What made him so cheerful this morning?

When she saw the Bible in his hand, she sat back in her chair abruptly. Jaydn? Reading the Bible? Was that for real? Or was he faking a desire to read the Bible for her sake?

There were times that she thought Jaydn was attracted to her—times when she wasn't second-guessing herself. She could feel the chemistry between them, but she didn't want him faking a relationship with God to get on her good side. She wanted…no, she *needed* him to have a faith in God because it was a personal, private experience, not because it might win him points with her.

She had to admit, though, when she looked at him, there was something different about him. There was a peace … a contentment … a deep understanding that wasn't there before.

Suddenly, her heart felt lighter than it had been since coming to the cabin. Maybe the Lord was working through this horrible situation, after all.

Jaydn pulled a cup from the counter and poured himself some coffee. He laid the Bible down on the table next to his plate and sat down.

Alana glanced at the Bible and then at him. She was sure he could see the question marks in her eyes.

He looked at her for a minute and placed both hands flat on the table. "Alana, I've done something I need to tell you about." He glanced at the black leather of the Bible beside him.

Alana held her breath—caution restrained the excitement building inside her.

"I was running around the property yesterday when I said a prayer about something. It's not important what the prayer was about, but I realized what I'd done—I'd *prayed* to a God I had tried to convince myself didn't exist."

She waited patiently for him to continue.

"I told myself that if I said a prayer, then it meant I had to believe, somewhere deep in my heart, that there was a God in heaven who heard my prayer. After a lot of soul searching and remembering what I'd learned about God from my college friends, I gave my life to Him."

The suspicions she had before were erased by the contentment shining in his eyes. She raised her head and smiled. It started as a grin then expanded to a full smile that transformed her whole face.

"Jaydn, that's wonderful. I'm so happy for you."

She reached out to him and held his hands with hers. "I think you'll find God a caring and loving Being who never leaves us, no matter what comes into our lives."

He nodded. "I'm sure I will, Alana."

"Morning."

Alana jerked her hands from Jaydn's and hid them in her lap.

Brad strolled into the room in his usual disheveled morning state. He was barefoot, and his shirttail hung out over his pants. Alana laughed at his half-closed eyes under his slightly ruffled hair.

"Good morning, Spot. Sleep well?"

"Fine. Wonderful bed. Good as home."

Jaydn and Alana shared a smile over Brad's sluggish speech and his closed eyelids. Naomi placed a cup of hot coffee in front of him and stood back watching, her fists on her hips.

When he smelled the strong liquid, his eyes opened a little wider. His heavy fingers reached for the coffee, and he took a sip from the white ceramic cup.

"Mmm, good coffee."

Naomi nodded in satisfaction and went back to washing dishes.

Alana patiently waited for Brad to gradually rejuvenate as the stimulating liquid awakened his senses. She wanted him to finish breakfast before she brought up the subject she knew would make him hit the ceiling.

When he ate two muffins and was finishing his second cup of coffee, Alana glanced at Jaydn and pushed her chair back from the table. A sense of dread descended on her shoulders, but she plunged into the sensitive discussion.

"Brad, you know what Monday is, don't you?"

Brad rubbed his chin with his fingers and closed one eye. "No, I can't say that I do."

"Brad, think! You know what Monday is." Alana looked perturbed.

When the importance of Monday's date penetrated his sleepy brain, his eyes opened wide.

"No way! I'm *not* letting you go. Leaving this protected location is out of the question."

"You know I have to go. I missed last week because of the hotel thing, and I lost so many of the pictures when my computer was ruined. They're already worried about losing their building and having to move. I can't disappoint them again. You know what my going means to the kids."

Brad shook his head. "No, Alana. I said no, and I mean it. It's not safe."

She sat up straight in her chair and turned her full gaze of resolve in his direction. "If God has taken care of me this far, He's not going to stop now. He'll take care of me there too. Jaydn reminded me of that this morning. Where's your faith? No one even knows I'm going. I can't see that there's a risk."

Alana and Brad were taught since childhood to have faith and trust God to protect them. Brad had to know she was right. She was hoping his admiration for her courage and faith would win the battle within him over his frustration at her stubbornness; then he would concede it was more important for them to trust in God. She was his little sister, and as much as he loved her and wanted to protect her, she was still hoping he would respect her wishes. He knew ultimately that her safety was in God's hands.

"All right, Alana. I'll consider letting you go, *if* I can plan ahead and *if* I can make it safe—not only for you, but for the kids as well. But, you have to wait until I can go with you."

"I have to go Monday, Brad. That's when the kids are expecting me."

His sigh vibrated across the table. "All right, Alana. I'll see if I can work it out. But, let me see if I can get off, okay?"

She nodded. "But, if you can't come, I'm still going. I won't disappoint them again."

Brad stared at her. She injected as much persistence, determination, and stubbornness in the look she returned as she could muster until finally, his scowl gave away the fact he knew he was beaten. "Maybe I can get Elliott to go along if I can't go."

Alana was a little embarrassed that Jaydn witnessed a private family squabble, but he sat quietly across from them, not saying a thing, until Brad consented—obviously against his better judgment. Then, it seemed his curiosity got the better of him. He looked first at one, then the other, and said, "What's all this about?"

Brad looked at Alana to make sure it would be okay to reveal her secret. She nodded her approval.

"Alana's been volunteering at the Bishop Orphanage every Monday, spending some time with the kids. She's been taking specialized photographs of them, a few at a time, and she missed last week because of the hotel thing."

Jaydn turned to look at her as if he thought she was crazy. His look confirmed her thoughts—he was shocked at her request. The threat of a negative reaction fanned a fire in her eyes, and she let him know silently she wouldn't back down. His deep controlling breath was infused with patience.

"I know what you're thinking, Jaydn, and it won't do any good to argue. It should be safe if no one knows I'm going. Those kids don't get much pleasure, and they need this little bit of fun in their lives."

His scowl communicated a clear meaning: *That fool woman! Doesn't she know someone's trying to kill her?*

Suddenly, it hit her. Someone *was* trying to kill her. Would she be safe away from this bubble of protection in the woods? What in the world was she about to do?

FIFTY-FIVE

JAYDN SAT ACROSS THE TABLE from Alana and stared at her. Was she crazy? Risking her life to go see a bunch of kids at an orphanage. He sat there shaking his head in indecision until he said slowly, "All right, Alana. But, if you go, I'm taking you in my car—it's tinted. No one will be able to see you."

Alana turned her head and looked out the window. He could see she was resolved. If she let him come along, it wouldn't make a difference, but if he stopped her from going, he'd have a battle on his hands.

She nodded her agreement. "Okay. You can drive."

Jaydn stood up and stretched before asking, "What did you mean when you said they might lose their building?"

"Their landlord sent them word he wants them to move. He wants to tear down the building to build a parking garage for the town."

Jaydn paused. "Don't they have a lease?"

"Yeah, but the landlord's lawyer found some kind of loophole. They're afraid they'll have to move—they have no place to go. It's a privately-owned orphanage, so the state will step in if they can't move all the kids to another location. They'll be separated. Some of them are siblings, and that scares them to death. Right now, they're just one big family."

During her speech, the hair on the back of Jaydn's neck tingled. Something in what she said created an uneasy surge up his spine. Steve's words, "just some non-profit group," emerged from the back of his mind.

"Where did you say the orphanage is located?"

"Right in the middle of downtown Bishop."

Jaydn held his breath. Was he about to evict a bunch of kids from their home? For what? A money-making parking garage?

Shame boiled in his gut. The color in his face must have blanched white because he felt every drop of blood drained to his middle. Thankfully, it was all lost on Alana as she rambled on about the kids and their relationship to each other. By the end of her long explanation, Jaydn had called himself every bad name in the book.

No wonder Alana hated people with money. If she found out he was the one evicting her friends, it would add fuel to her harsh opinion of wealthy businessmen.

He'd been narcissistic and self-serving about so many things lately, but this orphanage thing was the icing on the cake. Finding a solution for this problem would be difficult. The kids meant every-thing to Alana. They filled her life so full that there was no room for a "rich, arrogant business executive"—something he was—like it or not.

Jaydn's thoughts were interrupted by a defeated mutter from Brad. Leaning across the table, Brad planted his elbows firmly on the shiny, aged wood.

"All right, Alana. I have to let you go, but I don't like it. I'm going home this morning, but call and let me know what time you're coming on Monday. If I can't go with you, I'll make sure one of the guys will."

Alana nodded, grinning at her victory.

She might be happy because she won, but Jaydn saw something else in her eyes: fear. The person trying to kill her had seen through her disguise and discovered her move to his apartment—he might do it again. Would she be safe?

Alana sighed, and then Jaydn saw her features covered with a wave of peace like a warm blanket. She was remembering some-thing she had already told them both: God would protect her.

FIFTY-SIX

AFTER HIS CONVERSATION WITH THE lab, exhaustion and excitement made Brad hold the phone for a minute before returning it to its cradle. He sat down in his office chair, perplexed.

The black hair found at the last murder scene was a perfect match to DNA they found in the elevator of the hotel where Alana was abducted.

Didn't this prove that Alana's kidnapping and the murders were connected? A small voice in his head had been telling him all along that they were, but the connection never materialized until now. The murderer must have thought that Alana had seen something incriminating at the murder scene. That's why she was followed to the hotel, kidnapped, and sent into the lake.

Unless, someone in the dark SUV had followed her to the hotel from Landeville for a different reason.

For whatever reason, it was likely he used the elevator to get to her room and carry her body to the car. It would have been hard to carry her body and her luggage down the stairs in the middle of the hotel walkway without someone seeing or hearing the commotion.

Now maybe the judge would give him a search warrant. He'd get DNA samples from every guest and employee at the hotel that night. It might take a while, but if it panned out, they'd have their murderer and Alana's kidnapper—all in one fell swoop.

Of course, there was a chance the kidnapper wasn't a guest or employee at the hotel, but they all needed to be contacted anyway. Someone might have seen the SUV or even the person driving.

He had to get some sleep. Then hopefully—maybe—all the

pieces would fall into place.

He wrote notes on what the lab told him and filed them away in his briefcase for the morning when he'd meet with his men. If they got together and brainstormed about the facts, maybe they'd finally be able to put pieces together and solve this puzzle.

Brad got busy the next day. After calling Judge Collins on the phone, he hoisted up his expanding briefcase and stepped into Bo's office. Bo was leaning over his desk—pushing a stack of paperwork around to make room for the steaming cup of coffee in his hand.

"Bo, I've got a job for you tomorrow."

Bo finally shoved several large folders off on the floor to make more room on the cluttered desk.

"What did you say, Brad?"

Brad frowned and repeated his last statement. "I said, I've got a job for you tomorrow. I want you and Kent, or maybe Elliott, to collect DNA samples from each of the guests who stayed at the hotel the night Alana was kidnapped. The ones from out of state will have to be collected from the local authorities."

Bo sat up alert in the chair.

"What's up, Brad?"

"The black hair at the last murder scene matches one taken from the hotel elevator. That means the two might be connected. Judge Collins is giving us a warrant to check DNA samples of all the staff and guests for the week before the kidnapping."

"Wow! You really think the two might be connected?"

"Don't know for sure, but if they are, the murderer might be the one who kidnapped Alana."

"Yeah, you might be right. I know Alana will be glad to find the person who tried to do her in." He took a sip of his coffee, noticed a ring left on his desk, and wiped it with his shirt sleeve before setting his cup down. Rubbing his jaw thoughtfully, Bo said, "You know, I don't think you ever said where you moved her to."

Brad stood unmoving for a moment before aiming a narrow-eyed look at Bo. "I'm keeping that information to myself. I'm not telling anybody. Somehow, it leaked before, but this time I'm keeping my trap shut."

Bo pushed back from his desk and stood up—his face red with irritation. "Well, if you don't trust me, then—"

"It's not that I don't trust you, Bo, but these things have a way of leaking out. When it means Alana's life, it doesn't matter who it is, I'm not telling." His jaw tightened. He didn't want to hurt the feelings of his friend, but he also had a responsibility to his sister. It was as important as her life.

Bo faced Brad and spoke, not bothering to hide his anger. "Let me know if you need my help protecting her—if you can trust me, that is." His tone was full of sarcasm.

Brad rubbed his face with his hand. He turned to walk away from Bo's office and almost tripped over Kent hovering behind the door. "Hey, man. Watch out! What're you doing hiding behind the door?"

"Sorry. I lost my pen." The apologetic man stammered as he made a swipe at the floor and avoided eye contact.

Brad looked at Kent and remembered something. "Can I see you in my office a minute?"

Kent followed Brad down the hall and raised a curious eyebrow when Brad closed the door behind them.

Brad reached inside his desk and pulled out a piece of wadded up tissue.

"We found this in Chet's desk drawer with your name on it. Is it yours?"

Kent examined the yellow diamond ring. "Nope. Never saw it before."

Brad frowned. "I guess Chet must have meant for you to have it since he scribbled your name on it. It's yours."

Kent stared at the yellow diamond ring—something unreadable glowing in his face. "Wow. For real? I didn't know Chet could afford something so classy."

"I haven't checked it out, but I imagine it's paste. Chet lived like the rest of the other rookies—from paycheck to paycheck. There's no way he could afford a real stone like that. Do you know what yellow diamonds are worth?"

Kent shrugged and slipped the ring on his finger. "Wonder

why he wanted me to have it. It's not like we were best friends or anything—like Elliott. Why didn't he give it to Elliott?"

Brad shrugged. "Beats me. Listen, I never saw your report on the hotel investigation you and Bo did after Alana's attack. I wanted your opinion of what you saw that day ... the room, the walls, the carpet, etc."

Kent shrugged again. "I never made it to the hotel that day. Got called to a brush fire on Pine Road. Turned out to be a false alarm. Bunch of kid playing in a vacant lot. By the time I got the report filed, Bo was already back at the station. He handled the investigation and all the paperwork. You'll have to ask him."

Brad sat on the edge of his desk, perplexed. Bo never mentioned handling the hotel by himself. Knowing how Bo hated to do leg work, Brad figured Bo would have complained at least until Christmas. He shrugged and watched Kent admiring the ring on his finger.

"Don't let that ring go to your head, and don't let it hinder your work, okay?"

Kent stiffened. "You know me better than that." The tone of his voice could fry eggs.

Brad rubbed his forehead. He had to solve these cases in a hurry. If he didn't, he wouldn't have a sister or a friend left.

FIFTY-SEVEN

A LANA SAT INDIAN STYLE ON the den carpet—pictures and papers spread across the floor in front of her. Creepy sensations crawled across her skin as she flipped through the pictures of the bloody sheet. After studying the photos of the body from different angles, she grouped them together and hid them back in the envelope.

Out of sight, out of mind. She shivered.

Most of Saturday and Sunday was spent viewing crime scene photographs meticulously and repeatedly—with no success. Nothing in the pictures revealed anything out of the ordinary. There was no "smoking gun" to give them the name of the murderer—no revealing evidence—no "*ah-ha*" moment.

"It doesn't make sense."

Frustration drained her strength, and she sat back against the chair in a dejected huddle. Rubbing her eyes with the palms of her hands, she had a hopeful thought. Maybe Jaydn would be able to see something she was too close to the situation to see.

Thoughts of Jaydn hovered in front of her like the sunshine filtering in through the curtains. For some reason, he had withdrawn from her. The warmth that radiated from their relationship two days ago had cooled to a frosty breath of air.

Something she did must have disappointed him. Maybe it was that kiss. She'd been too eager.

Knowing he pushed her away hurt. He had locked himself in his office to emphasize the separation in spirit, and had emerged only a few times from behind the heavy door. When he came out to eat or sleep, his face was pinched and drained.

She could have forced her way into his office and his attention, but it would have been a fatal mistake. Every minute she spent with him only increased the longing for more.

Obviously, his feelings toward her had changed. Instead of torturing her already-breaking heart, she tried avoiding him as well. Her resolve to keep their relationship on a friends-only basis strengthened.

Easier said than done!

Something about him made her knees go weak and her stomach churn with anticipation. Her strong resolve to remain friends and nothing more was hard to keep when her body refused to cooperate.

Keeping a firm distance was her only option.

She forced her mind away from thinking of Jaydn and began sorting photographs into piles. Pictures of the same area in each room were grouped together. After sorting them, she began flipping through each stacked pile.

Suddenly, she pulled out two identical pictures and stared at them critically. They were in the same grid of the search area, and yet something felt different. Her skin prickled as she stared at the two pictures.

"What is it about these two pictures?"

She scanned them carefully, hoping the solution would jump up and grab her attention.

The first picture was an angled view of the victim's feet. In the background was a man's hand stuffing evidence from the carpeted floor into one of the evidence bags. A golden wedding ring glinted in the camera flash.

Probably Vernon. He'd been married only five months.

She picked up the second picture and compared it with the first. It was the same picture, but from a different angle. The thing that confused her was the man's hand in the background. It was also picking up evidence, but the hand was different. There was no ring on this man's left hand.

She shook her head. Something wasn't right. She knew enough

about Brad's procedures to know he only allowed one person gathering evidence in each grid of a crime scene. No one was allowed back in an area that was swept unless there was a question later in the investigation or if there were problems with some of the evidence.

She stared at the second picture until the solution jumped out and struck raw nerves.

Bingo!

For some reason a second person entered that grid. But who? And why? And what were they stuffing into the evidence bag? In the first picture, the tweezers held what looked like a piece of lint, but the evidence in the second picture was a piece of something small and white.

"Lord, please help me figure this out."

She stared carefully at the second picture and tried to make out what the man held in his hand. Was it a piece of paper? A matchbook? It could be a cigarette butt. Without a magnifying glass or enlarging that section of the picture, it was hard to tell.

She ran her hands through her tangled hair.

A break was what she needed.

Picking up the two questionable pictures, she walked out the door. As she passed Jaydn's office, she heard him speaking to someone on the phone.

Probably his office.

She was grateful he could handle some of his work while away from the office, but each day he stayed with her, the concern he might be fired increased.

She headed toward the kitchen, where Naomi was finishing the dishes from supper.

"Would you like some hot chocolate, honey?"

"No, but I would love one of those muffins we had for breakfast, if there are any left, and maybe some coffee." She sniffed the coffee with a deep, appreciative breath.

Naomi pulled a bowl from the refrigerator and handed her a plate. "About twenty seconds in the microwave makes them taste like fresh baked."

Alana put two miniature muffins on the plate and stuck it into the microwave. She poured herself a cup of hot, black liquid, then took a seat facing Naomi and laid the pictures in front of her on the table.

"Jaydn's working hard today, isn't he?" she said absentmindedly as she sipped the soothing liquid. "I hope he doesn't get into trouble at work for being here."

Naomi grinned again. "Don't you worry, honey. Jaydn knows what he's doing."

FIFTY-EIGHT

JAYDN SAT AT THE DESK in the cabin's roomy office, staring at the wind blowing through the leaves in the oak tree outside his window.

There was only one way to fix this problem. He would call Steve about reversing the eviction order for the orphanage. If he continued his plans and Alana learned the truth, she would never forgive him for uprooting and dismantling the orphanage. She would hate him when she found out it was him—the big-time executive, forcing them to move.

He even hated himself.

"But I'm not that man anymore," he reasoned. "Surely if God can forgive the man I was, Alana should be able to forgive me as well."

He picked up the Bible sitting on the edge of his desk and opened it to the concordance in the back. Somewhere he'd read about becoming a new creature after giving your life to Christ.

Here it was: Second Corinthians, chapter five, verse seventeen.

He fumbled through the pages of the Bible until he found the verse he wanted and read it aloud.

"Therefore if any man be in Christ, he is a new creature: old things are passed away; behold, all things are become new."

That means I'm a new creature, Lord. There has to be some way to fix what I've already done.

He picked up the phone and dialed his office. A hard, nasal sounding voice answered the call.

"Jaydn Holbrook's office. Bobbie speaking."

"Bobbie, this is Jaydn Holbrook. Can you please give me the number of Steve Reynolds' cell phone?"

"I'm sorry, sir. We're not allowed to give personal numbers over the phone."

"Look, Bobbie … oh, never mind. Just give me his work number."

It seemed to take Bobbie forever to find the number. Jaydn wrote it down as she dictated, then called Steve's office. His secretary informed him that Steve was out of the country and wouldn't be back until late tomorrow.

Tomorrow. One more day wouldn't make a difference. Steve would reverse the damage he'd done to the orphanage, and Alana would never know—*if* he could keep it from her until everything was straightened out.

He'd been working in his office all morning, but hiding away from their uncertain relationship and pretending she was nowhere around wasn't working.

His inability to be honest with her about owning a successful company was frustrating, but more than anything, he missed her smile. She had worked her way under his skin—a dangerous place to be when there were doubts about their future together. Their future could be brighter if he could find the person stalking her.

He sat back and thought about the clues. Alana's attack at the hotel. Her apartment was trashed and bombed, yet nothing was stolen. Her attack at the apartment pool seemed to indicate that whoever this was wanted her dead, but why? Something she saw? *Someone* she saw? Was it related to the sheet murders, or had she made someone mad enough for revenge? Could it be Martin—trying to get payback? And, what about the last clue—the black hair?

Picking up the phone, he dialed Brad's number and was surprised to hear him answer so quickly.

"Jaydn?"

"Alana's fine, Brad. I just wondered if you'd had any luck with that black hair you found in the ring of the last murdered woman."

"We know the black hair at the murder scene has the same DNA patterns as the DNA left at the hotel elevator, but we don't yet know who the DNA belongs to. We're in the process of taking samples from all the employees and guests who were registered the week before her attack. The problem is that a couple of them live out of state. We have to get the local police to contact them, take the sample, and send it to our lab. That takes time. Something we're short of."

Jaydn tried to keep the excitement from coloring his words. "That's good news, though. Isn't it? Have you told Alana?"

"Not yet. I'd rather wait until we know for sure that the two are connected. If we find a DNA match from someone at the hotel, it'll prove they're involved with the murders. It will also give us a hint why Alana has been targeted. If the two scenes are connected, her being targeted probably has something to do with the murder scene she photographed.

"But … it could have been someone else following her from Landeville for a totally different reason. In that case, none of the DNA samples will match.

"There's something else I need to tell you, Jaydn. I'm worried there might be a leak in my department. The crooks seem to be one step ahead of me in this investigation. The hotel room where Alana was attacked was cleaned out and everything was replaced before my team got there. We put out an APB on Chet's neighbor, and he'd already disappeared before the alert was even announced. And of course, someone found out Alana was at your apartment in Ross. We still haven't been able to find the man washing his car outside her apartment building, but if he's legit, the only other person who knew where she was at that time was Bo. He said he mentioned it to several people working the murder cases, so most of the department knew she'd been moved. That means it has to be someone connected with the department. Only someone in the department could have known all these things to stay one step ahead of us."

Jaydn groaned. "No wonder you're having such a hard time."

"Just don't mention it to anyone until I let you know. There's one more thing—I wanted to go with Alana to the orphanage, but I really need to finish collecting these samples and get them to the lab. We haven't told anyone when she's going, so I think the risk is minimal. But, I'd feel better knowing you were there to keep an eye on her."

"Sure, Brad. You know how I feel about her—even though she may never feel the same way about me. You know I'd protect her with my life."

"Thanks, buddy. It means a lot. And listen, before you stop at the orphanage, take Alana by the Bishop police station. I'd like her to look at the mug shots of Gene Hollister to see if she recognizes him from the hotel."

When Jaydn hung up the phone, he sat back in his chair. He had a feeling his life would never be normal again—if there was such a thing as normal any more, now that Alana completely captured his body, mind, and soul.

FIFTY-NINE

Alana was about to swallow a bite of her muffin when Jaydn burst into the room.

"I found something different in these two pictures." He laid two pictures on the table, identical to the ones Alana was studying. Glancing at her two photos, he added, "Looks like we both noticed the same thing." He leaned over her shoulder to study the four photographs.

She nodded and looked up. That was a mistake.

His face was only inches from hers. Her gaze was captured by his eyes, as blue as the sky in the evening sunset. She caught her breath as they brightened to an even deeper blue. Words that were on the tip of her tongue caught in her throat. All she could think was *Wow, he looks good!*

"Alana?"

She cleared her throat and looked around the room, anywhere but at those eyes.

"I'm sorry, Jaydn. What were you saying?"

"I said it looks like we both have questions about the same two photographs."

Alana nodded, forcing her gaze from his rugged features to look at the pictures. Trying to pull her raveling thoughts into coherent sentences was almost impossible. She concentrated on the pictures to clear her head.

"I know. It's odd. Brad never allows anyone back in an area that's already been swept. It's strange that a second man would be picking up evidence in the same grid, and at a different time, too, according to the digital time the camera recorded."

Jaydn studied the four pictures. "Do you recognize either of the two men in the pictures?"

"The one with the wedding ring might be Vernon. He was just married, and the ring in this picture looks new. But, I don't know who the other man is. There's no ring or anything to tell us who it might be."

Naomi slammed the back door as she took the mop outside to shake it out and hang it up to dry on the wooden deck.

Jaydn leaned over farther to pick up two of the pictures and study them closer, his head just inches from hers.

The musky smell of his aftershave gave Alana's heart a jolt, and she wanted to close her eyes and enjoy the way it made her feel. The stubble of a day's growth of beard covered his square jaw, and she traced its lines with her eyes, swallowing hard when she reached his lips.

Her heart refused to beat its next turn, and she raised her gaze to those blue lagoon eyes. He glanced from the photos to her, and the yearning she saw there almost took away her next breath. She was hypnotized by the longing conveyed in his eyes. Their heads moved closer together until there was only a breath between them.

Alana's brain yelled at her. *Stop! This won't work. He doesn't feel the same attraction you do.* But, her heart could only think about the smell of his aftershave and the lips she tasted before … so close.

The back door broke the trance as Naomi returned from outside and closed the door. Jaydn lowered himself into a seat slowly and cleared his throat. Alana jumped when he spoke—his voice cracking with emotion.

"Can you ask Brad about who was supposed to be searching that area?"

Alana nodded automatically, not wanting to admit she had no idea what he just asked. She tried to pull his last sentence from her short-term memory.

"Uh, yeah. I'll check that picture out."

Jaydn stood up suddenly and smiled shakily. He walked to the door, then turned around and frowned. "I guess I need to get everything ready for the trip tomorrow. Are you sure we can't talk you out of visiting the orphanage?"

Alana wanted to agree to anything he asked just to see him smile again, but the faces of disappointed children won the argument. She shook her head, a determined look on her face.

SIXTY

J AYDN GLANCED AT ALANA AS they sat in his car outside the Bishop City Police Department. She took a deep breath and bit her lip. Jaydn knew Brad didn't realize, when he asked her to look at the picture of Gene Hollister, how hard it would be for her to look into the face of the man who might have attacked her in the hotel bathroom. She'd mentioned how those dark eyes had haunted her dreams and would for a long time.

"You ready to go in?" Jaydn asked, knowing she was dreading this stop.

"Yeah. Let's get it over with."

When they stepped into the large waiting room, the policeman at the front desk looked at them. "Can I help you folks?"

"Yes, uh … this is Alana Candler and she's here to look at the mug shot of …"

"Gene Hollister. Yeah, I know about it. Come on into the administrative office, and I'll get one of the guys to help you."

Jaydn and Alana followed him into a large room that had a conference-size table and several desks and computers.

"Have a seat at this table right here. I'll get one of our officers to bring the mug book out."

As Alana walked over to the table, a man standing in the doorway of an adjoining room turned around.

"Kent! What are you doing here?"

Kent look surprised to see Alana. "Hey! We're picking up DNA samples and doing interviews with some of the customers from the Lakeside Hotel."

Elliott walked out of the room, shook hands with Jaydn, and turned to Alana. "Are you here to look at Hollister's mug shot?"

Alana nodded.

A uniformed officer came into the room with a large black book and set it on the table.

"How do you do? I'm Officer Randall." He shook hands with the three men then put the book on the table. "We've got the page marked here with an eye witness form."

Kent walked over to the table and pointed to a man's face on the right side of the page. "That's him."

Alana bent to look closer at the face in the edge of the page then shuddered. "That looks like him. I could only see his eyes, but I remember the scar in his eyebrow, just like this one."

Elliott walked over to the book. "Are you sure, Alana? We don't want to accuse the wrong person."

Kent gave him a sharp look and then pushed the binding down farther so the picture was more visible. Something shiny on Kent's hand caught Jaydn's eye. A yellow diamond ring glittered in the sunlight coming in from the open window.

Jaydn tilted his head. He'd seen that ring somewhere before ... and recently. But where? It planted an uncomfortable knot in his stomach. It was unusual to see a ring that gaudy. Why couldn't he remember where he'd seen it? It would probably come to him eventually.

Alana leaned over the table and took one more look. "Yeah. I'm pretty sure that looks just like the face I saw ... at least the part I could see."

Officer Randall took out a piece of paper and asked Alana to sign it. She signed her name then turned toward Jaydn—her face a pasty white.

"Let's go now. The kids are waiting."

As they were making their way to the front of the building, Bo came out of a room filled with lockers. He was followed by another uniformed officer.

"Hey, you guys," he said. He stopped to shake Jaydn's hand and smiled at Alana. "How'd the mug shot turn out?"

Alana shivered. "It was him."

Bo nodded—his face was emotionless. "You could tell with just the eyes, huh? Good job. Gotta run. See you guys later."

Jaydn put his hand on Alana's elbow for moral support. "It's all over now, Alana. Maybe this will help them put Hollister behind bars, and you won't have to worry about him anymore."

"If they can find him." Her voice held a touch of doubt, and Jaydn felt the same way. So far, nothing in this investigation seemed to be falling into place.

SIXTY-ONE

JAYDN DROVE THE WHITE BUICK into the orphanage parking lot with a heavy heart. He closed his eyes when he saw the address engraved on the plaque on the side of the building.

The numbers matched the ones he gave Steve—the new location for the Bishop Parking Deck.

When Alana got out of the car and began pulling her photography equipment from the trunk, Jaydn pushed redial on his phone and waited for Steve's secretary to pick up.

"Reynolds and Anthony."

"Hey, Mattie, this is Jaydn again. Did you ever get in touch with Steve?"

"No, sir, I'm sorry. He doesn't seem to be answering his phone, or he's in a place with no service. I left him the message about the property in Bishop, but I don't know whether he received it or not. I also left a note to have him call you as soon as he can."

"Thanks, Mattie. Tell him it's important."

Jaydn hung up the phone rebuking himself. *This is what happens when you act like a big-time real estate tycoon. Now look at the predicament you've got yourself into.*

He got out of the car when Alana slammed the trunk and hurried to help her carry the equipment into the front door of the orphanage. When he stepped inside the doorway, the darkness of the walls made it hard to focus, but what he saw when things began to clear surprised him.

Laughing, shouting, happy children hurried to encircle Alana. She gave each of them a kiss and a hug, and each one hugged her back. Jaydn guessed their ages ranged from about four years old to ten or eleven, and he could tell they were overjoyed to see her.

The sense of belonging and acceptance transformed each little upturned face. They were all talking at once, making it hard to distinguish each conversation, but bits and pieces let him know how much they missed her visit last week.

The smile on her face was so genuine that it astounded him. It seemed to glow like the sunshine. It was obvious she loved children with an all-consuming love, and it was just as plain that the children adored her.

A little blond-headed girl hugged the wall with eyes lowered— far away from the other kids. When Alana saw the shy child, a sigh of kindness escaped her lips, and she rushed to give the slight form a hug and a smile. Carefully, she drew her into the ring with the other children.

Jaydn swallowed and leaned against the wall. One more thing to admire about her—she loved children. His heart was be-yond hope.

A short woman in her late fifties came hurrying through the door.

"Now, children, don't squeeze Miss Alana to death. Give her room to breathe." The children pulled away for a second, but then they were right back, touching Alana lovingly as if they were afraid she would suddenly be taken from them.

Alana turned to Jaydn. "Jaydn, this is Shirley Hamlin. She and her husband Darrell are the 'parents' of all these children. Shirley, this is Jaydn Holbrook, a friend of mine."

Shirley's eyes narrowed as she turned to stare at Jaydn. She glared at him.

"Why are you here, Mr. Holbrook?"

Without moving a muscle, Jaydn cringed inwardly. The pointed expression on Shirley Hamlin's face spoke volumes.

She knew who he was.

He let out a slow breath of air before replacing the flat expression on his face with the strongest smile he could summon.

"Shirley!" Alana seemed shocked. Shirley's tone was condemning and Jaydn could see Alana was struggling to understand.

"Mr. Holbrook brought me today because I had," she paused and looked around at the tiny faces watching, "uh … a problem last week with my car. He was kind enough to help me haul my photography equipment."

The frown on Shirley's face was replaced with suspicion, then an awkward confusion. Hesitation transformed Shirley's face, but she finally said, "Well, Miss Alana, the kids are sure looking forward to getting their pictures made today, but Darrell and I are working on a water leak upstairs in the girls' bathroom. We'll be able to help you later if you'd like to wait," she glanced at Jaydn's red face, "until a better time."

"Nonsense. Jaydn's happy to help me. That's what he's here for. He can help the boys, and I'll get the girls ready."

The children suddenly sensed there was a question about having the pictures made and started groaning.

"Now, kids," Jaydn said, raising a hand to get their attention, "see how quiet you can be, and we'll see who gets to be the first one in front of the camera."

Shouts of joy were suddenly replaced by little voices issuing the command, "Shhh … shhhh …"

Quite suddenly, there was silence.

Alana laughed and looked at Jaydn with a sense of awe. "Wow! Good job!" She smiled. "All right, kids, those of you who are in the third group for pictures line up here in the hall, and we'll take you into the cafeteria. The rest of you have to wait your turn."

Jaydn grinned at the mixed sense of happiness in the children's faces. There was a little pushing and shoving, but for the most part, the ones being left behind knew their time would come.

Shirley reached around the edge of the door to a key rack hanging on the wall. Instead of handing the keys to Jaydn, she stepped across the room and put them into Alana's hands. "Here's the keys to the cafeteria, sweetie. Are you sure you don't want me to come along?"

Jaydn heard the strained note in the older woman's voice as she stole an annoyed look in his direction. He could tell by her tone that the offer to go with them was not one Shirley liked making.

"We'll be fine, Shirley."

They ushered the children out the door and into the long hall-way. As they passed one of the large hall windows, Alana froze. The child following her bumped into her and stopped. Alana jumped back from the window and leaned against the wall—her face lost its color. She looked back at Jaydn. He could see fear in her eyes and wondered what was wrong.

"Okay, everyone, sit down on the floor for just a minute while Miss Alana and I discuss the, uh … procedures."

The children groaned but slid down onto the floor.

Two redheaded boys starting shoving each other across the wide hallway until Jaydn grabbed their shirts and planted each one on either side of the line. Giving them each a stern look, he strode purposefully toward Alana.

She pulled him close—not wanting to scare the kids—and whispered, "Jaydn, that's Martin's car outside, parked by the curb."

The memory of Brad's description of Martin pushing Alana's head against the wall set his jaw. He crouched low on the floor and peeked out the bottom of the window.

"Call 9-1-1 and then call Brad. Get Shirley to come down and stay with you and the kids. I'm going to slip around the back of the orphanage and see if I can sneak up on him from behind."

"What?" squeaked Alana. "No, Jaydn! He might have a gun. Please wait for help."

"I won't do anything until they get here—just call 9-1-1."

SIXTY-TWO

ALANA DUG HER PHONE OUT of her purse and dialed 9-1-1 to report Martin as she ushered the children back into the great room of the rambling orphanage. After handing them over to Shirley, she dialed Brad's number.

"Brad Candler."

"Brad, Martin's here at the orphanage."

"Call 9-1-1. They can be there faster than any of my men."

"I already did."

Brad mumbled something to someone with him, then his voice deepened, and his tone implied confidence. "Bo and Kent are right around the corner, Alana. Sit tight. Where's Strands now?"

Alana slipped back into the hall and peeked through the window at Martin's car. "Across the street, still sitting in his car."

"Are you in the building?"

"Yes, but, Brad, Jaydn went around the back of the building to … I don't know what he went to do. He said he was going to sneak up on Martin!"

"It's okay. Jaydn won't do anything foolish. Just sit tight. My guys should be there within a minute or two. Stay on the line with me, okay?"

Alana nodded absentmindedly, forgetting he couldn't see her response. "Brad, how did he know I was here?"

"You've never made it a secret that you visit the orphanage sometimes, Alana. He probably just hoped you'd show."

Alana stole another peek at Martin's car. It was still sitting in the same spot, but Martin was moving around like he was agitated.

When she picked up the sound of a siren in the distance, she realized he must have heard it as well. While she watched, he started the car with a grinding sound and barreled out into the street. She saw Jaydn run from behind the building across the street just as the patrol car came careening beside them. He pointed toward the gray car turning the next corner, and they followed without even slowing.

"He's running, Brad!"

"I know. I heard Kent's report on the scanner. They'll catch him, and then he'll have some explaining to do."

At the same time, the city's cruiser came barreling after them—its siren blaring and lights flashing.

The adrenaline rush left her, and she relaxed. Blowing out a sigh of relief, she spoke into the phone.

"He's gone, Brad." Her voice was shaky and distant.

"Are you okay?"

"Yeah, I just wish this would end."

"Maybe it will soon."

Alana hung up the phone as Shirley and Darrell hurried to her side.

"Are you okay, Alana? We heard sirens outside. Does that mean everything's okay?"

"Everything's okay now, Shirley."

Shirley looked relieved until Jaydn walked into the room, then her expression suddenly turned cold. "I'm glad everything's okay, sweetie. Come on, Darrell. Let's go see about the kids." The expression on her face as she passed Jaydn was wooden.

Alana turned to Jaydn with an air of confusion.

"I don't know why Shirley's acting so strange. I've never seen her be rude to anyone before. Please don't blame her. I'm sure there's a perfectly good explanation." She looked at Jaydn, silently pleading for understanding.

He smiled his reassurance and helped her gather the group of kids together again. When all the children were lined up, they once more headed toward the cafeteria—on the alert for more surprises.

SIXTY-THREE

JAYDN SAT WITH HIS ARMS hung over the back of a chair in the cafeteria, watching Alana pose a small black girl into the right angle for the picture. She patted the girl's head affectionately before stepping off the platform and behind the camera tripod.

His feelings for Alana, whatever they were, grew stronger with each loving touch she gave to the kids. Seeing her interact with them pollinated an emotional seed he didn't know what to do with.

Later, Alana helped the kids make pizza for lunch. Jaydn watched her laugh with them and giggle at silly little jokes they told. All the activity tired him out, but he was elated at the insight he'd gained into Alana's character. She was excellent when handling children. The day was a complete success, thanks to her spontaneous love for helping each one enjoy the day. His feelings for her escalated into something bigger than he could define. Knowing there might not be a future for them only made the knowledge that much more painful.

After Alana had loaded her camera equipment into the car, she started on her goodbyes to the children. Jaydn stood by and watched. A glance out the side window told him Bo was parked outside the orphanage. After chasing Martin down a side street and through a couple of traffic jams, both cars had lost him. Brad had called and said he'd instructed Bo and Kent to return to the orphanage and watch over Alana. He wanted to make sure Martin didn't return to cause more problems.

Jaydn opened the side door and walked out to the unmarked police car where Bo sat behind the wheel. Kent was outside—slouched against the bricks at the corner of the building. Jaydn lifted a hand to Kent and shook hands with Bo through the open window.

"Thanks for hanging around, Bo. I know Brad appreciates your being close by today."

"No trouble, man. We're glad to do it." Bo covered his eyes to block the sun. "Kent said Brad suggested we tag along behind you after you leave here … just to make sure no one follows."

Jaydn looked down at the ground. He remembered Brad's last warning: "Don't tell anyone where she's staying. No one!"

Could he trust Bo and Kent to keep quiet? Did Brad really ask Bo and his shadow to follow behind—maybe to keep an eye out for Martin? He was unsure what to do. These thoughts flew through his head in the two seconds it took him to make a decision.

Kent walked over to join the conversation.

"That's okay, guys. We're not going straight home. Thanks for the help, though."

Jaydn could see the look of indecision on the face of the police detective. Bo didn't like his refusal. Jaydn waited as Bo's gaze bore into him, but when Bo realized Jaydn wasn't backing down, he turned with a huff.

"If you're not going straight home, don't you need us to tag along and keep an eye out for trouble? Brad's not gonna like it if something happens to his sister."

Jaydn looked around the area as he contemplated his options. "I think I've got it covered. Thanks, though."

Bo turned red and turned to Kent. "Well, Kent. I guess Brad doesn't trust us after all. We've been dismissed." Bo's anger bled through his words.

Without saying another word, Bo cranked up the car. Kent's expression was unreadable as he slid into the passenger's seat and touched his hand to his head in a mock salute.

Bo gave an exasperated sigh and, with a twist of the key, he jerked the car in gear and screeched out of the parking lot.

"What was that all about?" Alana asked when she came out of the building to join Jaydn.

"Nothing," grunted Jaydn.

What if something happened and he *couldn't* protect Alana? What if Martin followed them back to the cabin?

After Alana was settled in the car, he pulled out his phone and dialed Brad's number. Busy! He'd made his decision. Now, it was too late.

Maybe Brad *had* asked Bo and Kent to tag along. If he did, Jaydn knew Brad wouldn't appreciate his interference. And if something happened to Alana ...

I'll just have to make sure it doesn't.

SIXTY-FOUR

O N THE WAY BACK TO the cabin, Jaydn made several un-
necessary turns that seemed to take them around in circles.
Alana knew what the evasive turns were for—he was making sure
no one followed them from the orphanage. She saw his clenched
jaw and felt the worry radiating from him. That tension reflected
the uncertainty of the situation, and regret for insisting on this trip
resurfaced to taunt her.

"Jaydn, I'm really sorry for—"

The vibration of Jaydn's phone interrupted her, and the sound
pulsed through her bones. Turning toward him, she saw his eyebrows meet as he listened to the voice on the other end of the line.

"You're kidding. Yeah, I'll tell her. We'll be careful."

Jaydn turned to her. "That was Brad. He said they have an APB
out for the hotel manager. His DNA matched the DNA sample
taken from the last murder victim's ring. That means he's probably
involved with the sheet murders. Brad thinks he might be part of
the same group that murdered Chet. After checking the FBI files,
they found a connection between the hotel manager and Chet's
neighbor—they're cousins."

"Did they arrest Chet's neighbor?"

Jaydn shook his head. "A few days ago, they found him floating in Lake Morgan with a bullet hole in his head. Brad found
evidence at Chet's house implicating him, so they're pretty sure he
was involved—especially since his *friends* made positively certain
he wouldn't snitch on them. He was probably murdered right after
he killed Chet. The hotel manager's missing, and who knows? He

might be dead too."

Silence in the car gave Alana time to think about Chet, and she slumped down in her seat. Poor Chet.

Jaydn sat silent, but a muscle in his jaw twitched. Alana's intuition told her there was something more. "There's something you're not telling me, Jaydn. What is it?"

"They can't find Martin. They said he just vanished into thin air. He hasn't shown up at his house, and his cars are still in the garage."

"Does Brad think Martin's the one who tried to drown me in my car?"

Jaydn shook his head but kept his eyes on the road. "He didn't say. He did say that Martin's still a suspect but maybe not the one in charge. Brad thinks Martin is too cocky to have pulled these murders off without making mistakes. He would have been caught before this. That doesn't mean he's not in it up to his eyeballs. Brad said there *is* one person he suspects, but he has to check out a few more things. He's a little worried there might be a security breach in the department."

"A breach? You mean a leak?"

"They always seem to be one step ahead of him. That's why he couldn't come with you today. He plans on being at the cabin tonight, though."

Alana blew out a frustrated breath. The word "breach" haunted her. She knew how much it took for Brad to admit there might be a dirty cop among his men—even to her and Jaydn.

If he could plug the leak, maybe he would get a break. At least Brad was making progress. Maybe this nightmare would soon be over.

"Do they have any idea where Martin is now?"

Before he could answer, he glanced into the rear view mirror. What he saw there caused an involuntary sharp intake of breath. His sudden death grip on the steering wheel turned his knuckles white.

"What's wrong?" Alana's voice sounded thready.

Carefully watching the rear view mirror, Jaydn made a wrong

turn onto a road leading away from the cabin. A brown sedan several hundred feet back made the same turn. The feeling in his gut was confirmed.

"We're being followed."

The simple statement sent shivers up her spine. Icy cold waves of fear traveled back down again. She turned to look behind them. "Can you lose them?"

"I don't know, but, I'm gonna try."

"Should we call 9-1-1?"

"Hold off for a minute."

With the last statement, he made a sharp right hand turn into the parking lot of a gas station. Twisting through the cars waiting their turn at the pumps, he made his way around to the back of the station and charged over the culvert covering the back driveway.

The car jerked up and down, protesting the rough treatment, and leveled out onto the back road. Alana held onto the door handle and gritted her teeth as she slid from side to side. She glanced back and saw a brown car plow through the gas station and turn in their direction. Saying she was scared was not strong enough of a word. She was petrified.

After screaming through several turns and down a long stretch of highway, Jaydn relaxed a little in the seat. He quickly made an unexpected turn into the circle of a new subdivision.

"I think we lost them."

Construction crews were putting finishing touches on one of the new houses they were building. Two of the homes had cars in the driveways and curtains in the windows. Jaydn careened down one of the side streets, and turned sharply onto another. He said nothing, but pushed the gas to the floor until he reached the end of the residential street, then slid the back tires into the driveway of a newly built home. The windows were bare, and the house looked empty.

He pulled the Buick up close to the doors of the garage and sat watching the road they'd just traveled. After several minutes of silence, he finally spoke. "I think we lost them, but I'm not taking any chances." He reached into his glove compartment and pulled out another cell phone.

Alana leaned back in the seat and tried to control her shaky nerves. Even her fingertips tingled with emotion. Her mouth opened in surprise when she heard Jaydn barking orders for another car to be driven to their location. Where would he get another car?

Her mouth snapped shut when he turned to look at her. "What's the name on the street sign at the corner? Can you tell?"

Alana leaned over until she could just make out the words. "Chase Street." As she said the words, she looked at Jaydn, and they gave each other a pointed look.

How appropriate!

SIXTY-FIVE

T HE INTERROGATION ROOM WAS HUMID, hot, and stuffy, and Martin's shirt revealed fresh armpit stains and a ring around the collar. Without his father's protection, he was a bundle of nerves and bluster. He leaned forward and banged his fist on the table.

"I told you, Candler, I was with somebody the whole evening."

"Yeah, you told me—Sandra Temple. What does her cat look like, Strands?"

"Her cat? How in the world am I supposed to know? I don't even think she has a cat."

Brad looked at Vernon who stepped forward. "Sandra said you and her cat didn't get along."

Martin slumped against his seat. "Oh, yeah … uh … she's right. The stupid cat bit me."

From the sidelines, Brad watched Vernon lean in until he was sure Vernon could smell the sweat on Martin's face. "He bit you, but you can't remember what he looks like?"

Martin became agitated and twisted in his seat. "Look man. I told you, we just had a beer … then we watched a movie. I don't care about the stupid cat."

Brad stepped forward. "Sandra said *you* had a Coke, and *she* had a beer."

"Oh, yeah, that's right. She had a Coke, and I had a beer…I mean, I had a Coke and she had a beer. Just like she said. What does it matter, man? I already told you, I was with her the whole night until about midnight."

"Yeah, you told us. Only Sandra Temple said you and she shared a different set of *activities* than the one you described. We also have several witnesses that say she waited on them at the Roadster Café that night. So how could she be in two places at one time?"

Sweat dripped off Martin's face and fell with a plop on the table. He leaned back in the chair and mumbled under his breath. "Stupid broad ..."

Brad tried to hide a grin. He glanced at Vernon. They were thinking the same thing; Strands should have asked Sandra if she'd been home that night before using her as an alibi, and he was helpless while his father was away.

"Okay, Candler. Here's the truth. I was with somebody else—all night long—that's why I lied. Alana wouldn't understand. I was trying to protect Alana."

Brad felt his ears burn with fire—in disgust. Sarcasm colored every word. "Yeah, right. I'm sure it was *Alana* you were trying to protect. I think you were trying to protect your own hide, you bum. You didn't want Alana to know you were cheating with someone else when you were trying to get her back."

"That's a lie."

Brad leaned across the table and stuck his nose right in Martin's face. "Strands, you're about to go down as an accomplice for attempted murder and maybe murder-one if you don't start telling the truth. What's the woman's name you were with all night?"

"I'm tellin' the truth, man."

"Then give me a name."

Brad leaned away from the table and walked to the other side of the room, never taking his eyes from Martin's face.

Martin struggled with himself before blurting out. "Okay, her name is Jasper Jenkins. Just don't tell Alana, okay? She won't understand. Jasper and I've had a date every Friday night for the last few months—at the Comfort Inn in Reeds. The hotel manager knows my father. Call him and he'll tell you. I was there last Friday night and every Friday night. The maid that works on Saturday morning saw us leaving. She can tell you too. Call her."

Martin's whining only disgusted Brad. As tough as Martin acted, seeing him reduced to a whimpering child made Brad sick.

He nodded to Vernon standing in the corner, and they both walked out the door. One of his men stood guard outside the door as he turned to Vernon.

"Call the hotel, Vernon. Talk to the manager and get the maid's contact information. Then call this Jasper Jenkins and see what she has to say."

Vernon nodded and left Brad standing outside the two-way mirror watching Martin sweat through the tinted glass. If he was telling the truth, then he couldn't have kidnapped Alana or been involved with the murders. The last two murders were on Friday nights.

Fifteen minutes later, Vernon came into Brad's office. Dread had Brad holding his head in his hands.

"Bad news, Chief. The hotel manager confirmed what Strands said. He checks in every Friday night with the same woman— Jasper Jenkins. I called her number and got her roommate, who confirmed she goes out every Friday night with Strands and never comes home till morning. The hotel maid said she saw them leaving late Saturday morning—the night after Alana was kidnapped."

Brad sucked in a defeated breath between his teeth and puffed it back out again. "Let Strands go, Vernon. Tell him not to leave town until we say so. I'm gonna call Jaydn. I need to let Alana know Martin's not involved with her kidnapping."

Brad leaned back in his chair to add this new information to his list of clues in this investigation. Lately, he'd been going one step forward, then two steps back. Now it seemed he was back to square one.

SIXTY-SIX

JAYDN SAT WITH ALANA IN a navy blue Honda Accord and stared out the window. After an hour of trading cars and making one unexpected turn after another, he was comfortable making the final turns toward the cabin.

Alana was silent. She had been quiet since his men brought them a new car in the cul-de-sac. Was she finally curious about what he was doing? The apartment. The cabin. The multitude of plush "company" cars he summoned with one phone call. The unlimited access to a helicopter. These events *had* to make her curious. Had she finally pieced together the facts?

Even as he formulated these thoughts in his head, she turned in the seat to face him. Curiosity seasoned her words, and confusion sharpened her tone.

"Jaydn, I'd like to ask you some questions."

Dread made him feel as though his face might crack. His eyes never left the road, but his breathing slowed.

He quietly replied, "What's that?"

"You told me the apartment in Ross belonged to your company. What about the helicopter, and the cars you've been driving? Do they belong to your company as well?"

Jaydn nodded warily. "Yes."

She looked at him for the longest minute of his life.

"And?" She waited patiently for him to supply an explanation, but when none was forthcoming, she pushed for more. "What aren't you telling me?"

The air seeped from his lungs like a deflating balloon. The

moment he'd been dreading since the trip to her apartment in Ross was here. He had to tell her the truth.

"Alana, the company does own all those things, but what I haven't told you is … I own the company."

The statement was flat and without emotion, but Alana jerked back as if she had been burned. She slowly nodded. The next question took forever to leave her lips.

"What's the name of your company, Jaydn?"

"International Enterprises."

She shook her head. "I should have realized. The expensive office building. The luxury cars. Helicopters summoned at your command."

At first, she seemed surprised, but then he felt her tense. The truth hit her like a tidal wave, and he could feel her anger in the air.

"You lied to me."

"No, Alana. I never lied. Legally, the company does own it all. I just didn't tell you that I own the company."

"Not telling me the whole truth is the same as lying."

The words sizzled in the air. Her face was red. He was sure it was both from anger and embarrassment. She was angry that he kept the truth from her and embarrassed because she exposed her heart to him. She confided the pain of her past experiences with rich, aristocratic bosses to someone who obviously fit into the same mold.

"So you own International Enterprises." Her lips puckered as if the statement was bitter when it rolled out of her mouth. The next sentence she spat at him as if it burned her tongue. "International Enterprises!" She turned to glare him down. "You own the building the orphanage is leasing?"

Jaydn flinched. The strongest wish he had at that moment was to be someone else. To be able to say, no, he knew nothing about the lease with the orphanage. The shame and anguish of having to answer was nothing in comparison to the humiliation of her knowing the vile and greedy thing he'd done.

"You're the one forcing the orphanage to move."

She wasn't expecting him to answer. Her tone implied she already knew the answer. All her past relationships would have warned her about the type of man he was. In her experience, wealthy businessmen were only concerned with making more money—not the people's lives they damaged while filling their bank accounts.

"I don't know what to say, Jaydn. Except that after this is over, I don't want to see you again. You're not the person I thought you were."

If his face could have felt any hotter, it did at that moment. Pain and shame burned inside of him. He pulled the car off the road onto an overgrown gravel driveway and turned to stare out the window. He couldn't look at the accusations in her eyes.

"I'm sorry, Alana. I promise I didn't know the people renting the building were running an orphanage." He blew out a frustrated breath. "I will admit, I told my lawyer to check into seeing if we could get the tenant to move, but I didn't know it was an orphanage."

She crossed her arms and threw him a pained expression. Her stance proved she was dying a slow emotional death.

"I didn't want to lie to you, Alana. You made it no secret that you despise wealthy business owners. They're 'tyrants in suits,' remember? After hearing you rant about it, are you really surprised that I didn't mention it?" He shook his head regretfully. "I felt a closeness to you I've never felt with anyone before. My heart seemed to bond with yours, but I was afraid to tell you that I … have a successful business. I was afraid it would influence your opinion of me."

Alana glared at him. "Do you think?"

The silence in the car grew deafening.

She turned to him and studied his face. Then, unexpectedly, she sighed deeply.

"Jaydn, I'd be lying if I said I don't feel a special attraction when you're near, but I just can't get past the way you deceived me. Relationships are built on trust—not deception. The experiences I've had with rich businessmen have never turned out well. They've always used money for power and personal *projects*, not caring who it would hurt. And now, it seems you fit right into that mold, just like all the others. I can't handle going through another relationship like that."

He said nothing but put the car in gear and pulled back out onto the road. His jaw line tightened with each mile.

Regret weighed heavily on him. He had tried to keep the truth from her to protect what they might feel for each other.

Who are you kidding, Holbrook? You kept the truth from her for purely selfish reasons. Now, you've hurt her.

A quick glance to the right revealed the pain etched deep in her features. The pain he felt radiating from her traveled across the seat and into the center of his heart, but there was nothing he could say to make it better.

SIXTY-SEVEN

T HE INSIDE OF THE CAR was static with tension as the two men watched the red lights of the distant car in front of them disappear around the bend. The driver's breathing was suppressed —as if he thought their breathing could be heard by the occupants of the car in front of them.

The younger man turned to the driver and said in a low voice, "How'd you know where to find them?"

"The boss dropped a tracking device in the lady's purse." After they turned the corner quietly and slowed the car to a crawl, the passenger spoke with suppressed anger. "I don't like this kidnapping idea. Why can't we take 'em out, then go some place the cops won't find us—like we planned?"

The older man glanced at the curly black head of his partner.

"You mean take them out like you did at the Ross apartment or the pool?" Sarcasm dripped from his speech like molasses from a spoon. "The boss don't like mistakes, and you made plenty—like Gene. The boss wants it done this way."

The younger man shivered. Gene's face came to mind. He didn't like it when he was compared to Gene. "I'm just sayin' that we have enough. Why can't we leave now? Like we originally planned."

"You and I both know somebody'll figure out he's involved eventually—there's too many copies of them pictures—thanks to Gene. If he gets caught, we get caught. Do you wanna go to prison? If we get money from International Enterprises, we can disappear where they can't bring us back—another country, even. The boss already has plane tickets. This'll work. You'll see."

"You better be right." The younger man's voice sizzled with meaning.

"Just shut up and keep your eyes on those lights. The boys are ahead of us and waiting."

SIXTY-EIGHT

A LANA LISTENED TO THE TINY whitecaps crashing on the tall
pillars of the bridge underneath her as they crossed the bridge
to Jaydn's cabin. Shadows of the bridge fanned out across the water
in the evening sun.

Sitting next to Jaydn, she was reminded of all he had done for
her. He protected her with his life—several times. Her anger melted
like plastic in flames. In his presence, she felt safe and secure, and
the warmth of that security flowed through her veins.

Jaydn eased the car off the bridge and followed the gravel pathway around the house. Slowing the car to a crawl, he suddenly
tensed and jerked the car to a stop.

Alana shifted toward him, his stillness feeding her fear. Rippled
lines of worry or panic, she couldn't tell which, creased above his
brow. The way his eyes kept scanning the lake shoreline made her
uneasy. His body language spoke volumes.

"What's wrong?"

"I don't see any guards." The statement was whispered yet
sounded to her ears as if he shouted it from the mountaintops.

He jammed the car into reverse and threw gravel from the
driveway into the yard as he slid the car around and back toward
the bridge.

He picked up his cell phone from the console and threw it at
her.

"Call 9-1-1, then Brad."

When they rounded the corner of the house, Alana gasped when
she saw what was in front of them.

A box truck blocked the entrance to the bridge, and two men stood at each corner. Each of them held long, nasty-looking guns, and they were pointed straight at the car.

Alana quickly punched in the emergency number before she realized there was no phone service.

"No service!" Panic laced her voice.

Jaydn jammed the car into reverse and took off in the opposite direction. Shots were fired in quick succession, and the back glass shattered. Alana screamed, and Jaydn pushed her head down low.

"Stay down!"

He twisted the car from side to side, trying to avoid the bullets popping all around them.

God please help us. Alana prayed as she grasped the handle on the door and was jerked into the seat belt.

"We've got to get to the boat," said Jaydn through gritted teeth. "It's our only chance." He spoke as he plowed the car between two crape myrtle bushes and slid to a stop two feet from the lake dock.

"Hurry, Alana! Get into the boat!"

Alana gasped when she saw Jaydn pull a pistol from under his seat and point it toward the men rounding the corner of the house. She heard two loud pops, and the men following them scrambled for cover.

Jaydn pushed Alana toward the boat. "Untie the ropes and get in!" He took cover behind the car and aimed several more shots toward the men hiding behind the oak trees in the yard— his shots protecting her as she ran.

Alana's heart pounded inside her throat. When she reached the round wooden post of the dock, she slipped and fell down on one knee. Crouched in a half-sitting position, she struggled to untie the mooring rope holding the boat to the dock. Her fingers, numb with fear, worked shakily as she glanced back at the car and saw Jaydn clicking in another cartridge. He ran toward her, firing more bullets as he ran. Finally, the rope loosened enough so she could lift it up over the top of the large post.

Jaydn ran to the second boat moored at the dock and pulled the key from inside. It made a plopping sound as he threw it into the lake. Just as he reached the boat, Alana felt a zing as a bullet flew past her and lodged in the lip of the boat.

Jaydn roughly pushed her over the side of the boat and jumped in behind her.

"Stay down!" he shouted as he pushed her further down onto the rough wooden floor.

Splinters pressed into her knees as she bent over double and tried to get as low as she could in the small motorboat. From the corner of her eye, she saw Jaydn wrestling with the key that started the motor.

Another pinging noise bounced off the side of the boat and sent wooden splinters in all directions.

The motor sputtered and then came to life. Jaydn pushed the gas handle as high as it would go. He steered the boat away from the dock—his body bent low but his hand gripping the steering wheel with a death grip as he turned them away from the cabin.

What Alana saw when she peeked over the blue-trimmed edge of the white boat made her heart jump into her throat. A man in camouflage stood several feet from the lake with a rifle raised to his shoulder. The other man jumped into the second boat moored at the dock.

"Good luck starting that boat without a key." Jaydn's voice was quiet but sang with a touch of victory.

As the boat inched further away from the shoreline, the shots grew less intense. She glanced upward and blew out a breath. Slowly, they were pulling away. Jaydn still crouched in the boat but turned to look into her frightened eyes.

"There's a beach just around this strip of land—lots of people swimming. If we make it there, we should be safe. They wouldn't dare do anything to us in front of so many witnesses."

As they made a sharp turn around the rocky point jutting into the lake, Alana felt the motor give a sick shudder, then die.

"What happened?" she asked, turning toward Jaydn.

Still bent over in the boat, he turned toward the motor housing. "I think they got the gas line. We're leaking fuel."

Alana's nose picked up the startling smell of gasoline. Jaydn rushed toward where she huddled in the boat.

"Jump, Alana! Jump!" He pushed her into the water before climbing onto the edge of the boat himself.

Panic consumed her as the dark water closed over her head. She tried to control her shaking limbs and reach the surface. Struggling to tread water, and gasping for a breath that was both ragged and unstable, she heard Jaydn shouting her name and glanced wildly around for him. Then, her hearing was shattered by a loud explosion that accompanied a blinding flash.

Alana felt as well as saw the shock waves of the explosion as the boat blew into large fragments. The air that rushed past her was filled with water and debris from the boat.

Frantically, she tried to see Jaydn in the middle of all the chaos. She ducked when a piece of the windshield flew past her, but she couldn't avoid an aged piece of wood from the stern that slammed into her head with a blinding pain. Then, as if in a dream, the world around her slowly disappeared.

"Hey! Look at that!"

A crowd formed on the side of the popular sandy beach and watched pieces of Jaydn's boat flying through the air. One young mother grabbed her two small children and tucked them protectively under her arms.

"Must've had a gas leak." A tall thin man shook his head. "Better call 9-1-1."

"Oh! Wait! I've got a phone," yelled an elderly woman as she reached into her flowery beach bag and dialed the number.

A short man dressed in jeans and a casual shirt rounded the hill between the lake and the road, watching the crowd. He wasn't dressed for the beach and seemed alarmed. Sunglasses covered the frown hidden in his eyes, but somehow his agitation was apparent in his gait and stance.

"Move back, please," he said gruffly as he parted the crowd

and stepped closer to the shore of the lake. "I'm with the police department."

The crowd parted and watched with mouths open as he hurried to the scene of what they believed to be an accident.

SIXTY-NINE

ALANA FELT SOMETHING MOVE BESIDE her. The gentle swaying movement of the water penetrated her dazed senses, and she felt something hard poking into her ribs. Without opening her eyes, panic made her grab for the floating object and hold on. The rough surface bit into the exposed flesh on her arms, and she grunted in pain.

Her shoulder felt like it was on fire, and she felt a trickle of something running down her face. She swiped it with her fingers. It felt warm and sticky. It took all the strength she could summon to make her brain respond. She tried to open her heavy lids to confirm it was blood traveling down the side of her face, but her lids felt weighted down.

When she finally forced her eyes open, her world spiraled downward in a matter of seconds. Everything around her was black. With shaky fingers, she touched her eyes to see if they were open. The stinging sensation confirmed her fears.

She was blind!

She drifted on the boat fragment, moving in and out of consciousness with her head barely above the lapping water. It seemed ages before she even cared where she was or why she was floating around the lake on a splintered piece of wood.

The image of a man's face kept appearing before her darkened eyes as if beckoning her to remember. Then suddenly, the memory of what happened returned in a rush to her rattled brain.

Jaydn! What had happened to Jaydn?

She opened her mouth to call for him, but the memory of him

flying through the air at the time of the explosion made her throat constrict, and no sound escaped her lips. Tears fell unheeded into the water. It was all her fault. Jaydn was either hurt or—she had to find him.

"Jaydn!" She tried to ignore the agonizing pain that shot through her head when she shouted. "Jaydn, where are you?" Her hands splashed the water around her in a feeble effort to find Jaydn's body in the water.

She paddled around in weak circles, tremors wracking her cold body as she mourned his absence. Numbness from shock hindered her tired limbs from responding to the instructions her brain was giving them. She felt herself slipping away and couldn't stop the detached sensation that was claiming her thoughts.

"Alana!"

The muffled sound unscrambled itself and made sense to her stunned senses. The sudden burst of happiness she experienced when she thought it was Jaydn calling her name was dashed immediately. These words were coming from a scratchy tenor voice, not Jaydn's rich baritone. Without lifting her head, she waved in the direction of the voice.

"I'm here."

"Alana! This way! Swim this way!"

She heard several voices calling her name as the beach crowd cheered to find that someone survived the horrible explosion. They all yelled at her and encouraged her to kick harder. Her tired limbs pushed with all the strength she could muster.

"Alana! Kick! I'm coming."

She pushed and kicked until the voice seemed almost at arm's length. She felt the water around her moving in waves.

"I've got you." She felt someone tug on the wood she clung to. "I've got you now. Are you okay?"

"Kent? Is that you?"

The crowd cheered when she felt the sandy beach under her legs, and they knew she was safe.

Kent touched her face. "Alana?"

She shook her head and tremors wracked her body. "I can't

see, and Jaydn is out there somewhere. Please, Kent, can't you find him?"

"It's all right, Alana. We'll look for him. Help is on the way." Kent helped her out of the water and then picked her up and carried her to the road—it seemed like just a few feet.

"Kent, please. Find Jaydn. He must be hurt. He didn't answer me." Her mumbled words were lazy and sluggish. Inside her troubled thoughts, she hoped he could understand her.

"It's okay, Alana. I'll take care of you now."

He carried her for a minute or two. Then he shifted her weight and stood her up until her wobbly feet touched the ground. She heard what sounded like a car door open. He helped her into the seat and called to someone down the road.

"Up here!" Through the heavy cloud that descended on Alana's heart, she heard shoes make scraping sounds on the pavement as Kent walked away.

A few minutes later, she heard someone bark the order. "Let's move her. Then help me find the other one." She must be dreaming. In her dream, they moved her to another car. She rested her head on the back of the soft seat cushion and let her thoughts race. Jaydn might be dead. His tanned features danced before her sightless eyes, and tears welled up, threatening to fall. She felt as if a hand was squeezing her bruised heart to take all the life away.

At that moment, she knew she cared deeply for Jaydn Holbrook. No matter who he was or how much money he had, the rest of her life would have no meaning if she couldn't share it with him.

Dear Lord, please let him be okay. Please help Kent find him.

The jackhammer in her head refused to go away and made her sleepy. She laid her head back against the seat and closed her eyes. The sense of awareness slowly slipped away, and her head slid sideways on the seat. Right before she lost consciousness, she heard a familiar voice.

"I've got him. Let's go."

SEVENTY

ALANA'S TONGUE FELT LIKE COTTON, and her world was spinning in orbit. She forced her dry tongue to swallow and tried to remember where she was and what she was hearing. Muffled voices rumbled from somewhere behind her.

"I don't like all this waiting around. Why can't we take care of it here?"

"I told you! He has to make the call first, stupid. Then, after we get the money, we'll make sure no one finds the bodies. You're lucky you didn't kill either one of them—you and your trigger-happy finger. We need 'em alive for now. All we have to do is keep 'em quiet for a couple of days. Then we're outta here."

Someone opened the door, and Alana felt the car dip as something heavy was placed beside her. She wanted to ask where she was, but the words got all tied up around her tongue. Confusion twisted her speech in knots, and her mouth stayed shut. Her head rocked back as the motion of the car jerked her in the seat.

She lay on the back seat in a daze, trying not to think about what she just heard. It didn't matter anyway. Without Jaydn, life wasn't worth living. He must have died, or he would be with her now.

When the car stopped, Alana remained still. Rough hands lifted her out of the car and carried her a short distance away. A coarse bed creaked under her, and she felt a tiny prick on the upper part of her arm. She lay still and listened to their conversation grow quieter as they walked away. Only snatches of conversation penetrated her already declining awareness.

"How come you didn't tie her up too?"

"She's blind, stupid. Didn't you hear? She ain't goin' nowhere."

"Well, I don't like hanging around here. It's dangerous. They'll be looking for 'em both."

"Look, they're safe here. They can't connect us with this warehouse, so we're okay for now. Calm down. Do you wanna end up like Gene? Don't make the boss angry. We'll get the money tomorrow, and then we'll take care of 'em both."

Alana heard no more. The sounds and smells around her receded into the distance.

SEVENTY-ONE

JAYDN MOANED AND THEN WINCED as the sound made his head throb. He wondered why his fingers and arms tingled but quickly discovered that his hands were tied behind his back. A wadded up piece of cloth filled his mouth and tasted like something dead. His stomach roiled as he fought the nausea.

His head felt like it was exploding!

Slowly, the faces of two men he'd never seen before emerged from his memory. They had taken him to a room with a phone and called his office. He remembered speaking to his manager before a swift, sharp pain in his head knocked him unconscious. The last thing he saw was circles rolling around in his head before everything went black.

Alana! What happened to Alana?

He glanced around the dark room, but the shadows were eerie and distorted. He waited until his vision cleared and then searched the room for Alana's small form. He finally saw her heaped onto an old pile of bedding, but she wasn't moving. The gag kept him from calling her name.

Lord, please let her be okay.

She must be alive, or she wouldn't be here. He pushed at the wad of cloth in his mouth with his tongue. The fabric stretching around the back of his head tightened, but the gag wouldn't budge. He grunted his frustration.

He had to get free!

He strained and twisted on the ropes around his wrists, but there was no room in the knots to work with. If he could wake up

Alana, she might be able to work the knots free.

The ropes around his legs kept him from standing, so he dug his heels into the aged wood and dragged himself a couple of inches at a time across the floor toward her sleeping form.

SEVENTY-TWO

D REAMS OF HER SPIRIT CIRCLING around in the air and coming to rest in her body scared Alana to wakefulness. What happened to make her feel she had been run over by a truck?

Her drugged brain remembered only snatches of images. She saw the boat with Jaydn standing on the side, and she jerked when she remembered the explosion.

Jaydn! What happened to Jaydn?

Then, suddenly, disturbing images flashed in front of her, and she could feel once again the emptiness of death. What was it she felt? Pain? Resolve? Jaydn was dead. She was blind. And, there was nothing she could do about either.

Her head felt mashed and sore, and her arms weighed a ton. She reached up and felt the rough surface where her head rested, but a sharp pain in her shoulder stilled her movement.

Was she in a hospital? It was nothing like the starched sheets she remembered from her previous visit.

Her clothes were dry from the lake water, so she must have been here more than a few hours.

She opened her eyes and saw light shadows swimming around her. Was it night? Or day? The images were blurry, but she could make out various images. Her vision was returning.

Snatches of conversation rolled around in her memory, and what she remembered filled her thoughts with fear.

They were going to kill her.

For what, she still didn't know. For something she saw. But what? A recollection of her trip here surfaced. Was it Kent who brought her here? Was Kent the one trying to kill her?

She rubbed her head and tried to make herself think. Kent found her in the lake. He took her to a car and left her to find Jaydn.

Had Kent kidnapped her?

She remembered voices when she arrived. None of them sounded like Kent. Tears formed as panic wrapped around her heart.

She had to get out of here!

She tried to sit up on the chunky bedding and fought the nausea that filled her stomach.

I can't make it by myself. Lord, please help me. These people are going to kill me if I don't get out of here.

And yet, even as she prayed the words, she knew she couldn't leave this place without help. The area around her was too dark to see well enough to escape. She might walk right into the arms of her kidnappers.

Her head throbbed with sharp stabbing pains as she raised it to listen for sounds around her. A smell like sulfur penetrated her nostrils. Somewhere in the distance, a bird squawked. A strange, thumping sound shook the floor close to her head. Frowning, she turned her head toward the back of the building. Were they coming to get her?

Panic tightened her throat even as she heard a soft muffled word.

"Ana."

Lifting her head tenderly, she listened carefully. She heard the thumping sound again, coming from behind her. She turned her head toward the sound.

"Ana."

Dared she hope? The strangled word she heard sounded so much like Jaydn that tears once again burned the back of her lids.

Could it be true? Was he alive?

She pushed back on the pile of cloth to sit up and strained to hear sounds of someone approaching.

When she told herself she must have imagined the whole thing, she felt something touch her arm. She jumped and turned toward the object.

"Ana."

The smell of lake water was strong, but it could not drown out the faint smell of Jaydn's aftershave. She could barely make out the shape of a dark-headed figure.

"Jaydn," she whispered and threw her arms around his neck.

Jaydn leaned toward her and touched her face with his briefly. Then leaning back, he mumbled something unintelligible, and it dawned on her that he was gagged.

Alana pulled at the fabric tied around his face with her hands. The stretchy material finally gave way and pushed over the bottom of the gag.

Jaydn spit the gag out on the floor and the fabric around his mouth went slack and fell to his neck. He turned and spit several times on the wooden floor.

Softly, he kissed her on the cheek. "Alana." The word came out whisper soft and wrapped around immense emotion.

Alana wrapped her arms around his neck and held tightly, fighting tears. It felt so good to hold him close when she thought she had lost him forever.

Jaydn pulled back and spoke barely above a whisper. "Listen, Alana. I heard them leave a while ago. We have to escape before they come back. See if you can get these ropes loose."

Alana heard the urgency in his voice, but she whispered, "I'll try, Jaydn, but I can't see very well. It's so dark in here, and the explosion did something to my eyes. I'm not sure how much help I'll be."

"Try, sweetheart."

She bent over the back of his hands and tried to feel the knots in the coarse rope. She twisted and pulled until the rope began to loosen. After several minutes of straining, she finally felt the end give and pull through the loop.

When the ropes went slack, Jaydn pulled his hands free and loosened the bindings around his legs. She saw him stand up and flex his legs. A quiet moan escaped his lips as the returning circulation triggered a stinging sensation. He turned to Alana and softly touched the blood on her face.

"Alana, are you okay? Did you say you can't see?"

She couldn't speak, so she nodded. He didn't say a word but leaned over and lifted her into his arms. "Let's get out of here."

Alana lay quietly in Jaydn's arms, breathing in his male scent. The danger around her was forgotten, overshadowed by the fact that Jaydn was still alive. She felt him working his way across the warehouse.

"Where are we going?" she whispered.

He pointed with his head to a corner of the building. "There's an outside door over there. If it's not locked, we can get out before someone finds out we're gone."

She could barely hear his hushed voice, and his shuffling steps were almost silent. Maybe he was worried the kidnappers left a guard to keep an eye on them.

After what seemed like an eternity, Jaydn stopped. She could barely make out the outline of a metal door.

When they heard a scraping noise outside, Jaydn moved quickly behind a wooden crate and stood Alana next to the wall and tenderly touched her lips with his finger. His whispered "shhh" was like a gentle breeze fanning her face. Alana felt the tension in his muscles and wished she could see him in the darkness.

Jaydn glanced around desperately. Quietly picking up a club-shaped object, he waited as the doorknob turned gently and the door slowly opened. A sliver of light grew as the door opened wider, and the area was bathed in light.

Jaydn lifted the object high over his head and waited for the figure to emerge.

Alana saw the gun first.

SEVENTY-THREE

WHEN A TALL, THIN MAN rounded the edge of the door, Jaydn swung the small bronze statue he held down—aiming for the gun in the man's hand. The man jerked to the side, and the blow only grazed his arm. Turning on Jaydn, the man raised his gun for a blow to the head when light from outside the building illuminated Jaydn's face.

"Jaydn!"

Taking advantage of surprise, Jaydn grabbed the gun from Kent and turned it back toward Kent's chest.

"Freeze, Kent. Don't move, or I promise I'll shoot."

"What are you doing, Jaydn? I'm here to rescue you." Kent's voice was low and controlled.

"Yeah, right! Just put both hands on the side of the building and spread your legs."

"Jaydn. Listen to me. You're making a big mistake."

"Do it!"

The panic and anger in Jaydn's voice made Kent surrender and do as he asked.

Alana cowered against the crate and tried to follow the path of Jaydn's actions.

"Jaydn?"

"Alana, remember the yellow diamond ring in the photos Brad brought to the cabin of the stolen items? Kent was wearing it at the police station. Brad said he suspected someone in his department but had no way to prove it. It must be Kent." Jaydn stared at Kent with disgust. "He's the serial killer."

Kent laid his forehead against the building. "Jaydn, please," he whispered hoarsely. "Chet left that ring in a box with my name on it before he died. He must have stolen it from this warehouse and was leaving it as a clue when they killed him. The ring belonged to—"

"Me."

The single word came from twenty feet behind them. The hair on the back of Alana's neck tingled when she saw Jaydn freeze. He kept the gun pointed at Kent but slowly turned his head to find Bo standing behind him.

Bo's magnum was aimed directly at Alana's head.

"Drop it, Jaydn, or she dies, here and now." Bo's voice was electrically charged.

Jaydn slowly lowered the gun to the floor and let it fall with a thud.

Alana blinked—not believing her ears.

"Bo?"

The truth wouldn't compute in her head. Bo was the murderer?

"Poor little Alana—sweet little sister. You just couldn't figure it out, could you?" Bo once again turned to Jaydn. "Now move over beside Kent, Jaydn, and put these on his hands." He pulled a pair of handcuffs from a bag by his side and threw it on the floor at Jaydn's feet.

Jaydn leaned over to pick up the cuffs, never moving his eyes from the gun pointed at Alana's head. The shock on his face was as real as the gun in Bo's tight grip.

Alana peered in Bo's direction.

"Why, Bo?"

Bo grunted. "Cuz I'm sick of working 24/7 for *nothing*. No promotions. No raises. Doing your brother's dirty work without the pay that goes with it. I'm *sick* of it all. But not any more. After this last haul, I'm set for life. The money from International Enterprises should be delivered," he said, glancing at his watch, "just about now. And you three … will have signed your own death certificates."

Kent shook his head. "You're crazy, man, if you think you're gonna get away with this."

"Shut up, Kent. I've already gotten away with it."

Bo's laugh was high-pitched and raspy. He held the gun out closer to Alana's head.

"The whole department's stupid—just like you, Kent. None of you would have even gotten close if Alana here hadn't taken that stupid picture of me picking up Gene's stupid cigarette butt. I told him not to bring that thing in the building. But, no ... he just had to have his nicotine fix."

Alana shrank back at the disdain in his voice. This was a side of Bo she had never seen before. He turned toward her.

"You just had to be early that day, didn't you? If you had minded your own business, everything would've been fine. Now it's gonna cost you your life." He took two steps toward her, his gun still pointing directly to her head.

"Everything wasn't fine for all those widows you murdered."

Alana could hear the disgust in Jaydn's voice.

"They're better off. They had no family. No friends. I checked. Just a lot of money and no one to share it with. So, I let 'em share it with me."

Bo's voice became electric. "Do what I tell you, Jaydn. I'm the best marksman in the whole department. If I shoot, I won't miss." He straightened his arms, holding the gun toward Alana's head.

Alana was terrified.

She watched his fury grow until she heard Jaydn clear his throat and twist to the side beside Kent. Bo turned his attention back to Jaydn.

"No funny stuff. Get going with those cuffs. I wanna be outta here when the boys get back. They think I've got plane tickets for all of us, but they're gonna be happier with the surprise I left them."

Jaydn was stalling. Alana could see him fumbling—pretending to cuff Kent—when she saw a movement several feet from where they were. Jaydn must have seen it too because he froze and, without turning his head, glanced toward the corner where Brad crouched behind a large container. Brad put his finger to his mouth and made a chatting movement with his other hand—letting Jaydn know he needed to keep Bo talking.

Jaydn looked up at Bo. "Was it you that stole Alana from the hotel?"

Bo laughed and lowered the gun just a bit. "That part was pure luck. Sam recognized her when she pulled into the hotel. Him and Gene took care of that little job. If you hadn't pulled her out of that car, none of this would be happening. You just had to play the hero, didn't you?" He shrugged. "It doesn't matter. Your good works will be rewarded. Isn't that what the Bible says, Alana?"

Alana couldn't understand what she was hearing.

"It w-was your idea to k-kill me?" Her voice was just above a whisper.

The regret in Bo's voice nearly did her in. "I'm sorry about that, Alana. I hated giving Gene that order—Brad being my best friend and all. But … it wasn't personal—just business."

Alana was horrified. Bo had wanted her dead all along! Nothing personal? Just business? Tremors raced through her body, and she collapsed to her knees—her legs too weak to hold her up.

Jaydn struggled to take Bo's mind off Alana.

"What about Chet's neighbor, Gene Hollister? Did you murder him too?"

"It was a shame about Gene. He was a good security man. He knew everything there was to know about disarming a security system. He got careless, though. He had to be punished. Now, get those cuffs on—you're stalling." He raised the gun once more toward Alana's head.

Jaydn had no other choice but to place the cuffs on Kent's hands.

"You're crazy, man, if you think your *friends* are going to bring that money back here. What makes you think they won't skip out and leave you with a kidnapping charge and the blame for all those murders?"

Bo's laugh filled the metal rafters—his voice laced with sarcasm. "I've already told my *friends* that if they leave me here, I have evidence to prove they committed all the murders. I'll just turn it all over to the police and pretend I found you *after* they murdered you. Who do you think they'll believe? Me—one of Landeville's finest— or the story of some lowlife scum? Besides, I have a flight chartered with only one ticket ... and a bomb planted somewhere my *friends* will never find. After they bring me the money, they'll all get into the car to travel to the airport, and—*kaboom!* The beginning of my retirement."

Alana opened her mouth in a silent scream. Bo was mad!

"Enough talking. Get those cuffs on, or little Alana's gonna have a mighty big headache."

Bo moved to the right to watch Jaydn's hands and stepped directly in front of where Brad was crouched.

Brad leaped from behind the container and pounced on Bo, sending them both to the floor. Kent twisted to help Brad as much as he could with his hands in cuffs, and Jaydn grabbed Bo's hand— trying to pull the gun from Bo's death grip.

Bo pulled himself back up, raised his left leg, and jabbed Jaydn in the stomach—knocking Jaydn to the floor. Jaydn hit his head on a wooden container and shook his head, dazed.

"Run, Alana!" Brad yelled at her as he hit Bo with the back of his elbow. Bo jerked around, and the blow caught him in the back, but he kept his footing.

Alana was frozen. The whole thing seemed to be happening in slow motion.

Through the struggle, Bo's eyes, crazed with rage, turned to find Alana's. Adrenaline surged through his veins, and with super-human strength, he raised both hands, lifting Brad and Kent off the ground, and turned the gun toward Alana.

Jaydn didn't hesitate. He threw his body between Alana and the gun.

Alana saw the flare from the gun and heard the explosion. At the same instant, she saw Jaydn's body flash in front of her. Her soul felt rather than saw the impact. In slow motion, she saw Jaydn crumple to the floor

"Jaydn!"

A second shot rang out. Alana felt the shock from a second

bullet as it hit her in the shoulder.

She watched as Bo—still wrestling Brad and Kent—summoned one last ounce of strength and turned the gun on himself. Alana felt the shot all the way to her soul and turned her head to avoid seeing Bo fall to the ground. She heard the gun fall to the floor a few feet away.

Alana winced from the pain in her arm, but knelt beside Jaydn. She could see blood already spreading from the wound in his chest. Tears flowed down her cheeks as she tenderly lifted his head and held it off the blackened wooden floor.

In the background, she could hear sirens blaring in the distance and her brother shouting, "Dispatch! We have shots fired and a man down. Ten-fifty-two! Immediately! I repeat. We have a man down!"

SEVENTY-FOUR

ALANA SAT UP IN THE hospital bed as Brad walked into the room.

"Hey, munchkin. How are you feeling this morning?"

Even though Brad tried to portray a positive face, the dark circles under his eyes revealed how rough the last couple of days had been. Losing a best friend was hard, but finding out he'd murdered so many people out of greed was devastating. Bo had been a family friend for a long time. It was shocking to find out how cold and deadly he had become.

"I'm okay, Brad. I still have a headache, but my vision has returned completely. I'm very thankful."

"How's the arm?"

Alana glanced at her shoulder. The wound, grazed by Bo's bullet, was wrapped in tight bandages and protected by a sling—painful, but it would heal.

"Much better. Just a little sore."

The events of the past week circled around in her head like a merry-go-round. Most of the shocking puzzle now made sense, but there were still pieces missing—such as why Chet was murdered. She looked at Brad and asked the question she dreaded the most. "Brad, did you find out who killed Chet?"

He nodded slowly. "Chet's next door neighbor, Gene Hollister. Charlie Suarez, one of Bo's men, confirmed that Gene's the one who pulled the trigger, but Bo ordered it. Hollister shot Chet, and then Bo killed him. We found his body in Lake Morgan several days later. He was shot with the same gun that Bo used to shoot you and Jaydn."

"That means Bo shot Gene himself, doesn't it?"

Brad took a deep breath and sat down in the chair beside her bed. "Yeah. The hotel manager, also one of Bo's men, confirmed it. He's singing his head off, hoping he'll get a lighter sentence. He said Chet followed Gene to the warehouse, and one of Gene's men recognized him. They followed him home, and Gene killed him—after he forced him to sign the suicide note. Chet might have been foolhardy and obnoxious, but he didn't deserve to die."

"What about the ring Kent was wearing? Jaydn said he saw a picture of the same ring in the group of stolen items from the robberies."

"Chet must have picked it up at the warehouse. My guess is … he planned to produce the ring to prove his suspicions. He'd been warned about jumping to conclusions. He'd been warned about a lot of things …"

Alana remembered the look of compassion on Chet's face after her kidnapping. "Poor Chet."

Silence filled the room. Alana shifted position uncomfortably.

"Are Evan and Sam okay?"

"Yeah, just a little embarrassed. The security guards had no way of knowing they were being lured away from the island by the ruckus Bo's men created across the lake as a distraction. When they left to check it out, Bo's men tied Evan and Sam up in the basement. My men found them about an hour later—a little sore, but okay."

"I'm glad they weren't hurt. How's Jaydn?"

"He's fine, Alana. The surgery to remove the bullet was a success, so now it's just a matter of time. He'll be as good as new before you know it."

"He still doesn't want to see me?" Sorrow bled into her question.

"Not yet, Alana. I think he's still distressed about the way you reacted to his being a *rich tyrant*."

Alana squeezed her eyes shut. "I shouldn't have called him that—even if he didn't tell me the truth."

"I know he wanted to tell you. He was scared you'd overreact.

He cares for you, Alana. You two seem like you were made for each other. You need to forgive him."

Silence was his answer.

"I have one more thing to say, and then I need to get back to work. The Bible doesn't say money is the root of all evil, in spite of what you might think. It says the *love* of money is the root of all evil. Bo showed us all what that looks like. But, Jaydn's different. Think about that, Alana."

He stood up and leaned over the bed, dropping a kiss on Alana's forehead.

"I have to get back to work, munchkin. The doc says you can go home tomorrow. Lisa and I will be here bright and early to pick you up."

Tears welled up in her eyes. "Thanks, Brad. I'll see you in the morning."

Alana gingerly leaned back on the hospital pillow. She wanted to force her way into Jaydn's hospital room to see for herself if he was truly okay, but embarrassment stopped her. She'd rejected him. In the worst way possible, she'd pushed him away and called him horrible names. She couldn't get the hurt look on his face out of her mind when she'd told him she didn't want to see him again.

All because of money.

The concern she felt about his lack of faith in God—that burden had been removed. But, the fact he was an important company owner with money at his disposal to force his ways on others gave her reason to halt their relationship. So many unwanted consequences piled up when money was involved.

Tom, the man she thought she cared for deeply, lived a lie in front of her until it was almost too late. He had harbored a carload of baggage that revolved around money. He hid his true self until he became so overbearing that he was impossible to be around. He was autocratic, self-serving, stingy, and obsessed with the need to make even more money.

But ... Jaydn was none of those things. The truth shouted at her. Deep inside her heart, she wanted to believe Jaydn was different—after all, the man kept saving her life—but fear wrapped itself around her heart and wouldn't let go.

Alana stared at the room full of flowers sent by her friends. She touched a white carnation her neighbor, Cynthia Beal, sent the day before. They reminded her of the white azaleas growing near Jaydn's boathouse. Her heart sank to the bottom of her stomach, the way it always did when she thought of Jaydn.

Lord, please show me what to do. I care for him deeply, but I'm afraid to trust him. Please take away the fear.

SEVENTY-FIVE

JAYDN CAREFULLY SCOOTED UP IN bed in order to reach the TV remote. Patricia left the television blaring when she huffed out of the room. She came to his hospital room in order to inform him dramatically that she'd found someone else. When Jaydn didn't seem to mind, she told him, with a lot of sighing and deep breathy apologies, that they were obviously not meant for each other. She was sorry, she claimed, but she'd found someone who better understood her.

Someone who would cater to her beauty and celebrity status, no doubt. Jaydn shrugged inwardly and pushed the "off" button. It didn't matter. They weren't suited for each other. There was only one woman who could see into his soul, and she wanted nothing to do with him.

It wasn't just because of his money—it was because he hadn't been entirely honest with her.

He knew she'd tried to visit his hospital room, but he'd made it clear to the hospital staff that he didn't want to see anyone—especially not the beautiful blonde from the room upstairs. He was not up to a scene regarding his mistakes—not when he'd apologized already.

The harsh words she'd flung at him still stung. The baggage she carried around from the past killed their chance for happiness—unless she forgave him completely and took him as he was.

Lord, help her realize money can be a gift from You and not always a curse. Please help me move on if it's not Your will that we be together.

SEVENTY-SIX

Y OO-HOO! ALANA, ARE YOU STILL here, honey?"
Shirley popped through the hospital room door and brightened up the whole room with her smile.

Alana's eyes lit up in answer to the infectious grin. "Shirley! Oh, it's so good to see you. Thanks for all the phone calls and prayers."

Shirley bounced over to Alana and took both hands in hers. She lowered herself gently on the bed with a satisfied sigh and gave Alana a kiss on the cheek.

"How are you feeling, sweetie?"

That question was hard for Alana to answer. Physically she was healing, but emotionally, she missed Jaydn. How could she explain her reluctance to form a relationship with the type of man who had saved her life more than once in the last week, a man who otherwise bore a strong resemblance to the type of man she swore never again to get involved with?

Her hesitation made Shirley jump to the wrong conclusion. She leaned around Alana and gave her a one-arm hug, avoiding the sling.

"I have some news for you that will make you feel better instantly."

Alana waited, amazed by Shirley's controlled excitement.

"The owner of our building sent his lawyer by this morning, and he brought the deed to the orphanage property."

Alana sat puzzled, unaware of the significance of that news.

"Alana, on the deed, the title of ownership has been changed to …" Shirley paused for effect, "Darrell and me."

Alana's jaw dropped. "I don't understand, Shirley. What did you say? The deed is in *your* name now?"

Shirley could hardly speak for giggling. "For some reason, our landlord had his lawyer deed the entire block—the building, and all the surrounding land—to us. It's ours now. He even donated enough money to add that playground we've always wanted! Isn't it wonderful?"

Alana stared at Shirley, unable to speak. Finally, the stunning message of the older woman penetrated through her shock. She reached with her good arm to hug Shirley.

"Shirley, that's amazing!"

Shirley bubbled with excitement. "I thought that would make you happy. No more worrying about finding a place to move. The building's ours now, and no one can tell us we have to leave. There'll be no more rental payments each month. There are so many things we can buy for the children without having to make those payments."

Shirley smiled as she stood. "Well, I gotta run, sweetie. Just wanted to pop in and bring you the good news in person. Would you please tell him how much we appreciate what he did?" Happy tears slid down Shirley's cheeks. "The children are so happy." She smiled through her tears and turned.

When Brad appeared at the door, Shirley patted him on the arm and gave him a beaming smile as she left the room.

Brad glanced out the door and laughed at the way Shirley floated down the hall. "What in the world has her flying in the clouds?"

"I don't believe it," said Alana, pressing her hands to her cheeks. "She told me Jaydn deeded the orphanage building and the whole block to her and Darrell—for nothing."

She dropped her hands to her lap and blinked at her brother. "And she asked me to tell him how much they appreciate what he did." The confusion turned to misery. "How am I supposed to do that, Brad? He won't even let me see him."

Brad sat down beside her and took her hands in his. He said nothing for a full minute. Then he said, "Alana, there's something I need to tell you. I'm not sure Jaydn would approve, but I can't keep quiet when it's obvious how you two feel about each other."

Alana braced herself for what was coming.

"Jaydn asked me last week about the orphanage. He wanted to know what kind of job Darrell and Shirley were doing, about the kids there, and when their lease was up. He asked if plans to move to a new location were in place. When I told him no, he seemed excited. He said he had to talk to his lawyer, and he mumbled something about you."

"Me?" Alana asked. "What did it have to do with me?"

Brad shrugged his shoulders. "He did it for you, Alana. He knows how much that orphanage means to you. He gave it to them because it would make you happy."

Alana was dazed. Never in her wildest dreams would she have imagined Jaydn using his wealth for something so wonderful. It certainly clashed with her opinion of the wealthy business owners she had known in the past. She had tried to convince herself he was just like Tom, but deep down in her heart, she knew Jaydn was different. He said he cared for her, and to prove it, he put actions behind the words. Tears blurred her vision.

"Lane, you know what the Bible says about forgiving others. Can't you forgive Jaydn for loving you too much to tell you the truth? You have to know that he would never do anything to hurt you like Tom did."

He rubbed the back of her hand thoughtfully. "There's another reason you should forgive him, sweetie. He saved your life—several times."

When she nodded, he looked deep into her eyes. "He took a bullet for you, Alana." Brad's voice broke. "In my book, that proves a love beyond words. How much more does it take to convince you he cares?"

A strangled cry escaped her lips, and tears overflowed and streamed down her cheeks. Visions of Jaydn jumping in front of her at the warehouse and falling to the floor with blood staining his shirt overwhelmed her, and the throbbing in her chest grew stronger.

"Brad, please," she moaned, reaching out to him as tears fell unheeded down her cheeks. "I need to see him. Will you help me? I have to tell him I'm sorry, that I was wrong."

Brad nodded and took her arm, smiling. "That's one thing I'd be happy to do."

SEVENTY-SEVEN

JAYDN LAY BACK IN BED and stared at the stained ceiling. When a knock sounded on the door, he waited until Brad stuck his head around the door.

"Hey, Jaydn. Do you feel like company?"

"I'll take your company over a boring hospital room any day, Brad. Come on in."

Brad didn't move but looked down at the floor. "Well, actually, it's Alana who's here to see you."

Jaydn grew quiet. Why should he suffer through her presence when it would only make him yearn for something he couldn't have? Her words echoed in his head constantly like a time loop. *You're a deceitful liar. I don't ever want to see you again.*

Jaydn ducked his head and felt the awkward uneasiness injected into the room between him and Brad. Brad stood quietly—waiting for an answer.

Jaydn raised his head to look at Brad and shook his head. "Not yet, Brad. I'm not up to facing her yet."

Brad stood up taller. "I really think you should see her, buddy. She has something important to tell you."

Jaydn's heart balked. *Yeah, right. Like I'm still a deceitful liar.* He shook his head. "I don't think so. Not now."

Brad nodded sadly and said as he exited, "All right, Jaydn. I'll be back to see you later, then."

Jaydn's heart eased into overdrive as he stared at the closed door. Knowing Alana's stubbornness, he wouldn't put it past her to barge into the room uninvited.

He actually *wanted* her to. *Needed* her to.

The unnerving tap of the clock on the wall pounded out the seconds as he waited. The anticipation was murder. When she didn't appear, his heart thudded to the bottom of his chest.

Guess that was his answer. Their future was set in stone. There was no future.

SEVENTY-EIGHT

ARE YOU READY TO GO home, munchkin?"
Alana stood forlornly and mustered up a smile, waving Brad and Lisa into the room. Lisa crossed the room and sat a vase of gorgeous yellow and white roses on the table beside the window.

"What beautiful flowers, Lisa. Thank you!" She included Brad in the smile.

"Well, we'd like to take credit for them, but someone else had them delivered to the nurse's station, and they asked us to make sure you got them."

"Oh?" Puzzled, Alana wrinkled her forehead. "And do I know this someone else?"

"You do," said Brad quietly. "It was Jaydn."

"What?" Now Alana really *was* surprised. "Why would he send me flowers? He won't even see me."

Brad shrugged. "I think he sent the flowers before you tried to visit him upstairs."

Brad stole a glance at Lisa, who sighed and added, "In spite of his refusal to see you, I think he really cares for you. Just give him some time."

"Lane, when I went back to see him last night, all he could talk about was you. He wanted to know how your arm was feeling ... if you were in pain ... if your vision had returned ... when you were going home. The guy's hooked, and I think you feel the same way about him."

Alana felt the blush rise from her cheeks to her hairline.

Brad grinned. "Bingo! A blush like that has to mean

something."

Alana looked at Brad, then Lisa, and then her head hung low. "Brad, you know money and I have always been enemies, and you know the reasons why I feel that way. It changes a relationship after a while. I'm afraid. I'm afraid he'll end up being like Tom."

Brad sighed softly and lifted her chin with his finger. "I know you've had it rough in the past, but Jaydn's different. I feel it in here." He patted his hand over his heart.

A knock sounded on the door, and Kent stuck his head into the room.

"Can I come in?"

Brad got up off the bed and motioned for Kent to come into the room. "Sure, Kent."

Kent's olive complexion turned ashen when he saw the flowers surrounding the bed. "Man, I should have brought flowers. I'm sorry." His embarrassment caused his gaze to drop to the floor, and his feet never stopped scuffing the tiled floor.

Alana walked over to him and put her hand on his arm. "Kent, please. You've done so much already. If you hadn't pulled me from the lake … I don't know what might have happened. I couldn't have lasted much longer."

"But I let Bo steal you away. I should have watched him more closely and stayed with him like Brad ordered me to do. Then maybe he wouldn't have taken you to the warehouse in the first place, and you and Jaydn wouldn't have gotten shot."

Brad spoke up. "Kent, I told you to keep an eye on Alana and Jaydn, and that's what you did. You followed Bo from town and discovered the location of the warehouse, didn't you?" His voice shook with emotion. "You called me and helped me find them. You saved my sister's life. I'll forever be grateful." He shook Kent's hand with a moving handshake.

Kent shifted from foot to foot, clearly embarrassed with the thanks. Alana gave him a hug. "Thank you, Kent. You're a great friend." She smiled and turned back to the bed. "Now, let's get out of here, okay?"

On the way home, they drove down the quiet street right in

front of Jaydn's office building. Suddenly, Alana sat up straight in the back seat.

"Brad, I have an idea. Do you know when Jaydn will be coming home from the hospital?"

Brad thought for a minute. "I think it'll be in a day or two, the way he talked. Why?"

Alana grinned to herself. "I think I know how I can see Jaydn, and there's no way he can stop me." Her eyes were bright and full of hope.

SEVENTY-NINE

TWO WEEKS LATER, ALANA STEPPED out of the elevator and murmured a heartfelt prayer.

Lord, please let this work.

Her shoes tapped across the wooden floor until they sank into the oriental rug in front of the massive desk. Greeting the secretary behind the stylish desk, she gave her an uneven smile.

"Are you Florence?"

The middle-aged woman rose with a smile and walked around her desk to greet Alana. "I'm so glad to finally meet you, Alana. You're just as pretty as I pictured you over the phone." She gave her a kiss on the cheek.

"I hope this works."

"It has to, dear. I've never seen Jaydn like this before—moping around like a dog that lost his master. I don't think I can stand all this meekness any longer—humility *oozes* out of his pores. Something has to give." She smiled to take the edge off the criticism.

"When do you expect him here in the office?"

Florence looked at her watch. "In about twenty minutes. He's been coming in a little later since he got out of the hospital. Come on over. I'll help you get set up."

Twenty-five minutes later, the elevator door opened and Jaydn stepped out, talking to a tall, thin man beside him. The man stayed in the elevator, waiting for Jaydn to finish his instructions.

"See which of the three properties suit the town of Bishop, Ward. If they like either one of them, we'll develop that one for the parking garage. And, let me know when it's done." Jaydn nodded, and Ward pushed the button. As the elevator doors closed, Jaydn turned and stopped in mid-step.

The back of the woman standing at the filing cabinet behind the secretary's desk didn't look like Florence at all. In fact, she bore a striking resemblance to Alana—but then, everyone did these days. His heart sped up when the woman turned and faced him.

"Hello, Mr. Holbrook. Here are your messages." Alana picked up a small pile of notes from the desk. "The typed letters are ready to leave in the afternoon mail, and you have two messages about the building going up in Medville and three appointments before lunch. Your coffee's on your desk along with two perfectly heated chocolate doughnuts, and," Alana paused and finally looked up at him then, "you have a young lady waiting for an interview about an apology."

Alana smiled at him then, and the sun came out from behind the clouds. Jaydn stepped forward for the messages she held out and stopped beside the desk—his system gradually coming to life.

"And where is this young lady waiting for an interview? Does she have an appointment?"

She smiled at him shyly and shook her head. "No, but I had to see you, Jaydn. I know why you wouldn't see me at the hospital, but I had to say I'm sorry. I misjudged you." Alana could see into his heart, and what she saw brought tears to her eyes. "I'm so sorry, Jaydn. I tried to stuff you into the same mold as someone who had a completely different personality. Someone whose only concern was himself. Someone who used the money he inherited to make life miserable for everyone else. Can you ever forgive me? Will you please give me a second chance?"

Jaydn could stand still no longer. Setting aside the papers in his hand, he closed the space between them. Taking her hands in his, he stared into her eyes. "Alana, I've already forgiven you. I've missed you so much. You are the sunshine of my life. I think I fell in love with you the first time I ever saw you standing beside this desk. Do you think you could ever love a bull-headed, rich business executive like me?"

Her sparkling laughter filled the air. "Oh, Jaydn, I could never love anyone else."

He kissed her then, and it was nothing like he remembered. The fireworks in his head were louder and brighter than he ever felt before.

EPILOGUE

JAYDN REACHED AROUND THE CLOSET door and pulled his blue tie off the hanger. Wrapping it around his neck, he stared into space and thought about how complete things turned out in his life. He had a wonderful God to fill his heart with peace and contentment and a beautiful bride to fill his life with companionship and love.

No one but Alana could have filled his life with such joy. She was perfect for him. The one God chose for him.

A knock sounded, and Brad stuck his head around the door. "Are you ready, brother?"

Jaydn's smile stretched across his face. "More than ready."

"Well then, if you're ready and I'm ready, let's see if Alana's ready." He grinned. "I'll go get her, and we'll meet you at the front of the chapel."

Jaydn just nodded and beamed. He had been waiting for this special day since first meeting Alana. In just a little while, his dreams would come true. They would have the rest of their lives to spend together, and it really would be a happily-ever-after ending.

Alana smiled at all the little faces around her.

"I'm sorry, Miss Alana," Shirley said. "The children just had to see you before you walk down the aisle."

"It's okay, Shirley. I don't mind." Alana bent over and gave each of them a hug, not minding how many little hands touched her white, lacy, wedding gown. Shining faces radiated their happiness. In the last few months, they spent many hours with Jaydn and came to know him well. The smiles and touches confirmed their approval of the marriage between two of their favorite people.

After she assured each one of her love, Shirley led them out of the room. A wink and a smile traveled with Shirley to the door. "Brad's waiting. I'll send him in now."

Alana nodded and turned for a final look in the mirror. Her face was radiant, and she knew why. Jaydn's idea to get married in the orphanage chapel still warmed her heart. He was not Tom, and it was proven many times over in the last few months.

Thank you for Jaydn, Lord, and that he's a child of Yours. Thank you that we can spend our lives together using the money you've given us to help others and to honor and glorify You.

The money she was so afraid of before now became an instrument of doing good for others—all with Jaydn's leadership.

"Wow, munchkin, you look beautiful! Absolutely gorgeous."

"Oh, Spot, I'm so happy."

Brad's throat tightened, and he cleared his throat. "Well, sweetie, you look it too. I have something for you."

Alana looked puzzled. "You and Lisa already gave me this beautiful wedding dress."

"I know, but this gift is from Jaydn and me. Just call it a special gift from the special men in your life."

Alana tilted her head to the side and looked at the square box he pulled from behind his back. She carefully stripped off the bow and opened the box lid. Inside was a camera, just like the one her parents gave her.

"A camera! Oh, Brad. Thank you." She took the camera out and looked at it carefully. When she saw the little nick on the edge of the camera housing, she drew back in surprise.

"This is just like the one …"

"No, Lane. It's not *like* the one Mom and Dad gave you. It *is* the one Mom and Dad gave you. Jaydn found this little repair shop in downtown Ross, and we had it repaired. We both knew how much it meant to you."

A tear trickled down Alana's face. "Oh, Brad. You're the best brother anyone ever had. You and Jaydn are wonderful. I feel so blessed to have you both in my life. Thank you."

Brad's eyes were moist as he used his handkerchief to wipe the tear's trail down her cheek. "You're welcome, munchkin. Now, let's get you out of here before all this blubbering messes up your makeup. You don't want Jaydn marrying a raccoon, do you?" He held out his arm for her and smiled.

Alana laughed and grabbed his arm.

He kissed her on the cheek. "Are you ready?"

She didn't answer, just nodded with moist eyes.

He led her out of the room and to the double doors at the back of the chapel. When the wedding march started, the ushers opened the doors, and she saw her dear Jaydn standing in front of the chapel. His eyes glowed with pleasure when he saw his bride, and the delight in his face made her beam. She had much to be thankful for—a husband who loved her enough to put his life on the line for her, and a God who loved her enough to give her Jaydn. Now, her life was complete.

For more information about
JOANIE BRUCE
&
ALANA CANDLER, MARKED FOR MURDER
please visit:

Web site: joaniebruce.com
Email: joaniebruce@gmail.com
Twitter: @joaniebruce
Facebook: www.facebook.com/joaniebruce

For more information about
AMBASSADOR INTERNATIONAL
please visit:

www.ambassador-international.com
@AmbassadorIntl
www.facebook.com/AmbassadorIntl

www.ingramcontent.com/pod-product-compliance
Lightning Source LLC
Chambersburg PA
CBHW070219260626
47160CB00002B/603